Coding Slave

Version 2.10

By Bob Reselman

© 2003-2004

Coding Slave
Version 2.10

Published by NewTech Press
www.newTech.com
12730 Pacific Avenue
Los Angeles, California, 90066
Copyright © 2004 Bob Reselman

ISBN: 0-9749804-0-4

Published in the United States

Technical Editor
Brian O'Neill

Senior Copy Editors
Michele McCarthy
Alexandra Gründl
Richard Showstack

Associate Copy Editors
Brian Amick
Cathy Dobson
Martha Damerell
Dan Emehiser
David Imber
Dorothy Lifka
Alexandra Lifka-Reselman

Printed by The Printing Studio, Venice, California
www.printingstudio.com

To Brian, my brother in spirit,
who got me into this mess and to whom I will be eternally grateful.

All characters depicted in this book are purely fictional; the situations, less so.

Table of Contents

Prologue: Katherine Makes a Decision

"Fuck 'em. Send the code to India."

A momentary silence filled the room as the impact of her statement settled on the faces that surrounded the table. Walt, the face closest to her spoke.

"Katherine, do you know what you're saying? This is not New York, or the Bay Area, or even Austin. This is the deep Midwest. People are going to get more than a little upset at the idea of putting high-paying *American* programmers out of work and sending their jobs off to *India*, of all places. This is going to piss a lot of people off. Programmers are not the only ones that are going to feel the impact. These guys don't make minimum wage. They make real money and spend it here. We're talking about classic trickle down, Katherine. This will set a real precedent. A quarter of the people in this town are involved in some sort of technology work. This is going to hurt an awful lot of people."

Walt's comment provoked Katherine. She had not slept for the past two nights and was beginning to show the irritability that accompanies sleep deprivation.

"Walt that goddamn system controls us. This has got to change. The only module that is working is Payroll; not the General Ledger, not Inventory, not Purchasing, not Sales, not HR — just Payroll. Walt, we have just spent 5.2 million dollars for a fucking Payroll module that I could have bought from QuickBooks for ninety-nine dollars. This is unbelievable! We have a horde of programmers downstairs doing God-knows-what at an astronomical burn rate and all we have is *fucking Payroll!* That goddamn system is supposed to help us be more competitive, not drive us into bankruptcy."

Katherine realized that she was losing control. She was using profanity out of anger and frustration rather than to make a point. This was a sure sign that sleep deprivation was setting in.

"You want to keep the jobs here and still bring the implementation in on budget, Walt? Tell you what — get everybody at this table to take a thirty per cent cut in salary for starters. Get that to happen, Walt, and we have the beginning of something to talk about."

The other faces around the table looked to Walt. Walt was about to say something and then stopped. He looked down and began to scribble on his yellow, legal-size notepad. "Sorry Katherine," he said, "This is a bit of a shock. It's going to take some getting use to."

The faces looked away from Walt and started to scribble too, as if the Scribbling Fairy had visited Walt first and then one by one cast a spell upon each of them, allowing them to share threads from a common well of a single thought. Each face scribbled away in his own handwriting, contributing to the common, current event, to which he would be party and to which he would make every effort to avoid responsibility.

The decision had been made and Katherine Limeleaf was just the one to make it. This was not her first implementation. She had suffered sleepless nights before. All she had to do was get the burn rate down, she thought to herself, "Then I'll sleep again. Seen one ERP, you've seen them all."

Part 1: Convergence

Chapter 1: Ajita Escapes

Ajita Orhtihawamein looked out over the tarmac, watching the white lines of the runway grow smaller as the plane began its ascent toward Heaven. She was escaping Delhi, her mother, her father, her three brothers and one little sister. She was going to ascend as far as she could in the time that her H1 visa allowed. If she had anything at all to say about it, she was not coming back, never — not for love, not for honor, not for the death of her father or for her brother's wedding. She was a certified computer programmer. She was going to New York City and she was going to code.

Ajita, the daughter of Ramda Orhtihawamein—a lower middle class, dispatch supervisor, four years from pension at NDPL, India's premier power company—was twenty five years old, five foot two, one hundred and ten pounds, a little pretty and born to make software. She had the gift. Where others saw bank accounts, invoices and purchase orders, Ajita saw patterns of numbers and text that were obvious, known and well-formed. And, just as Plato saw his world as the shadows of ideas on the wall of a cave, Ajita saw her world as the shadows of the code that controlled it. In a world that appeared to others as random ambiguity, Ajita saw predictable structure. To her it was all related, relevant and grand. And because of this, Ajita was without fear. She knew the code and she knew that she was the code. She knew that the code had liberated her. She knew that the code would continue to make her free.

Ajita was now in the employ of StarTex Associates of New York, New York. StarTex, an international, high tech consulting company specializing in custom software development and technical labor fulfillment, had found a cute little niche in which to play. StarTex's deal was pretty simple: buy coders cheap and sell their services to American companies, particularly banks and other financial institutions, at below market rates. Buy cheap, sell cheap, keep a good margin. StarTex made a lot of money.

All of StarTex's programmers came from India. StarTex kept agents in various cities throughout the subcontinent who were always on the lookout for talent wanting to escape. Once a "resource" was identified, the standard pitch was made. The coder would sign a contract that bound him or her to StarTex for a period of two years. The coder was contracted out. While the coder was working, he or she was paid a salary of forty thousand dollars a year, a sum that an Indian coder right off the plane perceived to be a very large amount of money. If the coder was not working and "on the bench", his or her salary dropped to $19,000 a year or $365.38 a week.

Each coder was expected to bill a client at a minimum rate of forty dollars an hour. All coders were expected to work forty hours a week, fifty-two weeks a year, which translated into two thousand and eighty hours. StarTex paid no vacation, sick days, overtime or holiday time, but did pick up health insurance. Thus, each coder brought in revenue of $83,200 a year and produced a profit of $35,000, after salary, airfare and health insurance. If a coder was on the bench for more than two weeks, his or her H1 visa was revoked and the coder was sent back to India. Coders returning to India in disgrace were expected to pay StarTex back the cost of the airfare. StarTex had ninety coders at work in metropolitan New York City, five in Rochester, NY and six in New Haven, CT.

The previous year StarTex made a net profit of $2.7 million dollars, which was divided up between the Four Brothers and a Cousin who ran the company. One of the brothers and the cousin had gone to Rutgers University, each taking a BA in Information Technology. Both had spent two years working the back office at a big bank up on Park Avenue. The cousin had become friendly with a Human Resource manager who was looking to contract ten programmers for six months for a big project that was under a hard deadline. The cousin and brother called up the other brothers in India to come over to do the contract. The brothers in India called up eight friends. The hourly rate for which the other brothers and their friends were willing to work was so far below market average that the big bank made the H1's appear almost overnight. Thus, StarTex was born.

In practically no time at all the Four Brothers and a Cousin had forty coders in the big bank, another twenty coders in another bank, two agents in India and a waiting list of coders wanting to escape. StarTex made money. The banks saved money. Everybody was happy.

Even Ajita was happy, today anyway. She had escaped. She was no longer a lower-middle-class, unmarried, Indian woman in her twenties beholden to her father and her brothers or whatever husband they could find for her. She was a certified computer programmer who was on her way to do some serious coding in New York, New York.

After the plane leveled off at thirty-five thousand feet, the flight attendants began cabin service. A gorgeous, young, well-groomed young man with short blonde hair, clothed in the latest airline fashion — blue trousers, white shirt, red tie, and blue vest with wings over the front right pocket all protected by a three-quarter-length blue service apron with convenience pockets — came toward Ajita. The attendant was pushing a beverage cart filled with a variety of free beverages: coffee, tea, juice, and soft drinks as well as beer, wine and other alcoholic beverages all available for an additional cost of four dollars American.

Chapter 1: Ajita Escapes

Ajita was enchanted; she had never seen a man with blonde hair in real life. She'd seen plenty of them in the American movies and magazines, but this was her first encounter with a real man with real blonde hair.

The Adonis-like attendant stopped in front of Ajita and asked her what she desired. Ajita's heart was pounding. Using all the courage she muster, with four hundred nautical miles of distance behind her and seven miles of airspace below her, Ajita took four newly exchanged dollar bills from her purse and, with a polite but deliberate gesture, ordered her first beer. The attendant popped the top of the can open and poured its contents into a small plastic glass, which he then handed over to Ajita along with a bag of salted peanuts and the can containing the remains of her purchase.

Ajita brought the beer to her lips and took a small sip. She opened the bag of peanuts, drew one out between her index finger and thumb, put it in her mouth, chewed and swallowed. She repeated the sequence again and again — one sip of beer, one peanut, one sip of beer, one peanut, beer, peanut, beer, peanut, beer, peanut, until the bag was empty. Then she poured the rest of the beer from the can into the plastic glass and with one gulp finished it off.

As she put the empty glass on the tray in front of her, she let out a little belch, which brought a disapproving stare from an old red-dot Brahmin-caste Indian lady sitting in the window seat next to her. Ajita returned a little smile of feigned innocence. The lady turned away.

Ajita picked up the headphones from the seat pouch in front of her, directly underneath the tray upon which the emptied packages of her drink and peanuts lay. She put the headphones on and inserted the plug attached to the headphone wires into the corresponding holes in her seat's armrest. She turned the channel indicator on the armrest to the numeral six, the channel for in-flight music of the classic rock style.

Ajita pushed her seat back and listened to the music while she drifted off into a beer-induced sleep. The headphones emitted a soothing tune sung by Janis Joplin: "Me and Bobby McGee." Ajita liked the words of the chorus a lot.

Freedom's just another word for nothing left to lose....

Chapter 2: Albert Has a Headache

Albert Shulberg, a.k.a. "`BigDick6969`," looked out over the swimming pool, gazing miserably at the collection of skinny preadolescent boys and ripe adolescent girls as they taunted one another with screeches of hormonal excitement. The boys splashed water on the girls hoping to garner as much attention and rapture as they had imagined the night before while under the sheets, enthralled in mid-summer masturbation. The girls simply gave the boys the finger.

Albert reclined back into the cheap, white, plastic sunbed at the side of the pool. His head hurt. The hurt wasn't the hangover type — excruciating, head pounding throbs of ache at the back of the neck, coupled with the beer shits, in which his rapidly dehydrating body caused the blows of pain in the back of his head to accumulate into such agony that the only relief at hand was for his bowels to release a torrent of diarrheic discharge that cataloged every abuse he had committed upon himself the night before. No, this pain was that annoying hum in his eyes and forehead that came from too many hours pounding a keyboard, fondling a mouse and gazing endlessly into a too small computer screen.

Albert had been up all night making his presence known in an adult chat room. Albert's ploy was to capture one-liners being exchanged between chat members and redirect the sentences hundreds of times back into the chat room. The effect of Albert's work looked like the following:

```
Honeybabe>> Hey, WildStallion, what are you doing tonight?
WildStallion>> Honey,I'm looking for a female to suck my dick.
BigNHorny>> Any women out there want to do some hot chat?
CoupleFromNJ>> Couple, wife bi, looking for bi-female
Honeybabe>> Wild, you got a monster on you or what?
WildStallion>> LOL, you wouldn't believe.
BigDick6969 has entered the room.
BigDick6969>> Hi room, watch this...
Honeybabe>> Hey, WildStallion, what are you doing tonight?
WildStallion>> Honey,I'm looking for a female to suck my dick.
BigNHorny>> Any women out there want to do some hot chat?
CoupleFromNJ>> Couple, wife bi, looking for bi-female
Honeybabe>> Wild, you got a monster on you or what?
WildStallion>> LOL, you wouldn't believe.
Honeybabe>> Hey, WildStallion, what are you doing tonight?
```

Chapter 2: Albert Has a Headache

```
WildStallion>> Honey,I'm looking for a female to suck my dick.
BigNHorny>> Any women out there want to do some hot chat?
CoupleFromNJ>> Couple, wife bi, looking for bi-female
Honeybabe>> Wild, you got a monster on you or what?
WildStallion>> LOL, you wouldn't believe.
Honeybabe>> Hey, WildStallion, what are you doing tonight?
WildStallion>> Honey,I'm looking for a female to suck my dick.
BigNHorny>> Any women out there want to do some hot chat?
CoupleFromNJ>> Couple, wife bi, looking for bi-female
Honeybabe>> Wild, you got a monster on you or what?
WildStallion>> LOL, you wouldn't believe.
Honeybabe>> Hey, WildStallion, what are you doing tonight?
WildStallion>> Honey,I'm looking for a female to suck my dick.
BigNHorny>> Any women out there want to do some hot chat?
CoupleFromNJ>> Couple, wife bi, looking for bi-female
Honeybabe>> Wild, you got a monster on you or what?
WildStallion>> LOL, you wouldn't believe.
Honeybabe>> Hey, WildStallion, what are you doing tonight?
WildStallion>> Honey,I'm looking for a female to suck my dick.
BigNHorny>> Any women out there want to do some hot chat?
CoupleFromNJ>> Couple, wife bi, looking for bi-female
Honeybabe>> Wild, you got a monster on you or what?
WildStallion>> LOL, you wouldn't believe.
Honeybabe>> Hey, WildStallion, what are you doing tonight?
WildStallion>> Honey,I'm looking for a female to suck my dick.
BigNHorny>> Any women out there want to do some hot chat?
CoupleFromNJ>> Couple, wife bi, looking for bi-female
Honeybabe>> Wild, you got a monster on you or what?
WildStallion>> LOL, you wouldn't believe.
Honeybabe>> Hey, WildStallion, what are you doing tonight?
WildStallion>> Honey,I'm looking for a female to suck my dick.
BigNHorny>> Any women out there want to do some hot chat?
CoupleFromNJ>> Couple, wife bi, looking for bi-female
Honeybabe>> Wild, you got a monster on you or what?
WildStallion>> LOL, you wouldn't believe.
Honeybabe>> Hey, WildStallion, what are you doing tonight?
WildStallion>> Honey,I'm looking for a female to suck my dick.
BigNHorny>> Any women out there want to do some hot chat?
CoupleFromNJ>> Couple, wife bi, looking for bi-female
Honeybabe>> Wild, you got a monster on you or what?
WildStallion>> LOL, you wouldn't believe.
Honeybabe>> Hey, WildStallion, what are you doing tonight?
WildStallion>> Honey,I'm looking for a female to suck my dick.
```

```
BigNHorny>> Any women out there want to do some hot chat?
CoupleFromNJ>> Couple, wife bi, looking for bi-female
Honeybabe>> Wild, you got a monster on you or what?
WildStallion>> LOL, you wouldn't believe.
Honeybabe>> Hey, WildStallion, what are you doing tonight?
WildStallion>> Honey,I'm looking for a female to suck my dick.
BigNHorny>> Any women out there want to do some hot chat?
CoupleFromNJ>> Couple, wife bi, looking for bi-female
Honeybabe>> Wild, you got a monster on you or what?
WildStallion>> LOL, you wouldn't believe.
Honeybabe>> Hey, WildStallion, what are you doing tonight?
WildStallion>> Honey,I'm looking for a female to suck my dick.
BigNHorny>> Any women out there want to do some hot chat?
CoupleFromNJ>> Couple, wife bi, looking for bi-female
Honeybabe>> Wild, you got a monster on you or what?
WildStallion>> LOL, you wouldn't believe.
Honeybabe>> Hey, WildStallion, what are you doing tonight?
WildStallion>> Honey,I'm looking for a female to suck my dick.
BigNHorny>> Any women out there want to do some hot chat?
CoupleFromNJ>> Couple, wife bi, looking for bi-female
Honeybabe>> Wild, you got a monster on you or what?
WildStallion>> LOL, you wouldn't believe.
```

Albert had marginal fun messing up the chat room. The hack just wasn't that hard. But watching the flames that resulted from his technical acumen produced enough gratification to keep him up and interested through the night. After all, it was only the Internet and it wasn't like he was going to get laid or anything. Anyway, a good barrage of flames was better than cyber-sex any day of the week.

Where for others it was a way of life, for Albert, intruding into the text stream of a chat room was nothing more than a professional amusement, an aside, a way to pass time, sort of like twiddling your thumbs while waiting for your number to be called at the Department of Motor Vehicles.

Albert spent a good deal of his after-work hours passing time in the chat room. Albert had come to this God-forsaken, family values hellhole of a hotel near the Magic Kingdom as a layover during a period of cash flow adjustment. Albert was a Systems Architect. His going rate was $1500 a day, plus expenses. With the money he was making working for the Magic Kingdom for twenty-six weeks, he didn't give a shit about the kids, the hotel, or the absence of real sex in the chat room. It was all noise to be attenuated. Once the first check arrived, Albert planned to move out of this hellhole into a real hotel, one that served fresh croissants in the morning, filet mignon in the evening and had both male and female masseuses on call twenty-four hours a day as well as a concierge that could get you *anything*. No more of this pancakes, pizza and self-service crap.

However, right now he was living on savings, so this splash-me-splash-you, last-one-in-the-pool-is-a-rotten-egg, family style hotel was the best he could do given his current cash reserves. Albert found solace knowing that this would all change once the real money started to come in. And as far as chicks went, if he could not meet and dine a female into his bed, at $1500 a day Albert could buy himself a real woman. Even two, if his heart so desired.

So Albert got up from the cheap plastic sunbed, collected his tanning lotion, towel and stack of technical journals and stuffed them into his briefcase. Tomorrow was Monday. Albert had just finished a week of fact finding. The powers-that-be in the Magic Kingdom were waiting to learn how he was going to solve the problem for which he had been hired. Albert, ever one to be on top of things, had indeed devised a plan for the Magic Kingdom to be delivered first thing in the morning.

He walked around the pool full of skinny boys and ripe girls and proceeded to his room. Midway about the pool he got an idea — to create a computer game in which you were situated at a hotel window overlooking a swimming pool full of people. The object of the game was to shoot as many boys and girls in the pool as possible, points off for killing grown-ups. He called the game, "Gonna Git Me a Kid". It would be easy to produce, most kill games are.

Yet, Albert knew that such a game, in addition to being kind of horrid, had limited appeal within the general market. And, the proper niche might not be that big anyway. So Albert Shulberg, a.k.a. "BigDick6969," stored the idea in the back of his mind along with all the other hare-brained schemes he'd conjured up in the past in order to relieve himself from the reality of the present. And, with a tinge of benign resolution, he headed up to his room hoping to ease a developing case of pre-presentation jitters.

Albert planned to take a shower, order up some pizza and beer from the take-out joint down the street that passed itself off as room service and then watch some pay-per-view porn.

Porn always calmed him down after a while. With so much riding on tomorrow's presentation, the calmer he was, the better it would go.

However, Albert knew that the presentation was the easy part. Once the powers-that-be accepted his idea, he'd actually have to do something.

Albert sighed as he put his key card in to the card reader on his hotel room door. Making a buck in the Magic Kingdom was not all it was cracked up to be, even for a System Architect such as Albert Shulberg, a.k.a. "BigDick6969."

Coding Slave

Chapter 3: Frank Conducts an Interview

Frank DiGrazia looked out over the sea of interview cubicles that made up his corner of the Rochester, NY, office of the Internal Revenue Service. The first round of taxpayers, notification form letters in hand, began to wash in from the outside waiting room, taking the first available seat, waiting to begin the dance-like ritual of paying unpaid taxes.

Frank knew the dances and he knew them well. His taxpayer would conjure up stories, excuses, notes-from-the-doctor, tears, fears and anguish explaining why s/he couldn't, wouldn't, shouldn't, thought s/he had, really wanted to pay the tax but didn't. Frank would sit opposite his victim, calculator in hand, tapping in numbers that described the fiscal reality behind the stories, excuses, notes-from-the-doctor, tears, fears and anguish that the taxpayer brought to bare. During the entire process Frank would never, ever smile, although deep within himself he was rolling on the floor, laughing his ass off.

Frank lumbered his way over to Interview Cubicle #6 to do his first victim of the day. Interview Cubicle #6 was identical in every way to the other interview cubicles on the floor. The cubicle consisted of a grayish white desktop thirty inches in width, raised thirty inches off the floor, bounded by a wall on the left and a wall on the right. Both walls were covered with dark gray noise-suppressing cloth. Two chairs were placed opposite each other. If this interview cubicle were in a prison, there would be a pane of bulletproof Plexiglas placed on the desktop between the two opposing chairs to prevent the exchange of contraband and bullets. But, this was the IRS. Thus no Plexiglas was required because the only things being exchanged today were form letters, tax returns, justifying documents, stories, excuses, notes-from-the-doctor, tears, fears and anguish.

Frank's first interview in the morning was a little Asian lady dressed in a fast food uniform. The uniform's baseball-like cap was way too big for her little head. In order to make it fit, the one-size-fits-all clasps on the back of the cap's headband had to be retracted to the last set of nubs and holes, making the cap's baseball-like brim seem like a platypus bill appended to her forehead. In her hand she held a form letter informing her that she had underpaid taxes for the amount of $438.24.

Her plight was common to those who worked multiple jobs where the gross hourly wage never exceeded $10. The gross income of her first job combined with her gross income from her second job produced a total gross income, which

- 19 -

bumped her up into a higher tax bracket and for which not enough taxes had been withheld from either paycheck. Had she filled out her W-4 to withhold an additional $10 a week, she would have been another lawful taxpayer who enjoyed the benefit of a small refund which could be used to buy a DVD player or some other form of recreational electronics. But, she had not and now she was Frank's.

Frank greeted the little Asian lady with a cordial but firm salutation. The little Asian lady went frantic. She thrust over the form letter as a sinner casts out Satan and began a high-pitched, rapid-fire yammering in an Asian language that Frank could not identify. Every so often she inserted the phrase, "I pay" in a way that gave metronome-like reliability to her Asian frenzy.

Frank knew that this dance would take most of the morning. The little Asian lady's language would need to be identified. A translator would need to be brought in. A payment agreement would be arranged. Her paycheck would be garnished. Yeah, it was a lot of work to make good on a $10 a week underpayment. Yet the integrity of the system had to be preserved, no matter how small the incongruity.

If Frank knew one thing it was this: You can play games with the police. You can play games with the courts. You can play games with your boss. You can play games with your spouse. You can play games with your teachers, guidance counselors and school administrators. You can play games with your parents. You can even play games with God. But, you can not play games with the IRS. The databases are too big and the computers are too powerful.

Chapter 4: Rafael Prays for Help

Rafael Martinez looked out over the pews of The Church of Our Lady of Perpetual Devotion and prayed to God to make him whole enough to pass the certification exam. Rafael Martinez, the oldest son of Ernesto and Maria Martinez, immigrants from a small village outside of San Sebastian, Guatemala, and presently line workers at the MidContinent Industries meatpacking plant in Pleasant Lake, Iowa, was all geek. Yet Raphael had something somewhat atypical for a geek. He had a girlfriend. Her name was Connie. Most geeks just had computers.

Rafael started programming young, in grade school, writing programs in Logo, at that time the programming language of choice for elementary school teachers. Rafael got the language down so quickly and so well that the teachers at Our Lady of Perpetual Devotion Elementary School came to him to solve their coding problems with the new-fangled classroom computers.

Rafael's programs were way cool. Instead of having simple Pac Man-like figures chasing each other over the computer screen, Rafael made frogs that chased worms. When a frog caught enough worms, it turned into a stick figure prince.

Later on in high school Rafael developed the frog-to-prince theme further into a full fledged, 3-D game in which the frog ascended to princedom through a series of complex, knightly tasks and, once transformed into a human, the frog-turned-prince got to hunker down with a gorgeous princess babe that looked amazingly like Connie.

For the programming god that he was, Rafael suffered from the at-least-one obligatory frailty that the divine seems to assign to any and all genius: Rafael was learning disabled. As a result, he did not test well.

When it came to computing and computer programming, Rafael's considerable abilities expanded current reality to new and unimagined dimensions. But, when it came time to answer a simple test question designed to figure out if Rafael could write a function to add two numbers together, the genius that guided Rafael to immortalize Connie as a goddess in cyberspace would make his mind go blank. He was too busy getting machines to add numbers together to figure out *how* to get machines to add two numbers together. Testing Rafael about coding was like asking Mozart to recite the rules of counterpoint.

And yet Rafael knew that certification exams meant serious business.

The history of computer programming had taken a vicious turn in 1979 with the advent of the personal computer. Before that time, not just anybody could have access to a computer, let alone program one. Mainframe computers, the gargantuan grandfathers of industrial data processing, cost big money. No one person could own one. They were owned by corporations and The Fed. Access to and use of them were subject to the rigors and privileges of a very well-defined institutional hierarchy.

The mainframe computer lived in a big, fluorescent-lit, removable-floor-tile, climate-controlled room and was guarded by very serious men who wore ties and white lab coats. The only way you got to touch the logical innards of the machine was through, and with, these men. The concept of the computer programmer as a tie-dyed, counter culture renegade was not yet an imagined idea let alone an accepted personality.

Then, after Woodstock, the Evacuation of Saigon, the Resignation of Nixon, Star Wars and the Son of Sam murders, along came the Personal Computer a.k.a. the PC. Anybody with $5K and a copy of BASIC could learn to program—*anybody* at all, regardless of age, race, creed, color, sexual orientation and nation of origin. All that you needed was the brains and the time.

Whereas brains can be found evenly distributed among all age groups, time runs bountiful with kids. So while everybody else was out trying to make a living, the kids played with The Box, as the personal computer came to be called in Geek. And they became very, very good with The Box. The kids built The Box, sold the Box, and programmed The Box. Within ten years the kids with time bountiful on their hands and a Box with which to play became The New Captains of Industry.

Then things started to get out of hand. With the reality of a computer on every business desktop and one in every family room came the overwhelming demand for more coders to make The Boxes go and more powerful programming languages to make the coders go. The world needed more coders than existed.

Thus, becoming a computer programmer became akin to becoming Muslim: all you had to do was make the declaration that you were one. Learning to actually write code became a subsequent activity of confirmation, sorta like praying five times a day, not eating pork, fasting at Ramadan and making it to Mecca before you die.

Some learned to write real code, many didn't. The landscape became filled with a lot of bad code and a lot of crappy coders. But nobody noticed. The volume of software sales diminished not one iota and the industry kept booming, despite a noticeably large amount of programs of questionable worth written in some pretty bad code. So much for quality being job one.

Observing that the discipline of computer programming was becoming filled with lemons, The New Captains of Industry saw an opportunity to make lemonade. They got into the technical education business.

Over time, a sorta weird thing happened; colleges no longer became the arbiters of knowledge when it came to digital technology. Many of the New Captains of Industry were kids who didn't bother to finish college, if go at all. So where in the past the battle cry of success was "Get a college education and get a good job", the clarion call of the Age of Personal Computing was, "Learn to code and have a ball".

The new arbiters of knowledge were the companies that were founded by The New Captains of Industry. These guys understood that programming knowledge was the only real power left in the world. They knew also that getting programmers to program in a language that they owned, on a product that they made, was the ultimate power over the powerful. These guys thus went from being arbiters of knowledge to Dealers of Knowledge. The guys that made programming languages became the pushers and casino operators of the digital world, in which the first thirty days of tech support was always free and as long as you kept the coder using your language and tools, it was only a matter of time before all that was his was yours.

Still, the bad code got worse. In fact, bad code became so prevalent that it became the accepted standard for good code, for a while anyway. But as any kid who has ever been to school knows, at some point the teacher comes back into the room and wants to know what you've been up to while she's been gone. The Dealers of Knowledge needed a way to prove to those who didn't know how to code that those who said they could code could indeed actually write good code. If the New Captains of Industry didn't do it, then that huddled mass of intellectual chaos called a Standards Group would step in, which would be about as bad as government intervention and free software for all. The New Captains of Industry needed to protect their property, their *intellectual property*. And so, verily, from the womb of anarchy, freedom and low cost computing, certification was born.

The Dealers of Knowledge got into the certification business and it was the dream of every salesman with a quota and a Cadillac — the captured customer. Not only did the Dealers of Knowledge make the programming languages that the coders used, they made the certification exams that the coders took in order to prove to those who did not know how to code that the coder could code. Also, the Dealers of Knowledge provided the study guides and courseware that helped the coders pass the certification exam. They even provided certified certification preparation seminars delivered by certified professional trainers to prepare the coders for the certification exam. And, at every point in the certification food chain, the Dealers of Knowledge charged for the product and service.

Of course, none of the real coders thought that certification produced better code. Certification was one of those annoying rituals you went through to have a job, similar to having to be at work promptly at 8:00 AM, after having fallen asleep for three hours after a night of writing real code, not that pansy-ass purchase-order-and invoice stuff.

Certification was noise for coders in general and for Rafael in particular. Except for Rafael it was a very loud, continuous noise that drove him crazy with fear and dread.

Despite the fact that the thought of the certification process terrified him into losing fifteen pounds and many nights of sleep, Rafael accepted the fact that he had to get certified. Rafael had applied a few weeks previous as an internal candidate for a job as an Associate Programmer Analyst at the same MidContinent Industries plant where his parents worked. At the present time he was working in the office of the Processing Department as an Inventory Controller, Second Shift, an hourly position at a rate $10.82 per hour. An Associate Programmer Analyst was a daytime, salaried position that paid $37,500 a year.

The hiring manager told him that given his experience work history, he could have the job as long as he was certified. The next day Rafael sent in the money order to take the certification exam.

It was a quiet night in the pews of The Church of Our Lady of Perpetual Devotion. Two old ladies were over in the chapel at the side of the church lighting candles and talking to Heaven in whispers.

Rafael leafed through the certification review book that he had bought at the mall, answering sample questions as he went along. Leafing and answering correctly provided him with small pricks of comfort that soothed his heavily stressed psyche. Outside of the moments of comfort that leafing and answering brought, the only solace left was to pray to God to that he would pass the certification exam so that he could get the Associate Programmer Analyst position that he so desperately wanted.

Rafael wanted the job for two reasons. The first reason was that he wanted to get a home for Connie and himself. The increase in salary would allow him to buy one of those nice new *homes* with an attached garage that allowed you to go from vaulted ceiling living room to driver-side front seat without having to traipse through snow in the very cold Iowa winter. The second was that at last, after thousands of hours spent pounding the keys and fondling the mouse, he, Rafael Martinez, would get paid to code.

Chapter 5: Albert Gets Afraid

Albert Shulberg, a.k.a. "BigDick6969," looked out across to the runway-stage that was the centerpiece of the Sea Light Lounge and Gentleman's Club. Sitting at the perimeter bar that surrounded the stage, Albert watched the most exquisite pair of ankles in the world promenade before him, past the line of empty bottles and glasses that he used to mark time on the barstool.

This was Albert's first night at the Sea Light since coming down to the Magic Kingdom. Like all tittie bars, the Sea Light had a universal simplicity that Albert found relaxing and enjoyable — you walked in, put your money on the table and the company of beautiful, young women was but a ten dollar table dance away. And, as an added bonus, the Sea Light, and bars like it, offered Albert two commodities that were hard to come by in the pursuit of beautiful women: choice and certainty.

In the outside world, even if dinner went well *and* he said the right thing *and* he did not act overtly like the salmon swimming upstream to spawn that he was, Albert might get lucky enough to view the unclothed body beautiful of his evening's companion, if indeed his evening's companion's body was indeed beautiful beneath the obligatory layers of designer fashion that shrouded her frame.

Life in the Sea Light was nowhere near so uncertain. The Sea Light offered a willing variety of bodies beautiful for view, all in various stages of undress, all available on demand. All that Albert needed to do was pay a little cash and to pay a little respect to the opportunities before him. It was that simple.

The Sea Light experience was abstracted into a little dance of erotic Show and Tell from which each girl derived her specific implementation. Albert called it The Act.

The Act was wonderfully uncomplicated. The girl came to your table and for an agreed-upon ten bucks or so tossed on to your lap the one piece of evening gown that packaged her wonderful form. Then she caressed her tits in an act of self-arousing ecstasy and gyrated her ass in your face, all the while giving you a "Fuck Me, Fuck Me" look that couldn't be beat. And, if you showed appreciation for her efforts by putting dollar bills in her garter, which was the only article of clothing she wore after shedding her initial covering, The Act got much, much better.

The Act was effective and efficient. The entire interlude took the length of the ZZ Top tune that the DJ blasted from the club's crotch-throbbing sound system. The Act wasn't long and it wasn't tactile. But, it sure was fun.

The Sea Light had a look-but-don't-touch policy. Once in a while a girl touched you suggestively on the shoulder, letting her hand drift down over your chest in a way that made your nipples curl. Other times a girl might tap between the knees of your lap to separate them so that she could do The Act between your seated thighs. But, over all, touching was a no-no, which suited Albert just fine.

Albert didn't really care that much about touching or being touched. He liked to watch and he liked to smell. He loved the part in The Act when the girl pushed her head into his face so that he could smell the baby powder freshness of her hair. When Albert was in the rapture of such delirium he became a venerable tipping machining, inserting dollars into a girl's garter with controlled, respectful strokes.

The ability to conjure ecstasy by basking in the fragrance of a beautiful young woman's perfumed coiffure was one of the many traits that Albert admired about himself, the skilled professional that he was. Besides, nobody ever got AIDS from sniffing the follicles of a beautiful woman's head.

No touching policy or not, the girls at the Sea Light got around, even the ones who were marketing majors "just" working their way through college.

Fear, masked as its ubiquitous impersonator, loneliness, brought Albert to the Sea Light that evening. Albert was not what anyone, including himself, would call a people person. He claimed to find most people boring and a majority of them spineless. Albert conceptualized the human condition not so much as dog eat dog but rather as the blind leading the blind.

Albert was pretty mad at and about mankind, particularly that segment of the population that crammed itself into ten-by-ten cubicles, forty hours a day, fifty weeks a year, with five sick days, accrued at a rate of 3.4 hours a month.

And yet behind his madness was a profound sadness about so many lives wasted. As much as he tried to hide it, deny it and defy it, Albert cared about his fellow man. In fact, he *really* cared. As self-seeking, as self-absorbed and as crude as Albert seemed on the outside, the inside guy was an overly sensitive teddy bear who crushed easily, required a lot of affection and, in a perversely inverse way, was capable of bestowing large amounts of attention and affection on others, on an order of magnitude greater than that which he received.

Thus, as much as he detested the human condition in the abstract, he craved the company of others in the here and now. He needed others not so much for the casual recreation that the unpredictable stimulation of their presence provided but rather to intermittently reinforce two notions within himself. The first was that the world around him was not some sort of imaginary rendering of his own making and the second was simpler, more primitive: that he existed as a distinct being separate from others, as an ego.

Without such reinforcement, Albert suffered episodes of ego panic which produced extreme depression. Such depression transcended an easy definition or an easy defense and manifested itself as the most fundamental of feelings beyond words: sexual longing. So, when Albert got lonely, he got horny, and the best place for his distinct being to be was in a place like the Sea Light with a pile of money on the table and a pair of exquisite ankles on the runway. It was that simple.

And still, although the ankles before him were exquisite, as was the body to which they were attached, Albert was anxious and very afraid. He was failing. The system architecture for which the Magic Kingdom was paying him 1500 dollars a day, plus expenses, and by which he would promote his expertise as well as justify his rate to his next client was crumbling around him. Today he knew it and soon so too would the client. And, as much as he wanted them to, the booze and the girls wouldn't make the terror go away. Albert needed to do something to fix the mess that was unfolding before him, outside of the Sea Light. And, for the first time in very, very long time, he didn't know what to do.

Chapter 6: Katherine Has a Plan

Katherine Limeleaf looked out over the stack of purchase orders that lay on her desk. One of the first policies that she had instituted upon her arrival as Chief Operating Officer was to require that her signature be on every PO over $1000. Before she got there, MidContinent Industries had been a fiduciary free-for-all in which waste was as rampant as water was wet. Any manager could and would spend just about any mount of money for anything. The company had twenty-two-year old, third shift managers in Shipping trying to make time with box folding chicks in the Packing Room by taking them to trade shows in Tulsa and charging the expenses back as line items under Professional Development. Thanks to Katherine, such shenanigans were now a thing of the past. Yeah, there was the occasional villainous rumor, such as the story about some guys down in Advertising trying to buy a Harley through a very cooperative media vendor, using twenty PO's of varying amounts not exceeding the $1000 limit, all of which described the nature of the purchase as "sound effect recording." But, for the most part, the $1000 PO limit put everybody and everything where Katherine wanted them: under her mighty, red fingernail polished thumb.

However, controlling purchases was not her most pressing problem today. Her real problem was three letters long, ERP — Enterprise Resource Planning. ERP software is the code that makes the world of very, very big companies go 'round. ERP software controls every aspect of a company's operation — sales, inventory, payroll, purchasing, accounts receivable, accounts payable, supply chain — the whole shooting match. In addition, the software has the ability to tell an executive wanting to be in the know what's going on in the company at any given moment. Want to know if the inventory levels are dangerously low with regard to sales? The software will tell you. Want to know if the last round of raises given to Associate Technical Writers was in line with Human Resource Guidelines? The software will tell you. Want to know if the sales force in Spokane is meeting its weekly quota? The software will tell you. And, in some cases, the software will make suggestions about what to buy, who to hire, how to ship and when to sell.

This software, called in industry parlance *the package*, is big and it is not cheap. Spending ten million US dollars to buy an ERP is not uncommon. And spending another ten million dollars to install and adapt it to work in your company is not uncommon either. In fact, a 1:1 price-implementation cost ratio is getting off cheap. Some companies pay consultants ten times the purchase price of an ERP just to get the goddamn thing to work. More than one C — CEO, COO, CFO, CIO — has ascended to corporate heaven or descended to corporate hell depending on the success of an ERP implementation.

The key factor in bringing Katherine on board as COO at MidContinent was that she had a professed and acknowledged history of successful ERP implementations at other companies. The powers-that-be at MidContinent Industries knew that in order to stay competitive in the vast conglomerate landscape that the company had become, the minutiae of operational details that made up the enterprise had to be unified under a common software system. GM, GE, ADM, IBM, TRW and every other corporate anagram and brand name in the world were going with an ERP. Now it was time for MidContinent to do so as well.

And yet, when it came to ERPs, it was possible to spend money for years without having a working system in place, ending up in the suckered position of having to throw good money after bad just to keep the hope of success alive.

Wall Street actually rated companies on the success or failure of an ERP implementation. (Good implementation=buy. Bad implementation=sell.) The risk of failure was so significant that no current executive at MidContinent was willing to risk life, limb and country club membership to boldly go where no one had gone before. So they had hired Katherine.

Katherine knew that she was not hired because of her arousing good looks, as pleasant as they were to be around. Although the majesty of her appearance had become somewhat faded with time, as happens to even the mightiest of women, she still managed to get more than one set of eye balls to lock onto her when she entered a conference room. But such presence came with a price. She had to spend a little more time on the treadmill to keep her posterior up and a little more effort on the nautilus to keep her breasts up. Her weight was steady and her hair still flowed when she gave that certain, "Today may be the day that I choose you" gesture that she bestowed upon a selected peer at the weekly C meeting.

One of the reasons that Katherine got what she wanted at MidContinent as well as at other companies in the past was that she intimately understood a key feature of being female: when it came to any manifestation of the mating process, it was the female who selected the male that got to plant the seed within that allowed the species to carry on. Thus, within the landscape of the male imperative, Katherine held the trump card. Men really, really like planting seeds and the female got to choose the lucky winner.

Whereas many other females, once becoming executives within the Corporate State, went through a sort of gender transformation in which they assumed the posture and sensibilities of a man forsaking that which was feminine, Katherine, to her benefit, assumed a bi-gender disposition: She sounded like a man but acted like a woman. She knew that ultimately her ability to control lay not in her power to command, but in her power to choose. She could choose policy, she could chose subordinates, she could chose her allies, she could choose her battles just as she could choose her mate.

Katherine rarely, if ever gave a direct command to anyone. She simply chose from among the people and opportunities continuously making themselves available to her. Katherine had it down. Being a feminine, desirable woman was worth the freezer full of Jenny Craig meals and twice a month $150 color and cut visits to Fabian's, the only decent salon in her part of the country.

Hiring Katherine was a safe bet. In the ERP implementation business, you are only as good as your last engagement. Therefore, should she fail, she would never work at MidContinent, or any company with more than 500 employees, again. Her failure would be known industry wide. Within the transcontinental corporate vista, she would be dead, seen but not recognized, known but not wanted. Firing her would be a token act. She would be all washed up anyway.

Killing somebody who is already dead is easy, even for the most spineless of executives. She knew it. They knew it. The execution of her termination would be standard for a person at her level: She'd receive a modest but honorable severance package, enough to open a real estate office somewhere warm.

Risks being what they were, Katherine was well defended. She had a plan. Katherine knew that there were two big unknowns in an ERP implementation: business rules and labor costs. ERP implementations tended to go out of control when business rules — how a job, process or task is actually done, logically and physically — were ill-defined or just plain unknown. If a rule was not crystal clear, then every time a new tweak was discovered, the ERP software had to be rewritten to accommodate it. Hence, a rise in labor cost.

Conversely sometimes a business process was well known and the ERP software just "didn't work that way". In such situations, a series of political battles erupted. One side cried, "We are not going to change the way we do things around here just to satisfy some software." The other side — the programmers — repeated over and over again as if in some sort of drug induced idol-worshiping trance that the ERP software "just doesn't work that way," all the while hoping that the force or annoyance of their chant would make their foes cave in and submit to the will of the software.

Needless to say, the labor clock ran on for the duration of hostilities and the implementation costs kept creeping up and adding up.

But Katherine had a plan. It was simple and twofold: She would control the business rules as Mussolini controlled the train schedules and she would ship almost all the programming labor to India. She'd done it before. She would do it again. Practice makes perfect.

Katherine was the consummate politician for the Corporate State — messianic on the outside, Machiavellian on the inside. Katherine believed that the modern corporation was really just a feudal state with telephones, computers, and subsidized cafeterias. As such, executive power needed to be perceived and executed as though it was the divine right of princes and kings. Being king would be good. But, if she couldn't be king, she needed to be the biggest, baddest princess around.

In order to acquire the power that she needed, Katherine drove the hardest bargain known to man before accepting the job of implementing an ERP at Mid-Continent. Whereas others in her position would have been content to enter Mid-Continent as Chief Information Officer, a relatively new title within the history of the Corporate State, Katherine knew that in reality the CIO was a vassal of the Chief Financial Officer. Therefore, the CIO's interest would never rise above that of the CFO.

Katherine's experience taught her that the only thing that a CFO cared about when it came to an ERP implementation was that the P/L, the profit and loss statements, showed profit. The details were the concern of the CIO. However, the last word was always with the CFO, with the CIO positioned as the scapegoat should the CFO mess up. Katherine knew of more than one instance when a CFO had completely destroyed an implementation out of sheer ignorance and stupidity. Such a fate was not to be hers. When it came to an ERP implementation, the devil was always in the details. There was no easy answer or painless implementation, ever.

Katherine had no intention of serving any CFO. She had done it early on in her career path and learned never to do it again. Since there was no realistic way for Katherine to enter as Chief Executive Officer, the liege lord of the CFO and a position granted only by God and the male-only Board of Directors of MidContinent, the only remaining option was to enter as Chief Operating Officer. In the Corporate State the person in the position of COO was kindred to the likes of Richelieu, Metternich and Bismarck.

The only problem was that MidContinent already had a COO and MidContinent wanted to hire Katherine as CIO. So Katherine did what almost fifty years of experience being a woman on this planet had taught her: She knew that she had the primordial advantage of feminine selection; that as long as she was attractive enough to bring powerful men to her and strong enough to bear what they had to offer, her wish, with a little show of executive cleavage, was their command. She used the power of persuasion, innate to her gender, to get the CEO to appoint the sitting COO to the open position of CIO. And, she did it without so much as a kiss. In the corporate world the promise of tomorrow is always greater than the reality of today.

Yeah, the old COO was pissed as all hell by the new arrangement, but after a couple of meetings in which Katherine turned on the "give me your allegiance and I'll choose you someday" vibe, Walt, the old COO, now new CIO, settled right in. Besides, Walt was fifty-eight years old and the only thing he knew was everybody at

MidContinent. At his age and with his skill set Walt had no place to go. He knew it and Katherine knew it.

Once named COO, Katherine not only had political power second only to the CEO, but all operational power — administrative and budgetary — as well. Katherine literally ran the people, policies and purse of MidContinent on a day-to-day basis. The CEO concerned himself with the big picture. Katherine concerned herself with everything else. Her rules were The Rules.

Having tied down the rules issue, Katherine moved on to the labor problem.

Katherine hated American programmers. Katherine liked Indian programmers. American programmers cost lots of money and liked things such as sick days, vacations, maternity leave, 401K's and company-paid technical training. And they were high maintenance prima donnas.

Indian programmers, on the other hand, cost about a fifth the price of American programmers and didn't know about things such as sick days or vacation time. If they got pregnant, they went home and weren't heard from again. If one needed technical training, he or she was fired and a new programmer with the needed knowledge was hired. They were manna from heaven, albeit manna from a heaven unfathomable to most Americans.

For Katherine and for that which she intended for MidContinent, India and Indian coders were like the North Pole and Santa's elves: a magic place where gifts were made by enchanted people. Every white kid in the world (as well as children of color in the United States, Canada, Mexico and parts of Great Britain) knew that there was a magical place somewhere "up there" in the icy North where Christmas gifts were manufactured. It was a delegation scenario. Nobody could actually get there, except the postman who was charged with delivering wish lists from every boy and girl in Western Civilization, and Santa, who delivered the gifts from the North Pole back to the world at large. That was his job, that and keeping track of who was naughty and nice.

So if Katherine had her way, and there was absolutely no reason why she shouldn't, having the code originate out of India would be like having Christmas originate out of the North Pole: magically wonderful. She would find a business analyst to act as the postman, delivering the wish list of user requirements to the Indian elves, and she, Katherine Limeleaf, would be Santa, delivering nice finished code back to the eagerly waiting throngs of Yuletide revelers at MidContinent. Nobody would actually ever go to India or see an Indian coder, just as nobody gets to go to the North Pole and visit with one of Santa's Elves. It didn't matter anyway. As long as working code showed up everybody would believe in the Magic of Christmas and the power of Katherine Limeleaf.

On the wired planet all things were possible.

The only possibility of disaster was a natural catastrophe such as a typhoon or nuclear explosion on the subcontinent or an unforeseen political miscalculation on Katherine's part here in the States. Katherine knew that she could not control nature or prevent a large-scale technical holocaust. Yet she *could* protect herself from an unforeseen political miscalculation.

So later that morning after authorizing most of the PO's on her desk, Katherine picked up the phone and called her favorite, most reliable, most loyal, most cost effective technical search firm, the Hyde Group, in order to take out an insurance policy.

Chapter 7: Ajita Gets a Call

Ajita looked out over lower Manhattan from the rooftop upon which she engaged in one of her new delights. She was smoking a cigarette.

Almost immediately upon her arrival in New York, New York, Ajita began judiciously and deliberately to acquire those practices, accessories and attitudes that she imagined common to a young woman free in the new world, not subject to the supervision, discretion and protection of a father, brother or husband. The practice of smoking, along with the fact that she wore underwear from Victoria's Secret, and drank the occasional beer, made Ajita feel more removed from her past, that she was on her way to becoming a more permanent fixture in the new scheme of things.

Ajita was not brazen with her practices, accessories and attitudes. When she smoked, she made sure that she did so with private dignity. While others more comfortable in their volition were happy to gather outdoors before the fronts of buildings or in designated smoking areas, demonstrating together as a nefarious, nicotine-dependent cabal, Ajita was content to go off on her own, preferably a rooftop, to savor the liberating moment of each puff and to avoid any semblance of audacity.

She took the same discreet approach with regard to her lingerie. That on a given day she might wear a black lace thong that made her backside appear as smooth as the shell of a soft boiled egg or a red satin bra with under wires that accentuated the cleavage of her breasts and made her nipples protrude slightly out over the cup (as was presently fashionable), for Ajita such information was best left for her sole consideration. Ajitas preferred that she appear to the world of New York, New York, as the typical Indian coder — ill fitted and awkward in wardrobe and language, demur in presentation. Yet as Ajita placed the filter between her lips and took one last drag of the cigarette before flicking it out across the gravel surface of the rooftop, she knew that she was neither ill fitted nor awkward, that her presentation was exactly as she wanted it to be and that in fact she was quite formidable. While all the other code around her was blowing up, the stuff that she wrote worked — consistently, continually and profitably, despite the best efforts of Quality Assurance.

The world of Quality Assurance is a cruel, carnivorous place. The QA tester has not yet been born who does not think that he can break any piece of code, made by any coder, at any time. Within the framework of modern software development, QA testers know themselves to be the last line of defense against the chaos of flawed intentions that any coder will perpetrate upon mankind were his code left unchecked and untested. QA testers believe that all code is crap because all coders are crap, and that it is their duty as well as their God-given right not only to beak the code but to break the coder was well. Coders make code; QA breaks code. When you break the code, you break the coder.

Although the relationship between the two was savage and adversarial, it could not have been any other way. The coders knew it. The testers knew it. The rational mind accepted Darwin a long time ago.

Yet Ajita's code did not break. This is not to say that every QA tester who knew her and knew of her did not try to expose her for the flawed specimen of human thinking that they insisted she be. Ajita had been singled out. She had been subjected to every manual and automatic testing regimen known to the industry. They had even sent her stuff over to Localization to see if they could catch her in Dialogs.

Many foreign coders had met their demise there. Foreign coders were particularly susceptible when it came time to write the simple warning dialogs that prompted a user to do a specific task or risk some sort of user input problem or machine failure. For example, it was not unusual for:

"Your printer is out of paper. Please add more paper:"

to be written as,

"The printer that you bought does not any paper in it to do the task that you require. If you want to continue, please find some paper and refill the machine according to the instructions in your manual."

Foreign coders prided themselves on their mastery of English, favoring verbosity and formality as the yardstick of achievement. Americans just didn't care. Less is best; ad space cost money. So in their desire to demonstrate competence above and beyond the call of duty, the Indians consistently blew up in Dialogs.

But Ajita didn't blow up. She survived and she thrived. She was formidable and almost magically American in her language and, in a way, mysteriously *un*-American in her comportment. She neither required nor demanded any attention whatsoever, for her competence or for her accomplishments. She was content to keep her need for recognition as private as her smoking, beer and underwear. To use American terminology, Ajita was her own best friend.

After finishing her cigarette, Ajita opened the roof door and descended down the stairwell two flights to the twenty-second floor landing. She walked across the landing, past the fire hose on the wall neatly folded like a serpent ready to leap, to the fire door that led onto the main development area. Then she pulled the door open and entered the vast expanse of floor, which housed the bulk of the coding team, and proceeded to the cubicle that she shared with Raji, her cube-mate.

Being a contract programmer and not an employee, Ajita, Raji and those like them were not subject to the OSHA requirements that dictated the minimum square footage that each employee of a company must be allocated as acceptable workspace. Hence the rule of thumb industry-wide seemed to be to pack as many monitors, keyboards, pointing devices and contract programmers into as little floor space as possible.

This current client really knew how to "pack 'em in." Cubes that held one full-time employee held two contract programmers.

Ajita and Raji were considered quite lucky. Sharing a cube was a sign of status, a location that you moved into. Most programmers were folding table coders. Around the floor there were open areas containing configurations of folding tables, ten rows of eight-foot folding tables, three tables placed side by side, a combined width of twenty-four feet. Two programmers sat at each eight-foot table, six programmers to each row, sixty programmers in a configuration that provided sixteen square feet of workspace per programmer, about a third the size of a stall for the average cow. When a contract programmer vacated one of the shared cubes a favored folding table programmer was honored with a promotion to that cube.

Ajita started out as a folding table coder. Within three months she was sharing a cube. Her cube mate, Raji, was a folding table coder for nine months. He had been sharing a cube for a year. Ajita arrived six months into his occupancy.

Raji was in the employ of StarTex from folding table to cube. He thought he was doing well for himself and let Ajita know it on a daily basis. However, Ajita was aware that entry-level clerical workers at this client were assigned, as a matter of company policy, to single cubes the size of which Raji and she shared. This fact that Raji took for real status was an illusion, which was not lost on Ajita. She felt about Raji the way she felt about her brother, another male of marginal talent, always on the lookout for opportunities to advertise his folly.

Ajita cared little if she were at a table or in a cube. The only important consideration for her about the space that she occupied was that she was in a location from which she could get to the roof without attracting any attention. For her, the pleasure of having a cigarette alone was a status infinitely more desirable than sharing a cube.

The phone rang as Ajita entered the cube. Raji answered it, as was the historic protocol of the cube. Raji always answered the phone first. His manhood demanded it.

He picked up the receiver, said a few words and then passed it to Ajita. It was one of the Brothers.

"Hello," said Ajita.

The voice on the other side talked for a while.

"OK" Ajita replied and then hung up.

"What was that about?" asked Raji. Not only was he the first to answer the phone; he believed that his illusionary status entitled him to know the contents and consequence of all of Ajita's telephone conversations.

Ajita replied, "I have been assigned to work in a company named MidContinent Industries in a place called Pleasant Lake, Iowa. I am to be there Monday and I am to bring a warm coat with me."

Chapter 8: Rafael Makes a Change

Rafael Martinez looked out over the night lit parking lot at MidContinent Industries Shipping and Receiving, watching a fierce game of forklift polo. Six Mid-Continent employees — third shift — commandeered six dirty yellow Clark forklifts, three to a side, for possession and control of a cabbage size ball made from wound up adhesive packing tape spray painted phosphorus orange. The drivers used hockey sticks brought from home to knock the ball across the parking lot toward their respective goal nets. The goal nets, large circular cardboard boxes, four feet deep, six feet in circumference, now turned sideways, were used to ship watermelons between field and market. The cardboard boxes, along with the watermelons for which they were made, were a gift to the third shift from a truck driver who had one load too many.

The dirty yellow, propane-powered monsters ran back and forth across the parking lot with their big, tusk-like front forks lifting up and down as if they were great mastodons preparing for primal battle. Every so often one forklift rammed the side of another, turning the assaulted vehicle on to its flank. The collision resulted in a loud thud as the forklift hit the pavement followed by a quick roar of its out-of-control revving engine. Then there was silence. And, as the great dirty yellow beast lay on its side, its driver emerged from the protected seat cage, reeking of beer and bearing the biggest shit-eating grin known to man, a grin that once again reinforced what every warehouse rat at MidContinent knew: third shift was the place to be if you wanted to party and get paid for it.

Rafael got sentimental as he watched the game. When he had worked nights, he too had been a player at Incontinent, the term that the warehouse rats used to reference their employer. But now that he was on days, all Rafael could do was savor the mindless excitement and drunken stupidity that had been an important part of his hourly employment. Of course, working days in Rafael's new line of work meant that he worked all the time — first shift, second shift, third shift — whenever he was needed, which was always.

As one of the forklifts zoomed past, the warehouse rat driving the machine carelessly whacked the ball straight at the loading dock where Rafael was sitting. Rafael caught the cabbage-like projectile with a longing reflex and then threw it back into play among the other forklifts. The offending rat forced his forklift into a fast turn, drove back toward Rafael, arm extended. Rafael extended his arm as well and met the hand of the oncoming driver with his own in a mutual, over-the-head slap known as a High Five. The rat then followed the ball back into the fracas as Rafael continued to watch the game.

Despite the moment of fraternal camaraderie, Rafael was not watching the third shift game as some kid coming back to the neighborhood for a reunion with his street corner buds. Rather, he was just running some reports that would take a while and he needed a break, so he had come down to the docks. That he was working into third shift, well... such is the life of a professional. Rafael had gotten what he asked for. He was getting paid to code.

Rafael's new position, Associate Programmer Analyst, was about as close to his background as a game programmer as a chicken is to a rock. Game programming requires a lot of really hard-to-learn-and-understand skills such as geometry, calculus and statistics, color and light theory, object-oriented analysis and design, and story development — really cool stuff in Rafael's book. All you needed to know to be an Associate Programmer Analyst is how to work a database at a very elementary level and enough programming to write functions for a spreadsheet, both of which are things that his kid brother could do. Oh yeah, another helpful, but not required skill was the ability to take direction without resentment from a crude, mindless moron who has sat in the same chair for the last nine years, has written about three lines of code in his life, all of it twelve years ago while taking his Masters in Information Technology with a specialization in Systems Administration and who doesn't know the difference between COBOL and C++ but is arrogant enough to believe that he can learn either over the weekend from a good book, written by a real IT professional. Such is the world of IT.

IT, Information Technology is the Personal Bodyguard in the Army of the Corporate State. An Associate Programmer Analyst has all the rank and privileges of a buck private, the lowest of all enlisted men. Programmer and Systems Analysts are the Corporals and Sergeants while Senior Programmer Analysts, Tech Leads and Systems Analysts are the lifer Master Sergeants. Project Managers are the Colonels, and Majors, while Business Analysts are the Captains and Lieutenants of the Officer Corp. The CEOs, COOs, et. al are the Generals who plan strategy; the Project Managers devise the tactics to support the strategy, the Business Analysts communicate the tactics and the coders march happily off into battle, keyboard in hand, risking life, limb and neurons to get the job done. At least that's how it's supposed to work. But if Viet Nam taught anybody anything at all, it's this: if you give an enlisted man a gun, some dope and some rock 'n roll and send him on enough idiotic, high-risk missions, it's only a matter of time before he takes his life back into his own hands and frags anybody giving any order he doesn't like. In Rafael's world, the PC was the gun; the code was the dope and the Stones still ruled. Command ain't what it used to be.

After the game ended, Rafael went back up to the second floor, right above the warehouse and returned to his cubicle in IT. The pages of the report were popping out of the top of the laser printer with sixty pages per minute efficiency, sorta like a miniature mechanical volcano spewing forth shards of paper lava. Rafael's supervisor showed up just as the last page of the report hit the catch tray.

"Hi Rafael," said the supervisor.

"Hey," said Rafael.

"I've got some news that you might be interested in."

"Oh?" said Rafael.

"There's a position that has just opened up that I want you to apply for."

"Oh?" said Rafael again.

"The position is titled, 'Project Specialist.' The guys doing the ERP implementation need someone from IT to work with the curry-head consulting company that's been brought in to do the nuts and bolts coding".

"Will *I* be coding?" asked Rafael.

"Well, it's really not a coding job, per se. The person taking the job will need to learn the package at a pretty detailed level so that the curry-head coders from the consulting company can make the required changes properly. It's sort of a project support type of job," said the supervisor. The supervisor was a bigoted man.

"I don't know. I'd really rather be coding."

The supervisor paused a moment before continuing.

"Rafael, look — you've been programming for us for about a year now. You're very good at it. But the way things are going, I think that you'll do better for yourself and for us if you think beyond programming. You're a pretty talented guy. I mean, do you want to be coding when you're in your forties? Besides the company really needs you there. You don't want the curry-heads to be running everything, do you?"

Rafael looked up from his monitor and said, "Hey, I really appreciate the suggestion. But I really like to code. It's OK with me if I don't move up the corporate ladder. As long as I am coding, things are cool."

Rafael's supervisor gave him a look a little more serious than solicitous. "Rafael, I like you. You get the job done. You give a hundred-and-ten per cent and you don't cause any problems. You're a team player. Look, I'm going tell you something that is very confidential. If you repeat it, I will deny ever having said it."

The supervisor continued, "There are changes coming for me and for all of us.

"I want you to do something for me. Stand up right now and take a look around."

Rafael got up out of his workstation chair and looked over his cubicle half-walls at the large expanse of floor that housed two hundred other cubicles, each occupied by a programmer. He sat down and looked up at his supervisor.

His supervisor kept going. "You see all the coders on this floor? In a year's time, none of them will be here, not a one. If you don't apply for the Project Specialist position and take it when it's offered to you, and it will be offered to you, then your fate will be the same as everybody else on this floor. You'll be gone."

Rafael glared into his monitor, trying to make sense of what he was being told. All the coders gone? The information was high impact, like a tidal wave: it came fast, leveled all in its path, and then left the destruction for others to clean up. Rafael was about to respond when his supervisor interrupted him.

"And, Rafael, I am serious about the confidentiality thing; nobody is to know. If this news leaks out, and even if you did not make the leak, I know two meat packers down in production who will be in real trouble. And, they both have a son named, Rafael. Get it?"

The next morning before going up to his cube, Rafael Martinez, Associate Programmer Analyst, stopped by the Human Resources office and applied for the newly posted position of Project Specialist, job reference: IT0909453-2.

Chapter 9: Albert Leaves Town

Albert Shulberg, a.k.a. "`BigDick6969`" looked out over the multi-colored rows of cars in the Rent-a-Car parking lot situated on the outskirts of the Magic Kingdom. The cars were arranged in Dr. Seuss fashion: There were red ones, blue ones, yellow ones, green ones. big ones, small ones, mid-size ones, dream ones.

Albert had a lot of cars from which to choose. His Rent-a-Car Platinum Membership allowed him to go to any car he wanted and just drive it off the lot. All he had to do was present the Platinum card to the guard at the gate and after a swipe of the card through the bar code reader, off he'd go. The machines behind the reader would take care of pairing Albert to the car.

However, as euphoric as it is to take a car on whim, today such freedom of choice was not a privilege that Albert really cared about that much. He would have taken a stripped down Escort without any air, power brakes and power windows as long as it went forward at a minimum speed of sixty miles per hour and only required refueling every three hundred miles. And he would have paid cash as well as filled out the rental form in as much detail as necessary. He would even have waited in line to be called "Next", just as long as he got a car.

Albert had missed the last flight out and was in a hurry to get to his next arranged flight, at the next available airport. Things were fucked in the Magic Kingdom. It was time to go as fast as the next, most available piece of transportation would take him.

The cause of Albert's problems was key chains, along with salt-and-pepper shakers, shot glasses, place mats, mouse pads, refrigerator magnets and tee shirts of various sizes, colors, styles and quality. The Magic Kingdom sold a lot of them as little pieces of branded memorabilia that would one day turn up on eBay or as intergeneration bric-a-brac generously bestowed upon an unsuspecting niece at some attendee's will reading.

Normally a high sales volume is a desirable thing for the Corporate State. Citizenship within the Corporate State is determined by what you buy, not where you live. Thus, more sales translate into more citizens, which is a good thing.

As desirable as a high sales volume usually is, in the Magic Kingdom selling a lot of key chains, et. al., was a problem — the more they sold, the less money they made. The freight cost of getting the souvenirs from the hundreds of distributors to the thousands of retail centers throughout the Kingdom was eating into the profit margin faster than a fat man at a State Fair pie eating contest. If the trend continued, the Magic Kingdom would end up paying its customers to take the stuff off its hands. In the Corporate State, you can't pay your citizens to be citizens for a very long time. Paying out a short time to get market share, you can do, but for a long time, no way José. At some point, tribute needs to be paid. The Magic Kingdom didn't plan on engaging in an extended period of loss leadership. It sort of came up out of nowhere and had to be addressed quickly, as in yesterday, so to speak. So the powers-that-be in the Magic Kingdom decided to do the wise thing. They decided to call in a consultant.

The rule of thumb at the Magic Kingdom was that if you have a really big problem that comes with a high degree of political risk and you want it to go away fast, you call in a consultant. The worst thing that will happen is that you will have some egg on your face for making a bad short-term hiring decision, which is a whole lot better than having someone find out that you are a technical nincompoop. Besides, the benefit of having someone to blame long after the culprit is gone is worth the egg-covered face.

The task of finding the right consultant was delegated down and about through the various layers of management and supervision within the Magic Kingdom for about a week and finally ended up with a call to the Hyde Group. The Hyde Group in turn contacted Albert for a finder's fee of $10,000, refundable in thirty days if Albert didn't work out. Thus began the association of system architect Albert Shulberg and the Magic Kingdom. Albert was hired as a 1099 contractor.

Albert worked under the rules of Federal Tax Form 1099. He billed the Magic Kingdom his $1500 a day directly, every two weeks. They cut him a check for that amount, usually within forty-five days without any taxes withheld. It was Albert's responsibility to pay taxes on a quarterly basis to the Fed, which he did after he took every deduction to which he and his certified public accountant thought he was entitled. He deducted his automobile lease, his motorcycle lease, sixty per cent of the mortgage of his three-thousand-square-foot loft condominium that he never saw and health club membership that he never used, his computers, his home theater, DVD rentals and CD purchases, his entertainment trips to the tittie bars, visits to his therapist and psycho-pharmacologist, anything which he and his certified public accountant could justify as a reasonable business expense for a consultant in his line of work. That his line of work happened to be anything he was doing at the moment was of great benefit.

This is not to say that Albert was a con on the make for a corporate sucker. Quite the contrary: Albert was a very good Systems Architect. System Architecture is the sausage making of software development. It's not a pretty profession and few people can do it well. You take a whole lot of outdated systems and poorly designed programs that were never intended to do what the current need requires and mix them together with a good amount of technical skill and a credible amount of marketing mumbo jumbo, the result of which is that you've taken yesterday's source of disappointment and frustration and made it into today's testament for exemplary software — something from which the client will derive value and for which you will get a very big, fat check.

At least that's the way it's supposed to work and usually does, except in the Magic Kingdom. The keychain fiasco was a whack out of nowhere, even for Albert who is accustomed to handling all sorts of weirdness within the Corporate State.

The Magic Kingdom was a textbook case of growth run amok by way of decentralized initiative. Somewhere along the line, as if by divination, the phrase, "frontline empowerment," became the Concept of the Day glaring from the top page of the Daily Calendar for Inspiration and Leadership that sat on the desktop of every executive in the realm. Delivered with benevolent decree, the new mission of the company became to push as much decision-making down to the lowest levels of management as fast as possible. Whether the reasoning behind the initiative was based on sound business practice or cowardly self-preservation is still, to this day, a hot topic of conversation in business class seats throughout the friendly skies. Yet, where inspiration leads, implementation and its trusty sidekick, action items, follow. Frontline empowerment became the action item of the day, the week, the quarter.

Buying key chains, et. al., became chaos. In a matter of months, every retail center in the Kingdom was buying key chains, et. al., from wherever it wanted to, when it wanted to. Because all the retail centers were selling a whole lot of key chains, et. al., fast, the stock needed to be replenished quickly. Delivery time became just as important as price, so much so that the distributors figured out that they could seemingly sell stuff at really low prices yet turn around and whack the retail center with increased handling charges on overnight delivery. For the vendors, it was shipping and handling nirvana. For the Magic Kingdom, it was a supply chain nightmare (no pun intended).

This is what Albert had to make better. So he had done what all consultants do when faced with a significant amount of systemic change: He arranged an executive retreat. Albert knew that an executive retreat would be about as technically useful as inviting the Joint Chiefs of Staff to a geisha house. However, it would give him an opportunity to get to know the political interests, emotional desires and inebriation habits of the major players, as well as an opportunity to create some interpersonal debts which he could pocket and then call in at a later date as favors when it suited his political purpose.

So there was Albert sitting in the bar at the retreat resort, surrounded by the powers-that-be from the various fiefdoms of the Magic Kingdom, looking and sounding really smart but not at all threatening like those other guys in IT with their technical jargon and pocket protectors.

Then he delivers the goods. He pulls the cocktail napkin out from under his Mai Tai and there on the cocktail napkin Albert diagrams the solution to the whole problem — tah dah! Needless to say the executives are really impressed because, even though they are "not technical," they get it. At least they think that they do. Anyway, no one will question Albert or discuss the matter with others because no matter what, not one of the executives on the retreat, as brilliant as he may be in many other areas of the Magic Kingdom, can admit to being clueless on matters of the software that runs his world. Such a revelation would be as devastating as Charlemagne admitting to anybody but his most trusted scribes that he could not read. A prince must always appear to be princely, regardless of the content of his character, the breadth of his cognition, or lack thereof. The State depends on it.

Albert's plan was quite simple and pretty standard in the world of distribution schemes. He sold and the Magic Kingdom bought the idea to build a Central Purchasing Facility. All retail centers would send in orders to the Central Purchasing Facility, which in turn would aggregate the orders into bulk purchases made from selected vendors. In turn the vendors would ship orders of significant size back to the Central Purchasing Facility, which then would send the smaller orders onto each retail center. The fact that the smaller orders would be sent via the same express carrier that had been moving goods all along was somewhat comical but operationally incidental. The profit was in eliminating the cost of handling, a seemingly small amount that had mushroomed to the size of Godzilla.

The most significant problem was getting the order information between the retail centers and the Central Purchasing Facility and then subsequently between the Central Purchasing Facility and the vendor. The fact that the idea of a Central Purchasing Facility was against every precept of "frontline empowerment" was completing ignored. In the world of Systems Architecture, today's obsolete system was yesterday's good idea, sort of like asking a woman who is on her fifth husband why she married the first: "It seemed like a good idea at the time."

The current idea was not brain surgery and, as such, should have worked with no problem at all. But it didn't. Why? Because the retail center grunts didn't want it to, that's why. They liked talking to the vendors and the vendors liked talking back. Albert and the powers-that-be at The Magic Kingdom had underestimated the power and allure of simple human interaction, from Monday morning bullshitting to the continuous pursuit of coital congress.

Albert had wanted to put a piece of software in place that would magically monitor cash register transactions to figure out how much in the way of key chains, et. al., were being sold. Then when inventory levels became too low, that same software would call up Central Purchasing to talk to its software in order to replenish stock. Then once the Central Purchasing software aggregated the small orders from the retail centers into the One Big Order, that software would select the best Vendor of the Moment — the guy with the best price and the best delivery turn-around. The Best Vendor of the Moment's software would be called and the Big Order would be placed. This was the system that was to propagate throughout the entire supply chain, express carriers included. It was a highly efficient system that would pay for itself in eighteen months. However, it was also a highly efficient system that you couldn't argue with, share today's misery with, or ask out on a date.

It turned out that there were hundreds of meaningful relationships of every kind going on between purchase agents at the retail centers and order takers on the vendor end. It was sort of a fringe benefit to doing business. You had romances of every sexual and asexual proclivity emerging. You had investment clubs forming, with the latest insider stock tips going back and forth. You had a robust Mary Kay network in play, not to mention a thriving marijuana exchange. A microcosm of human enterprise had grown within the substrata of the Magic Kingdom's retail centers. The vendors knew it. The retail centers knew it. But the powers-that-be at the Magic Kingdom were in complete denial.

In order to preserve this new community, the purchasing agents at the retail centers and order takers at the various vendors conspired to make the system not work. No matter how random and void of purpose an organization may be, all live to survive. No organization, organic, systemic or mechanical wants to die. Individual members within the organization might want to die, but the raison d'être of all organizations is survival, to stay in business.

En masse the retail center-vendor community just said no! The software interfaces were never fully implemented. The cash registers talked only to themselves. The vendors' systems always seemed to be down. Human intercourse continued to flourish in its myriad of manifestations. Machine-to-machine exchange went nowhere.

Like beta-max videotape and fuel-efficient cars, Albert's idea was one that everyone liked and no one wanted to use. The project went on for six months, cost over a million bucks, and had nothing to show for it except a Central Purchasing facility in disarray. And for Albert the real gut-wrenching tragedy was that the fucking software worked! But nobody used it no matter how hard the powers-that-be at the Magic Kingdom threatened. Freud and the Beatles had it right. In the human experience there is love and work and of the two, all you need is love.

The rule of thumb kicked in. Albert was the consultant. Like Isaac, the son of Abraham, executive retreat or no executive retreat, Albert was taken to the corporate altar for sacrifice, only God didn't step in at the last minute. Albert was fired and the Hyde Group was sued despite the thirty-day clause. Albert was sued, too. The Magic Kingdom wanted the $10K finders fee back from the Hyde Group and three million dollars back from Albert, treble damages for the cost of the system architecture he created and inflicted upon them.

Luckily Albert had errors and omissions insurance, which is sort of like malpractice insurance for geek-heads. But, given the dollar size of the claim, Albert's insurance company was as panic stricken as he was. The whole mess was going to take a long while to figure out and once the lawyers got into the act costs were going to skyrocket. As a precaution, the insurance company asked Albert to leave the Magic Kingdom with all due haste and never to return.

Albert was back on the streets again, with a $1500 a day lifestyle, a very bad reference and in need of enough cash to make his monster go. So he called the Hyde Group. Yeah, they had a gig for him. It paid about $7000 a week, good money, considering it was the Midwest, almost New York rates, almost as much as he needed. If he wanted it, he needed to be in the God-fearing Midwest by 8:30 AM the next morning and he needed to wear a tie.

Albert hung up the phone, packed his stuff and took a cab to the airport only to miss the last flight out. But the next airport over had a flight that left in three hours. He had time to make it if he didn't dawdle.

So Albert did what was natural for him. He chose the green Lexus, fully loaded.

Chapter 10: Frank Throws in the Towel

Frank DiGrazia looked out over the debris of parts that used to be a very expensive, very high end PC and with exasperated resolve began to reassemble the machine that brought him and his family so many hours of learning, creativity and fun. It also brought Frank a sense of structure, competence and wellbeing that he desperately needed in his life. Unbeknownst to most, Frank was a geek with a preference for hardware — the latest hardware, the fastest hardware, the cutting edge stuff. Frank prided himself on the fact that the box had not been built that he could not master.

So when his kid came to him complaining that everything was hung, that he could not play his favorite computer game, Mind Voyager featuring Iron Maiden, the exquisitely rendered, big breasted, high definition, virtual female babe who was the object of every thirteen-year-old boy's joystick controlled worship and desire, it was natural that Frank responded with a promise of paternal technical support that he made often, but delivered upon only once in a while. Yet, in this instance, Frank promised to look at the machine tonight after dinner, which he did.

Finally at 3 a.m. Frank threw in the towel. The machine was winning. No matter now much he tried, he couldn't get the machine to boot all the way up. It just hung at the brink of consciousness never to become fully awake.

Frank did the hardware assembly just fine. He got the video card, sound card and memory sticks properly seated into their respective slots without a hitch. All drive cables were new and properly connected. The machine saw the mouse, keyboard and other peripherals upon start up. The operating system even loaded, sort of, until it started trying to do the Internet dialup, then, wham, the machine went comatose. It just hung, displaying the mouse pointer arrow icon against a sky blue background.

Frank was at the end of his rope and the machine was one step from the window. Logical troubleshooting required that Frank start replacing parts one by one and reconfiguring the operating system after each part replacement, a process that took about fifteen minutes per part. This was going to take a long time: one part switched out, reconfigure the software, another part switched out, reconfigure the software, and so forth and so on to the exponential value that was mathematically possible given the number of parts available to replace. And even then there was no guarantee that the problem was going to be solved.

Some days computer repair relied solely on random magic and virgin sacrifice. Frank hoped that tomorrow would be one of those days.

So for tonight, Frank pulled the plug on the machine, turned out the light in his home office and went upstairs to bed. Mind Voyager would have to wait. Frank needed as much rest as he could get because the next day he was to begin the second day of work at his new position within the IRS. After years of exemplary service, Frank had been transferred from interviews to audits. Frank no longer spent his day in a little cubicle nickel-and-diming two-bit payment plans from taxpayers with form letter in hand. He was now in the land of audits, fines, liens and seizures. Now he was in a cubicle that was a lot bigger, in which he was the sole occupant. Now he was going after the creeps.

As he put his head to the pillow, Frank reflected upon his current case, a filing with a whole lot of 1099 income and a pattern of suspicious deductions. The taxpayer in question was one Albert Shulberg. As Frank drifted into unconsciousness, he rested easy knowing that troubleshooting Albert Shulberg was going to be a whole lot easier than troubleshooting the machine downstairs. Creeps, unlike machines, always made mistakes.

Chapter 11: Connie Gets Off

Connie looked out over the top of her computer monitor into the WebCam that lay atop her system, shed her clothes and turned herself into a piece of full motion video about the size of four good-sized postage stamps arranged in a two-by-two square. Connie was enterprise incarnate. She worked at home, set her own hours and was her own boss. She answered to no one but the WebCam atop and the monitor below. Her only operating expense was the cable bill that allowed her to connect her choppy little image to the Internet and spew it throughout the universe. The wired planet made all things possible. Were Connie a member of Junior Achievement, she would have made them proud.

Connie's little enterprise had started just after high school. Right after graduation she got a job working lunches downtown at Giorgio's Italian-American Restaurant while Rafael was working nights at MidContinent. Working at Giorgio's was OK. It paid her part of the rent and provided her life with the structure and social context she required to move forward in the day, which was good because Connie knew that people needed this sort of structure. But, on the whole, working at Giorgio's was a drag — it didn't get her off. Rafael got her off, big time! But he worked nights. The only time she got to see him was on weekends and once in a while on weeknights, for about an hour after he got home and before she went to bed. So on weekends she got off on Rafael big time, but during the week all she had was Giorgio's and Stacy.

Connie and Stacy were high school lesbians. They started playing around with each other senior year as a way to get off while their boyfriends were off drinking or doing their geek shit. Being lesbians turned out to be fun. Where in the past it was taboo, today there was little shame to it. Lots of their girl friends in Pleasant Lake were lesbians and had boyfriends too, just like Connie and Stacy. It was just like what you saw on MTV.

Connie's older sister used to be a lesbian, but at around twenty-two she decided to get married. Now she has two kids: a girl and a boy.

Connie didn't know how long she was going to be a lesbian with Stacy. She would hang with Stacy for a while or until she and Rafael got married. But with Rafael and his geek shit, marriage was going to be a long, long time coming.

Anyway, one day she and Stacy were hanging around after school in her basement. They weren't playing around or anything, they were just hanging out and watching soap opera reruns on videotape. Stacy mentioned that her cousin was making some good money on the Internet. Her boyfriend had set it up. The boyfriend found this company that paid girls to sit in front of a WebCam naked and get themselves off. You didn't have to see anybody, let alone touch them. All you had to do was sit at your desk or in your bedroom and get off. And for this, the company paid you $25 an hour. Once in a while you had to type some stuff into a keyboard to talk to the guys and girls who were looking at you, but that was it. You got naked, got off and typed into a keyboard. At the end of the week a check showed up in your mailbox. It was easy. She said that her cousin was making about $500 a week!

That night Connie called Stacy's cousin's boyfriend and got the email address of the company that did the WebCam stuff. Within a week a package containing a WebCam and CD was on her doorstep. Rafael helped her install the stuff. He assumed that Connie got the WebCam to keep in touch with her parents, her sister and her sister's kids, being that Connie came from a very close family and all — three sisters, a brother. Her mother and father were still married. The fact that they all lived in Pleasant Lake didn't make Rafael a bit suspicious. On the wired planet, all things were possible. WebCams were like modern telephones.

It took Connie about a week to get the hang of things. After the first check showed up from the WebCam company, Connie cut back on working lunches at Giorgio's to three days a week. She liked having a reason to get out of the house. Yet in the privacy of the office that she and Rafael had set up in the spare bedroom of their apartment, Connie was living the American Dream: She was getting paid to get off without selling her body to anyone. The only thing she was selling was a two-postage-stamp by two-postage-stamp, full motion video image of herself with her clothes off, getting off.

But change was in the air. Now Rafael was working days. Connie wasn't quite sure what Rafael would do when he found out that his girlfriend spent her evening hours in front of the computer with her clothes off, getting off. He might like it or he might freak. Anyway, Connie was in no hurry to give up the WebCam business, nor was she in a hurry to give up Rafael. As hard as things were getting, she decided to do nothing, for the time being anyway. Besides, Rafael was working more hours than he ever had. For now, things were cool.

So, for today, Connie turned her head up, lowered her hand down and, as she began to get off, thought with a small degree of melancholy that some days it was easier just being a lesbian.

Chapter 11: Connie Gets Off

Part 2: Bondage

Chapter 12: Ajita Has a Meeting

Ajita took hold of Rafael's neck, spread her legs wide and lifted herself across his lap. She lifted her dress up to her waist, moved the crotch of her Victoria's Secret string panties aside and put his exposed penis way up inside of her. It was a quick, face to face, silent effort. Rafael was in utter amazement. This was not the design session that he had expected when he penciled in the date in his Franklin Planner.

Manfred sat in the corner of the meeting room watching.

Ajita had been at MidContinent two weeks, sharing a cubicle with another consultant, reviewing code. She was pretty much left to herself to get up to speed on the project. "Getting up to speed" involved little more than sitting in front of a computer monitor looking through the pile of code that was supposed to be the customer transfer module for the Big System. The code was boring in its redundancy. But Getting Up to Speed was part of the assimilation process known as Coming on Board. Coming on Board and Getting up to Speed were important items in the Project Plan.

In Ajita's world, the Project Plan was all. The Project Plan listed work to be done, work completed, task assignment, labor costs, delivery dates, missed dates, project impacts and about any other piece of information that was necessary to assure that a project would be delivered on time and on budget, which it just about never was. All items in the Project Plan were sacrosanct, to be executed with all due diligence and sincerity. If an item was ignored, then the project ran the risk of missing dates and incurring cost overruns, which it almost always did. The fact that projects with Project Plans seemed to fail just about as much as projects without Project Plans did was somewhat irrelevant. The customer demanded Project Plans. Project plans provided a sense of safety as well as evidence of control and competence. Nobody ever got fired for creating a bad Project Plan. People got fired for *not* following a bad Project Plan.

So Ajita did as hundreds of consultants before her had done: she reviewed the code that she was to inherit. That the code was under-documented was typical. It seemed as if the developers who had created it were confronted with the usual set of pressures that go with any coding project that had a ten-thousand-dollar-a-day aggregate burn rate: get the code out fast and make sure that it sorta works.

Thus, in order to meet the daily production pressures, very little descriptive comments were included inline in the code. If a developer could get header comments written that indicated who wrote the code and an overall description of what the code was supposed to do, he or she was in good shape. Commenting code took a lot of time, however, and properly commenting code so that it could be understood easily took even more time. In the world of ten-thousand-dollars-a-day aggregate burn rate, such time was a luxury. The Project Manager told the developers to get the code into production first and then go back and do the commenting.

Of course, the developers never got a chance to go back. There was too much pressure to go forward. So part of Ajita's forward movement was to figure out, by reading through thousands of lines of computer language code, what had been going on in the minds of the developers who were supposed to have gone back and commented their work in order to make things clear in the first place. Ajita felt as if she was in multidimensional time, going backwards and forwards simultaneously.

After a week Ajita got enough of a grip on the code to start working with it. She told the Project Manager that she was ready to go. The Project Manager set up a meeting to introduce her to the development team. Rafael was the Project Specialist assigned to the project. In addition, there was a Database Administrator (a.k.a. DBA), a Business Analyst named Bridget and two supporting consultants, one of whom was Ajita. Ajita would be writing the code that manipulated the data that was kept in a database.

The Project Manager thought that it would be a good idea for the DBA, Rafael and Ajita to get together "off line" in order for her to get to know the database better. Rafael had been working with it for a while and with Ajita being a new team member, Rafael could give her some pointers. The DBA, some guy named Manfred who spent the meeting playing with his PalmPilot, agreed to show up wherever Rafael and Ajita decided, but that he "would only stay a few minutes. I have some other projects that need attention, too!"

Rafael and Ajita agreed to a meeting time and location, and penciled the meeting information into their respective Franklin Planners. Manfred asked them to request his presence electronically using the company-wide online calendaring system.

Ajita expected the meeting to be usual — meet Rafael, learn the ERD (Entity Relationship Diagram, the picture that described the structure of the database) and pay homage to the DBA.

Homage to the DBA by application developers is a standard ritual in the world of software development. DBA's like to think of data, *their data*, as being the raison d'être for all software development known to man; that the reason for any software application is to do no more than allow puny, unworthy and incompetent end users to interact with the invoices, credit card transactions, airline reservations and criminal records that their databases create, update and delete. DBA's believe that they are God, creating, maintaining and destroying the most vital part of the world of information technology at whim.

And to most people, particularly CFOs, DBA's *are* God and must be granted all respect and accommodation due to God. The executive has not been born who does not go bananas when deprived of the daily reports that feed their decision-making process. These reports are made from the DBA's data and are bestowed upon executives by DBA's in very much the same manner that the Ten Commandments were bestowed upon Moses by God. Without the DBA to intercede between the database and the executive, the world is a barbaric chaos.

So Ajita went to do her "meet and greet" with Rafael and Manfred the DBA. And then Ajita had the Epiphany. For reasons she understood, yet could not explain, Ajita knew that the next step in her life was to connect two seemingly disparate points in time and space with one overwhelming gesture from which there was no going back.

So she did.

When she entered the conference room, Rafael was standing before the conference table perusing the large schematic of the database that lay on it. Ajita walked over and placed herself between the table and Rafael. She put her hand to his chest and gave him a gentle push back into one of the conference table chairs that lined the perimeter of the table. Rafael's eyes went wide and his heart jumped as he sat back in the chair. Without saying a word, Ajita unzipped the fly of his trousers, placed her hands inside and fished about for his penis. After negotiating the obstruction of his underpants — plaid boxers she discovered — she found what she was looking for.

After getting Rafael into her, Ajita ran the show. Rafael took to Ajita the way a bee takes to a flower. He had no choice but to pollinate her. It was his nature. The fact that Manfred, an earlier arrival, was sitting in the corner of the room unknown and unannounced to Ajita, was of surprisingly little concern for Rafael. Manfred's presence was just an added element in the scenario, which was way beyond the conceivable. To Manfred the episode unraveling before him was just another thing to watch.

And so they fucked. After a few minutes of heavy breathing, hard kissing, with lots of tongue action and tight, athletic embraces, a mutual climax was reached.

Ajita sat on Rafael's lap for a few moments casually observing him from her dominant position. Rafael sat back in the conference room chair with his hands on Ajita's hips and his eyes closed trying to assign some understanding to the reality he had just experienced.

Ajita waited for her heartbeat and breathing to return to her normal, non-coital rate. When her observable vital signs returned to normal, she got off of Rafael's lap, adjusted her underwear and then her dress. She straightened her hair.

Satisfying herself as best she could that she looked presentable enough to get to the women's toilet without attracting attention, she left the conference room as she had entered it, quietly and directly.

Rafael put his penis back into his trousers and zipped his fly shut. He went over to the conference table and folded the database schematic to a size manageable for easy transport back to his desk. Manfred went back to playing with his PalmPilot. No words were shared between them.

Upon arriving at his desk, he sat down in his chair and opened his Franklin Planner. Rafael was terrible with names. He rarely, if ever, remembered the names of people with whom he met for the first time. The attendee of his last meeting was named, Ajita Orhtihawamein. He could not pronounce the last name, so he concentrated on remembering the first, Ajita.

Chapter13: Albert Takes a Drive

Albert Shulberg, a.k.a. "`BigDick6969`," took hold of the steering wheel with both hands in a desperate attempt to avoid smacking head on into the highway exit sign before him. It was no use. The rental car continued to move forward beyond his control.

Luckily Albert remembered some rule from some long ago Driver's Ed class that said if you have lost control of the steering in a skid, just let go, the car will come to its senses. So Albert let go of the wheel for a moment, just enough time for the car to come to it senses and avoid hitting the sign head on. The vehicle sideswiped one of the steel poles that held up the highway sign, which resulted in the loss of its left rear view mirror.

The car came to stop in a ditch that ran along the side of the road. Albert opened the car door and got out. The still falling snow was thigh deep, covering his black Johnson and Murphy shoes and dampening the trousers of his gray Brooks Brothers suit, the standard System Architect interview/meeting attire. It was dark, it was cold and the snow continued to fall. Albert was in the middle of nowhere, with no cell phone, no warm clothes and no way to get back to his hotel. Then the thought occurred to him: If someone did not come by to get him within the next few hours, he was going to die — alone in the snow, in the cold, in his black Johnson and Murphy shoes and his gray Brooks Brothers suit.

The snow came out of nowhere — BAM! It was if God had, on whim, decided to dump fourteen inches of it on the interstate, just to see what Albert would do. What had started out as a pleasant drive in a cold, bright Midwestern winter day had, upon return trip, turned into a catastrophe in a blinding blizzard.

A few hours earlier Albert had been at the airport renting a car to take the one hour trip north through Iowa farmland to MidContinent Industries in order to have a meeting/interview with Katherine Limeleaf, the company's COO. Katherine was in desperate need of a Systems Architect to repair an ERP implementation that was off-schedule and over-budget.

Although it was the middle of winter and the temperature was a little below zero, the drive was nice enough. The snow lay over the barn-and-cow-dotted countryside giving the surrounding landscape the feel of a benevolent Siberia. Albert needed to wear his Magic Kingdom sunglasses in order to see. The white of the snow made bright by the sun sitting in a cloudless blue sky was blinding.

Once in downtown Pleasant Lake, Albert followed the signs from the center of the town and drove another ten minutes to the Pleasant Lake Country Club. The meeting with Katherine was scheduled to take place over lunch in the Club House restaurant. Albert entered the building, walked past the Pro Shop, open but empty of customers, toward the hostess podium at the restaurant's entrance. Albert told the hostess, a portly blonde woman in her mid-forties with the name *Phyllis* engraved into her Pleasant Lake Country Club nametag, that he was here for a meeting with a Ms. Katherine Limeleaf.

Phyllis led Albert into the main dining room, past a myriad of tables. Each table was set with a white linen cloth and full table service. None of the tables had any diners seated at them, save one table by the window that looked out onto the eighteenth hole green, which was covered with snow and void of golfers. Katherine Limeleaf sat at the table looking out of the window that ran from floor to ceiling.

She stood as Albert approached. When Albert arrived, she extended her right hand to greet him. Albert accepted her hand and shook it cordially. In another lifetime, he would have kissed it. Katherine invited Albert to sit.

Phyllis gave Katherine and Albert the menus that she had brought with her from the hostess podium at the entrance to the dining room. Once the menus were delivered, *Phyllis* asked if there was anything that either of them wanted from the bar. Albert ordered a ginger ale with lemon. Katherine ordered iced tea. *Phyllis* said that she would be back in a few minutes with their drinks and left them to their privacy.

The conversation continued like this:

Katherine: How was your drive?

Albert: Good. Lovely country out here.

Katherine: Have you been to the Midwest before?

Albert: A few years ago, Chicago, to do some work with the Mercantile Exchange.

Katherine: Pleasant Lake is a little different than Chicago.

Albert: It seems nice enough.

Katherine: Yes it is.

Phyllis returned with the drinks. Both Katherine and Albert took a sip of their respective beverages. The conversation continued.

Albert: Have you been here long?

Katherine: I came out here about a year ago to facilitate the ERP implementation. It was around the time that MidContinent started engaging in a number of strategic acquisitions. They were bringing on companies faster than they could assimilate them. None of the IT systems fit. We had all these companies and no way to integrate data. Getting out a simple P and L was a nightmare. There was still a lot of hand workarounds being used to fix shortcomings among the systems. Wall Street took notice. The company's stock began to drop. The analysts said that without a unified system, we would implode. Our sales were great, but our business systems were too inefficient. The software infrastructure was killing us. So they got me, and here I am.

I spend most of my time at the office, so I don't really get to take advantage of all that Pleasant Lake has to offer. It's just as well. Between you and me, Pleasant Lake doesn't offer that much. When it gets warmer I plan to come here and play a few rounds. Do you golf?

Albert: I used to, more than I do now. Sort of lost interest in it over the years.

Katherine: Too bad.

Albert: Yes, in a way it is. I miss the relaxation.

Katherine: I hope that I am not insulting your intelligence or expertise by telling you this. In a way I feel as if I am preaching to the choir.

Albert: No, not at all. Please continue. This is good information.

Katherine: I get here and the first thing I find out is that my predecessors have already committed to an ERP, contracts are signed, consultants in place. The ERP is not bad, but it is not good, either. The various business units that make up Mid-Continent require the ERP to be customized — nothing unusual in the history of ERP implementation, so nothing to get excited about. But I snoop around and discover that things are more broken than I thought them to be. The amount of customization required is considerable. But, by this time, MidContinent has spent well over two million dollars and is under considerable pressure from Wall Street to get the thing on line.

It might not look like it, but even though Pleasant Lake is not a thriving metropolis, in the world of agricultural products, MidContinent is a very big player worldwide. So I have a decision to make: Start all over and go through the process of implementing a new ERP — you know, needs analysis, product evaluation, attending numerous sales presentations and other dog-and-pony shows. To start over would take at least a year, a year that we really do not have.

Or, do I take what we have, fix it and move forward at the same time?

The big problem with fixing a bad system is labor cost. The programmers have to learn the existing code, implement the new changes and not break anything that already works. It's like playing pickup sticks. Make one bad move and you break the whole thing. In no time you have one set of coders fixing problems that exist and another set of coders fixing problems that the first set of coders made. Things can spiral out of control fast.

Albert: Yes, I know your situation. I've seen it happen many, many times before.

Katherine: At the time I got here, getting the system up and running, or at least getting Wall Street to believe that we were getting the system up and running, was the priority — expense be damned. Time was more important than money. Our ability to raise money to continue the acquisitions relied upon the perceived success of the implementation. The banks would only continue to finance us if the Wall Street analysts kept giving our stock "Buy" ratings. And "Buy" ratings were directly connected to the ERP.

However, that was then and this is now.

The acquisition craze is over. Our internal financing is settled for a while and we have a system that is not working. Fixing it may no longer be an option. We may need to bite the bullet and start over.

Albert: I see.

Katherine: Which is why you are here, Mr. Shulberg.

Albert: Call me Albert, please.

Katherine: Albert, we need to have someone take a fresh look at our systems, someone with both custom development and package configuration experience. We need someone to look over all the systems among our acquisitions, to make a report on what we have, and then, once we have an idea what is going on, we need someone to help us find the right solution.

You come very highly recommended by the Hyde Group. And I have read your articles in *The Systems Architecture Journal*. You obviously know your stuff. We are a bit lost and we need someone to help us find our way. We think this "fresh look" will take about three to six months, and if you can come up with a good solution, we will probably need to extend your engagement through the life of that new implementation.

Are you available?

Albert: When do you want to start?

Katherine: We are under considerable pressure. I was hoping to get you on board as soon as possible. Do you have other commitments?

Albert: I have a few other things going on, but this sounds like an interesting project. I can juggle. I just want to make sure that I am the right person for the job.

Katherine: The Hyde Group speaks very, very highly of you.

Albert: How about I come back next week? Are you adverse to a Monday through Thursday work schedule? I can use Friday as a travel day.

Katherine: Monday through Thursday is fine.

Albert finished his drink.

As *Phyllis* approached the table to take their orders, Katherine's cell phone rang. She answered it in a business-like manner and listened for a minute, looking up and smiling at Albert intermittently. She spoke a few words and ended the call.

Katherine: That was the office. Something has come up. I need to return quickly. I am embarrassed that I have to leave so soon. We did not even get to eat. Do you mind?

Albert: No — not at all.

Katherine: Thank you for understanding. Here is the direct line to my office and my email address. I look forward to seeing you next week. I will have my Admin contact The Hyde Group to get an Engagement Agreement for you. Contact me as soon as you arrive next week. I look forward to working with you.

Albert stood up as she was about to leave and offered his hand for a departing handshake. Katherine accepted it, then took her bag and left the table.

Albert sat back down again and beckoned to *Phyllis* to come over to take his order. He ordered the Linguini with White Sauce and a House Salad. He thought about ordering a Martini for the drive back, but did not do so. There would be plenty of time to do some serious drinking once he arrived back at the hotel.

There was a lot to celebrate. He had just landed a six month engagement at $1500 a day, with hotel, rental car, meals and a round trip plane ticket home on weekends thrown in. The fact that he did not have a real home per se, having sold the condominium weeks earlier at a nice profit, was irrelevant. MidContinent did not care where he went on weekends as long as he showed up in Pleasant Lake on Monday morning. Thus, starting on his travel day, he could go to any destination in the continental United States that his heart desired. Also, he would be paid for his travel day too, $1500. Such is the life of a System Architect.

If he lived, that is….

Albert stood in the middle of the highway, alone and in the dark, with his cell phone back at his hotel, in his carry-on flight bag. In all his hurry to make the meeting he'd forgotten to bring it. Off in the distance, about a mile up the interstate, Albert saw headlights approaching him. As the lights came closer he raised his hands over his head and waved them furiously, more furiously than he had ever waved at anything before. His life depended on it. The car, a large one that looked as if it was made in the early 70's, stopped in front of him. He walked over to the driver side of the car. The driver lowered the window. He was a big, burly looking man, with a big beard on his face and a baseball cap on his head. He spoke.

Driver: How you doing, friend?

Albert: My car skidded off the road. Can you give me ride back to town?

Driver: Sure, get in.

Albert opened the rear door and climbed in. The car smelled old, the type of smell a vehicle develops after years of oil changes and much-needed repairs. The rear seat was tattered and beer cans were thrown about on the seat and floor. Albert sat back as the car started down the highway into the blizzard.

Albert: Boy, am I happy you guys stopped to pick me up. If you didn't I would surely be dead in a few hours.

Driver: You betcha, you surely would be dead.

Albert noticed that the big, burly guy with the baseball cap had a passenger in the front with him, another big, burly guy with a baseball cap.

Albert: What are you guys doing out on a night like this?

Driver: We are sportsmen. We are going to a Sportsmen Convention in town. We're looking to get a deal on some rifles and shotguns.

Albert: Even on a night like this?

Driver: Friend, we are real sportsmen. A real sportsman will go to a Sportsmen Convention no matter what the weather. Where you from?

Albert: The last place I lived was Florida.

Driver: Friend, this ain't no place like Florida, is it? You hunt?

Albert: No

Driver: No matter. You want a beer?

Albert: Sure!

And so Albert and the two sportsmen on their way to the Sportsmen Convention drove down the highway into the blizzard, drinking beer in a car from the 70's that smelled old and had a tattered back seat that was filled with empty beer cans. Albert was happy. He was unusually grateful he was alive. He figured, "How bad can it be spending a few months out here in the Midwest with men such as these, life saving angels disguised as the salt of God's good Earth?"

Chapter 14: Walt Gets It

Walt took hold of the mouse that sat on the MidContinent mouse pad perched on the rollout shelf. He was deep in the basement of his house. The mouse pad was an award that he had received from one of the many ongoing employee motivation programs that the Human Resource Department at MidContinent Industries ran hoping to improve employee morale.

Walt mused to himself that he seemed to be always buying cookies, paying to sponsor some cause, or purchasing a ticket to some sort of community dinner. Walt did not mind it so much. It's not as if supporting the Girl Scouts, curing cancer and recognizing the courage of public servants were not good things to do. He just wished that he received better gifts of appreciation for his contributions. Mouse pads were boring in their redundancy. He had a drawer full of them.

It was 10:30 on a Thursday night. A lone florescent light hung above him. Although he had a larger home, two thousand-plus square feet with four bedrooms, an eat-in kitchen *and* a dining room, den and family room, Walt preferred to do his surfing in the catacomb-like security of the hovel that he called his home office. His desk, situated underneath the stairs that led from the kitchen to the basement, was a workstation of modern design, bought at the Computer Furniture section of K-Mart—assembly required, but only hammer and screwdriver necessary.

A monitor sat on an eye-level platform that rose up from the desktop while the keyboard, mouse and mouse pad sat on a small shelf that rolled out from the middle of the workstation. The computer box and the connected printer were tastefully hidden from sight within the unit. If Walt wanted to print a document, all he had to do was open a door down to his lower left. On the lower right were two drawers stacked one on top of the other. The larger, lower drawer contained files. The upper draw was filled with an interconnected chaos of printer cables, power chords, network wires and little black AC power converter boxes — the type that you use to charge your cell phone and plug into CD players to avoid using battery power. Walt had a lot of stuff like this; items that were orphan accessories to some technological gizmo that was lost long ago.

Walt was getting ready for his weekly online date. His credit card lay on the rollout shelf to the left of his keyboard. He needed the credit card in order to get in to the video room designated for the rendezvous.

Nobody upstairs knew about the date, and nobody was really interested anyway. Interest in Walt — the person, the man, the walking container of newly discovered desire — had left the two thousand-plus square feet of living space long ago. In the world upstairs, all that was meaningful was his performance, his schedule, and his ability to get things done.

Walt was a train on the track of life. He went where the track took him. As long as he ran on time, left in the morning and came back at night, made his drop-offs and pickups, and required but the most minor of repairs, his purpose was complete, for himself and the two thousand-plus square feet of living space above him.

Until last week that is.

Up until last week, Walt was mad every waking minute of every waking hour of every waking day that it had to come to this: That some video image, somewhat interactive, somewhere in some far-off unknown place, somehow attached to some female human being, somehow aroused his passions, stirred his masculinity, made him feel alive, made him feel complete, and made him feel like a real man. And up until last week, as mad as he was, Walt knew that he was not a victim. He had made it this way.

Walt had started dumping his inner desires and passion a long time ago. He opted for The Show: the car, the house, the kids, good credit and the approval of his friends and family. He was all that others wanted him to be. He could sleep at night. Yet every waking day was an exercise in unfulfilled longing. Walt was horny. Every moment was a passion to be suppressed, a desire which he struggled to ignore.

And Walt's horniness made him fat.

There was a time, many years earlier, when Walt's horniness had made him feel sublime. When he was younger his desires and passions sang strongly to him in melodies that enraptured his soul and harmonies that embraced his person. He was slim and attractive. He listened to these voices intently and sang along as best he could. It seemed as if the act of singing with the voices provided enough exercise to keep his waistline trim.

Sadly, over the years Walt's fears grew stronger than his passions. After a while, his only desire was to not be afraid.

His stomach began to bulge.

His ability to dress deteriorated. Earlier in life, every night Walt had invested an hour, if not more, deciding what he was going to wear to his next professional day. Every night was an adventure in detailed design: the knot of the tie had to match the collar of the shirt, the tie had to match the socks, and all had to match the suit of the day. His attire was his message. Although Walt owned but two suits of impeccable fit, six ties of quality silk and ten shirts, none of which were white, his aesthetic provided him with enough choice to create an infinite wardrobe. Walt gave new meaning to the term "mix and match."

But that was then and this is now. As time went on and people and things owned him more, the time he invested choosing his daily wardrobe became equal to the time he invested in his professional day, which was no investment whatsoever, other than the awake-yet-unaware moments of his life.

As his desires ebbed and his passions went dormant, his belly grew fat. Each day the morsels of life unlived attached themselves to his midsection, increasing the size of his waistline. Walt did not have "love handles." He had *fat* and that fat, along with his daily attire of white shirt, dark suit and monochrome tie, one of three in his closet, made him ugly.

Walt hated his ugliness and found that the only source of relief from it and the life he had made to support it was the date every Thursday night, at 10:30 p.m., underneath a fluorescent light at the assemble-it-yourself workstation underneath the steps leading into his basement. There he found beauty.

Walt sat at the workstation and logged on to the website that hosted the video interface to his date, a woman named Connie. Walt had been "seeing" Connie for a little over a month. The framework to their interaction was simple. Connie sat at a desk in front of a video camera perched at the top of her computer monitor. The video camera projected Connie's images and actions over the Internet to a web page on Walt's computer. Walt could see Connie but Connie could not see Walt. Walt liked it this way.

At the bottom of the web page that contained Connie's video image was a little text chat box though which Walt typed messages to send to Connie and vice versa. At first the images and messages were casual. They talked about things they liked and things they didn't like and the state of something or other. For this sort of conversation Walt paid Connie a fee of twenty dollars, charged to his credit card.

Walt found Connie attractive and engaging. She was easy to talk to and stimulating in a very innocent sort of way. Connie paid attention to the little meanings in Walt's messages, the phrases he used to express excitement and frustration, anger and melancholy. Connie remembered Walt's birthday and associated it with his astrological sign, Capricorn. Connie talked a lot about astrology. Walt liked the attention.

On their second meeting Connie gave Walt a pet name. She called him, Winkie.

During the course of their fourth weekly meeting, Walt noticed that the content of the messages was changing. Connie started to ask Walt more personal questions: Was he married? Did he find her attractive? Is there something special that he wanted her to be wearing when they got together? Finally, Connie told Walt that she felt really comfortable with him, that she felt really close to him, so close in fact that she wanted to show him her body.

Walt found himself getting an erection.

At first he could not respond. But then slowly he prepared a message in the text box underneath the video image of Connie. The message said that, yes, he felt close to her, too, and, yes, she could take off her clothes. In fact he would like it.

The message lay dormant in the text box for two minutes before Walt mustered up the courage to express his desire and click the Send button.

Upon receiving the message Connie unbuttoned her blouse, removed her brassiere and revealed her breasts to Walt.

Connie told Walt, that showing her breasts was difficult, but that she really liked him and wanted him to see them. Connie asked Walt if he liked what he saw.

Walt answered yes, and at that moment it was if every inch of excess fat on his waist cried out to be cut from his midsection, by any means necessary — liposuction, surgical removal or butchery. At that moment in time and space, Walt felt just enough of Connie to want be whole again.

And it was too much. Walt thanked her for her time, told her that he looked forward to seeing her the next week and logged out of the site. He then went into the crude toilet-only bathroom that was in the basement next to the washer and dryer and masturbated, something that he had not done in years.

That night Walt lay in bed unable to sleep. His wife lay next to him, back to him, snoring softy. He had no desire for her. All he could think about was Connie, the way she called him Winkie, her innocent messages and the revelation of her breasts. He wanted to hold them, to kiss them, to adore them. He wanted to feel their warmth against his chest. Walt fantasized about Connie's flat stomach lying against his flat stomach. He imagined that he could look down toward his stomach and see the cut and bulge of his abdominal muscles. He wanted to feel Connie's breasts against his chest, a new chest with statue-like hardness. The feeling was strong, acute, like a blade of grass determined to make its way through a concrete sidewalk.

Walt felt tears come to his eyes. He was feeling desire unfulfilled. He wept quietly. He did not want to wake the other person in his bed. To do so would reveal more than he was willing to show. He did not want to answer the question, "Walt, why are you crying?"

This week was his fifth meeting with Connie. Walt got the browser up, logged in and provided the necessary credit card information. Connie came on screen. She was wearing nothing out of the ordinary. Their conversation went like this:

Connie: Winkie, hi!

Walt: Hi.

Chapter 14: Walt Gets It

Connie: How r u this week?

Walt: Good. And you?

Connie: Great, I have been looking forward to seeing u!

Walt: Yes, me too!

Connie: I was afraid that u would not want to see me anymore.

Walt: Why?

Connie: Well, last week was a little *hot*, if u know what I mean. ☺

Walt: Yes, you were *hot*. I thought about you all week.

Connie: Oh, that makes me feel good. I was afraid that u would think that I was cheap or something.

Walt: No — not at all.

Connie: Great! I was hoping that u liked last week.

Walt: I did, a great deal.

Connie: Great! Say, Winkie, do you mind if I tell u something personal?

At this point, Walt could see in the video image on the web page that Connie was fondling the upper button on her blouse.

Walt: No, not at all.

Walt could feel his heart begin to race a little faster.

Connie: Winkie, I need u to help me.

Walt: What can I do?

Connie: Winkie, I have a problem. Most guys don't really care about me. All they care about is my body. They talk to my chest and don't see me. They say things that are rude and crude. u on the other hand, u are gentle and thoughtful. u talk to me.

Walt: Thank you.

Connie: Usually I am really turned off to sex. But with u it's different. I feel very comfortable with u.

Walt: Again, thank you.

Connie: I think that I could really be satisfied by u. But I am afraid that once u hear what I want, u won't want to see me anymore.

Walt: No, I like you. I would not think of it. Please tell me what you want.

Connie: I want to reveal myself to u. I want to reveal things that I have kept inside for a long time.

Walt: I am willing to help the best that I can.

Connie: Can I tell u a secret?

Walt: Please do.

Connie: Winkie, I have a fantasy.

Walt: What is it?

Connie: I want to take off all of my clothes for u. I want to reveal all of myself for u. I want to think about u while I am doing it.

Walt: How can I help you?

Connie: Winkie, the fantasy is very detailed. I have been thinking about it for a long time.

Walt: What is the fantasy?

Connie: Winkie, have u ever played strip poker?

Walt: Yes, I used to play that at parties in college.

Connie: Well, this is sort of like strip poker, except a little different. I want u to buy my clothes from me. It is really important to me that u buy the clothes, otherwise I won't get off?

Walt: You want me to buy your clothes?

Connie: It won't be much, and then once they are all off, I will be sooooo hot that I will need to be satisfied and u can watch me.

Walt spent $75 that night and regretted not one cent of the expense. Walt was no longer mad that some video image, somewhat interactive, somewhere in some far-off unknown place, somehow attached to some female human being was a vital part of his life. He was grateful for the feelings that the image provided, regardless of its origin.

It was better to have an erection than not have an erection. It was better to desire than not to desire. It was better to sing to the music of life than to stifle it with the noise of the mundane. If Connie and the web page in front of him were the way to being whole again, then so be it. Walt remembered reading someplace that there are many paths to Enlightenment. Working out with Connie couldn't be any worse than The Show. He had done The Show and The Show wasn't that good.

And so Walt understood his situation as Oliver Twist understood his hunger. He wanted more.

Chapter 15: Frank Loses Money

Frank DiGraizia took hold of himself. If he did not regain control of himself immediately, there was no telling what would happen. He had to get out of the kitchen. The last time that he had been this angry, he had thrown things; dishes right out of the Formica cabinet above the dishwasher shattered against the wall on the other side of the kitchen. At first each hurl dissipated his anger a little more. Then, by the time he got to the sixth dish, he began to enjoy the sound of the crash of ceramic plates against painted sheetrock. It was almost as if he were playing the wall as a musical instrument, creating an ode to his rage. Before he knew it, he had broken every dish in the cupboard.

His wife had been terrorized by his performance. She called the police. They came, walked him handcuffed through the rubble of rose pattern debris and removed him from the premises. The next day she got a restraining order preventing him from entering the house, *his* house, ever again. He ended up spending two weeks in a Motel 6, calling her everyday, trying to ingratiate himself back into the big bed, which he did at the cost of a complete kitchen renovation to her exact specification and expectation.

Now, looking back, Frank could not remember what he had been angry about, but, whatever it was, it could not have been anything this bad. Frank DiGraizia's wife, Miranda, following the wisdom and good advice of her investment club, had just lost $60,000 of their money. Regardless of the stupidity of her actions or the amount of damage and setback that she had inflected upon him, he could not lose his temper, for in the Halls of Justice, when it comes to restraining orders, women can conjure them up faster than Prospero can summon Ariel.

It wasn't really a get-rich-quick scheme. It was more like a planned windfall. Miranda DiGraizia's investment club took a liking to a company named MidContinent Industries. The stock was priced at a steal, around six dollars a share. The company was an agri-business conglomerate located in the heart of the Midwest. MidContinent had its fingers in a little bit of everything — seed research, energy brokerage, nitrogen production, agricultural insurance — anything that had to do with keeping the planet alive and functioning. MidContinent's prospectus looked great. The company had been listed on the New York Stock exchange from the mid 50's. It had a great P/E Index and a healthy cash reserve. The company always paid dividends. In fact, things had been so good the stock had split twice in the last ten years. For all intents and purposes, this one was a winner. And, at six dollars a share, which even Wall Street was saying was very cheap for this stock, if the stock rose just a dollar, that would be a 16.6% jump, better than anything any money market or mutual fund was offering. This stock was set to go.

Frank sort of liked the investment club. It gave Miranda something to do, and over the three years that she had been a member they had made money. Granted, they had no more than five thousand dollars in play at any one time, but the profits had been good and they had been consistent. So, when Miranda suggested that they make a play on MidContinent, Frank went along. However, in this case "going along" to Miranda meant the purchase of sixteen thousand six hundred and sixty seven shares of MidContinent common stock, worth a little over one hundred thousand dollars, not counting brokerage fees, which were not that much seeing as how all the trades were done on the Internet.

Miranda was feeling particularly good and particularly lucky the day that she went downtown to their safe deposit box, took out the well-matured savings bonds that Miranda's parents had given them on their wedding day, cashed them in and bought the stock. The feeling of the purchase was so exhilarating that Miranda did not want it to go away, so she called her friend and fellow club member, Jeanine, on her cell phone and asked her to meet her for lunch at Blossoms, the trendy yet affordable California Cuisine restaurant next to the Marriot.

Jeanine showed up at Miranda's table a little after noon. Miranda ordered the first round of rum and Coke and they proceeded to drink the afternoon away. Miranda and Jeanine drank a lot of afternoons away.

Right after purchasing the shares, the stock went up thirty three cents that trading day. Miranda was ecstatic. She was not indifferent to the amount of cash that she had put on the line. The money meant a lot to her and she was quite pleased with herself that she had invested it wisely. Miranda liked doing things well.

The second day the price of the stock didn't fluctuate much. The third day the stock rose a dime. At the end of the trading week, the stock was up almost fifty cents. Miranda felt really good.

The following Monday the stock started out strong in morning trading, rising another dime, but by midday, the price was down forty cents. By the ring of the closing bell, the stock had lost another forty-seven cents. Tuesday was a loser too, as was Wednesday, and Thursday. Friday's closing bell rang forth with a price of four dollars and twenty-three cents a share, a new market low.

That Saturday Frank took their sons on a weekend camping trip near St. Catherines. Miranda stayed behind to see her sister, Denise, with whom she drank away the weekend.

Monday morning it was more of the same. Everyday was an added loss. On Thursday of that week a noted Wall Street newspaper released a story indicating that MidContinent was in serious trouble due to hyperactive acquisition behavior coupled with inadequate software systems. The stock closed at two dollars and thirty-eight cents, an even newer market low. What had once seemed so mighty now seemed so low. The stock for which Miranda paid a touch over one hundred thousand dollars was now worth less than forty thousand dollars. "No matter," thought Miranda, "we never used that money anyway," as she left Parkhurst Liquors, a cinderblock liquor store near downtown Rochester that had neither a vintage wine section nor wine consultant, just shelves upon shelves of good hard liquor as well as cases and kegs of beer, all at very good prices.

A traffic accident on Interstate 490 caused Miranda to arrive home after Frank that evening. She drove the car into her spot on the right side of the garage that adjoined the house, got out and entered through the door at the back of garage into the lower level of the house.

Before going upstairs, she made sure that she hid her purchase in a closet in the lower level room, on a shelf behind boxes of board games. A stack of Risk, Monopoly, Candyland, Clue, Boogle and Yahtzee cartons kept her bottle of liquor from common view.

She proceeded up to the main level of the house to find Frank in the kitchen holding an open envelope and its unfolded contents in his hand. He was standing still, feet planted firmly on the kitchen floor, yet shaking at the same time, mostly in his hands. The envelope was from the online trading website that they used to do their stock transactions. It was the monthly statement. There was no need for Miranda to ask what was the matter. She knew.

Frank walked out of the kitchen, downstairs to his home office on the lower level. He logged on to the online trading website to confirm the information that he had just read in the letter. It was all true. Somehow a hundred grand had been deposited into his trading account a few weeks earlier to buy stock in... what was it?... MidContinent Industries? And, now, that stock was worth forty grand. Frank was stuck with paper loss of sixty grand. And, if he cashed out immediately he would have a real cash loss of SIXTY THOUSAND FUCKING DOLLARS.

Frank sat quietly looking at the monitor for a few seconds of eternity. His hands were still shaking. He got up from his chair, turned to the door at the entrance of his home office and closed it. Then he returned to his desk and opened the right-hand side drawer. He took out the hammer that he used to hang pictures and do small repairs. It was a good size hammer, big enough to knock a two-by-four into place and small enough to tap a nail hanger into the wall.

Frank held the hammer firmly in his clenched fist and waited for his hand to stop shaking. Then, once his hand was steady, he raised the hammer above his head and with all the fury he could muster proceeded to smash his monitor, keyboard, mouse and computer to smithereens.

Chapter 16: Rafael Gets Fired

Rafael took hold of the Bug Sheet that sat on top of the conference room table and stared at its contents in continuing disbelief. Of the fifty-three priority one items open for resolution, his name appeared in the "Programmer" column of thirty-seven of them. In the scheme of things, Rafael's code sucked and today's bug report gave documented evidence to this fact. Rafael was getting the shit kicked out of him in Q/A.

Working on the Customer Transfer module was killing him and it was beginning to show. He had never experienced pressure like this before. He had never fucked up like this before. He was supposed to be good at this, for chrissakes, and now he was a dismal failure. Coming over to work on Customer Transfer had been a mistake, a big mistake.

Oh yeah, he was coding again. Programming had been added to his Project Specialist job description. They had had no choice. The project needed all the help that it could get. The programmers were running behind schedule and were very shorthanded. Every resource was needed to get the goddam thing to work.

Originally Rafael's primary responsibility was to create specs. In the beginning he spent his day talking to end users and managers in order to get an idea of what they wanted. Then he found out that they wanted different things on different days. Some days contradicted other days, which in turn destroyed days of previously written code. As time went on creating specs became a folly. Things changed too fast. Now the team needed more coders pounding more keys to keep up with the changes. Nobody on the team was reading the specs anymore anyway. They were all making it up as they went along. There was no time left to specify. It was all code—code, code, code, code. And it was all boring code. As much as he loved to code, Rafael was not very good at writing boring code. And it showed.

Every morning there was a meeting at 9 a.m., the purpose of which was to review the state of the project and to plan out activities for the day. The Project Manager went around the room and asked each team member which tasks were completed, which tasks were outstanding, and which problems were priorities. Then they reviewed the Quality Assurance Report, The Bug Sheet.

Every night after the programmers were through with their tasks and a daily build — all the code of the day compiled into a working program — had been made, the Quality Assurance Team, the Praetorian Guard of software development, tested the build to make sure that the code performed to whatever specification was in force. If the code did not work, the tester wrote up the error in the error tracking system. First and foremost the tester gave the error a severity number, an indicator of "just how bad it was." A "1" was a very, very, very serious error; one that took down the system, on par with an exploding engine on the Space Shuttle, for example. At the other end of the scale was a "5", a very minor problem, annoyances such as misspellings and rude error messages. A Number 5 was like bad snack food served during beverage service on a transcontinental flight — something that needed to be addressed at some point, but not something you would ground an airplane over. Then the tester filled in the column that described what part of the code the error was in and how to replicate the error. The following morning, the Technical Lead, the sergeant among the enlisted programmers, filled in the programmer who was responsible for the error.

Now the trick of good software development is that you want to generate as many errors as possible as quickly as possible. Errors that you know about are always better than errors that you don't know about, because if you know about them you can fix them and if you don't know about them, you can't. However, in the testosterone-driven world of software development at MidContinent Industries, errors were a sign of weakness, incompetence, a sure sign that the developer is a ninety-eight pound weakling. And, as every ninety-eight pound weakling has a bully to kick sand in his face, the developer with the most Number 1's is forever at the teasing mercy and blunt disdain of those developers for whom divine grace has spared the horror of bad numbers.

At MidContinent Industries, teamwork stopped at Severity Number One. A developer being bludgeoned by Q/A was on his own. And Rafael was very much on his own.

Some days Rafael left the 9 a.m. meeting close to tears. It seemed that every day something new was added or removed from the specification and every morning he was assigned to make a new, unanticipated change. And most times when he tried to make the change, he ended up breaking a whole bunch of code that had worked before. When he traced back through the code from the error in order to find the cause, sometimes he ended up in somebody else's code. Then he would end up having to physically locate that person because, due to lack of adequate commenting, he could not figure out what the original programmer was trying to do.

He might find the programmer at his desk; he might not. The programmer might be at a meeting, at "training" or on vacation. In some cases the programmer had quit or was fired.

In the event that he did not have the help of the code's creator, sometimes he would spend days trying to figure out what was going on in the code. Many times he would go through this whole rigmarole only to find out that the code that he had spent days trying to decipher was not the cause of his problems at all. Then he would end up at the 9 a.m. meeting having to say that he was behind in his tasks and get the "you are wasting the company's money" look from one-third of the table and the "you are the most lame person ever to walk the earth" look from the other third of the table. The final third just played with their PalmPilots, sending wireless email to one another mocking the whole spectacle in silent hilarity.

Rafael's Project Manager, some guy from some consulting company who was certified by the Project Management Institute, was taking a lot of grief from above. He was not unsympathetic to Rafael's plight. In fact, The Project Manager liked Rafael. The kid came early and stayed late. He had heart. But for the Project Manager, the Bug Sheet was not only hurting Rafael; it was killing him. The Project Manager was missing his dates. Missed dates meant lost money and lost money meant that a pile of executives, trained to find blame in order to assuage the stockholders and Wall Street analysts, would be looking for someone upon whom to pin the cause of the problem. When it came to assigning blame, Project Managers were cuts of tender, succulent sirloin to be quick charred over a bed of pure, red-hot, mesquite coals.

The Project Manager had to do something to mend the situation. One option was to send Rafael off for "rehabilitation" at some technical re-education center, née Technical Training. It was the humane thing to do. Rafael had a lot of potential; he had moments of brilliance; but overall his code sucked. A little more training might solve the problem. But, the type of courses that developers like Rafael attended were about a week long and cost over two thousand dollars, not counting the airfare that would need to be paid to transport him to the training site, as well as the money to keep him housed and fed once there. Also, Rafael would need to be paid for his time while attending the course and an additional cost would be incurred because the project would be slowed down by him not producing code. So when you added it all up, the price of treating Rafael humanely would add a little over seven thousand additional dollars to the project's budget.

Or, the Project Manager could remove Rafael from the project today, call a consulting company that specialized in staff augmentation and have his chair filled by the day after tomorrow. Granted, he would lose a week getting the new developer "up to speed". But, given how cutthroat the consulting companies were for business, he could probably get the new developer for nothing for the first week, if not the first two weeks. And, if he was really aggressive, he could probably get the consulting company to agree to send in two consultants to learn the code and keep only the one that he liked best.

Much to Rafael's eventual distress, the Project Manager decided to remove him from the project. If Rafael had been a consultant, he would have just been sent packing. But Rafael was a full-time employee of MidContinent Industries. The Project Manager was a consultant, on hire only for the life of the project. His only jurisdiction was the project and the personnel on it. He could fire all the other consultants that he wanted, but he could not fire Rafael. Only an employee of the MidContinent Industries Human Resource Department could terminate Rafael from MidContinent. In fact, nobody could be fired from MidContinent except by an employee of the MidContinent Industries Human Resource Department, under the strict observance of the Termination Procedures documented in the Employee Handbook.

HR did the hiring and firing, nobody else. A manager could not fire an employee; a Vice-President could not fire an employee; not even the Chairman of the Board could fire an employee of MidContinent Industries. Others in authority could recommend termination; but only a member of the MidContinent Industries Human Resources Department following the Termination Procedures documented in the Employee Handbook could actually fire an employee. The potential for lawsuits was perceived to be too great otherwise.

There were many instances at MidContinent of completely moronic incompetents being kept on salary rather than being fired, with their only task being to go to and from the toilet all day. Although keeping them around was idiotic in terms of morale, it was wise in terms of economics: the cost of keeping them on was cheaper than the cost of having to fight it out in court for years with some ill-dressed, contingency fee lawyer found in the Yellow Pages.

Toward the end of the day, the Project Manager walked over to Rafael and asked him to check in his code and come by his cube. Regardless of the fact that the Project Manager was responsible for the operational implementation and execution of a budget in excess of six million dollars of MidContinent Industries money, he was a consultant nonetheless, and he got what all other consultants got, a cube.

Rafael acknowledged the request and walked over with trepidation. He knew what was coming. The code check-in gave it away. Asking Rafael to check his code into the master library indicated that they wanted to make sure that they had his latest code on file and accessible to others. They were taking his code away.

Rafael approached the cube. The Project Manager invited him to sit down and began to speak.

Rafael remembered hearing the opening words, "Rafael, we have a problem…" Then the rest of the Project Manager's speech became a cloud of blah, blah, blah, blah, blah.

Rafael looked around the Project Manager's cube. He noticed a photo of the Project Manager standing behind a woman seated in a chair with a little girl in her lap and an older boy to her left. Rafael inferred that the photo was of the Project Manager's family. The woman was plain and it looked as if the whole group had shown up for the photo session dressed like employees on Dress Down Friday:

causal-not-blue-jeans pants, golf shirt and loafers. What was supposed to be informal appeared orchestrated. Oh, the children looked friendly enough despite the rigidity built in to any family portrait, but overall the spirit of the photograph was sterile. The passion that was supposed to have produced the two offspring in the photo was not apparent. Rafael had a hard time imagining the woman and the Project Manager doing it on the kitchen floor, let alone screaming and yelling their way to orgasm in a sun drenched bedroom in a Cozumel hotel.

Rafael's thoughts moved on. His attention shifted back to the Project Managers voice when he heard the words, "… so I am going to take you off the project, Rafael. I'm sorry."

He'd known it was coming, but he was traumatized nonetheless. He fought to hold back tears. The Project Manager told Rafael to report back to the HR Department in the morning and they would tell him where to go from there.

The Project Manager extended his hand. Rafael shook it and left the cube. Rafael went back to his cube and packed his few possessions into his briefcase. After he closed the briefcase, he paused a moment and looked at it. Rafael thought of his father.

His father had worked at MidContinent for close to twenty-five years and had never carried a briefcase to work. In fact, he never carried anything to work, not even a lunch bag. His father worked through lunch for the overtime.

Rafael picked up the briefcase and left his cube in the Customer Transfer development area for the last time.

The next morning, as he was walking down the hall toward the HR Department, Rafael ran into Ajita, who was on her way to the development area. Up to that point, Rafael and Ajita came into contact everyday, but their contact was never like that first meeting when Manfred the DBA looked on. A part of Rafael was still unsure if it ever happened. Ajita had never talked about it, denied it or repeated it. Day after day they did their day; they made software together. The fact that she had sexually engaged him, without his encouragement and without his permission, in a public conference room while a third party looked on seemed to have about as much relevance to the present day's chance meeting as did the Blue Plate Special that was served in the company subsidized cafeteria last Wednesday.

Ajita asked Rafael how he was doing. Rafael told her with a bit of embarrassment that he was off the project and that he was on his way to HR for reassignment. Ajita's only comment was this: "I am sad that you did not give the Project Manager what he wanted." Then she proceeded down the hall away from Rafael onward to the development area.

Rafael watched her walk away. He knew that he was going to miss Ajita, probably more than he was going to miss the code.

Chapter 17: Ajita Takes Over

Katherine Limeleaf took hold of a bran muffin from the pastry tray with a piece of disposable pastry tissue and placed it on a small Styrofoam plate. Then she poured herself a cup of coffee from the pot on the hotplate next to the tray. Next she poured a small amount of milk into the equally Styrofoamed cup that held her coffee and took both items, along with a gold foil wrapped pat of butter, over to her seat at the small round conference table in her office.

Albert Shulberg was seated at the table already. He too had visited the pastry tray and was busy trying to eat a jelly doughnut and drink his morning coffee. Both Katherine and he were waiting for the arrival of the Project Manager and the Technical Lead of the Sales System's Customer Transfer Module.

Try as he might, Albert could not eat the jelly doughnut with grace. Every time he took a bite, a dab of red strawberry jelly shot out of the center of the doughnut and oozed down his thumb. Albert had a stack of paper napkins next to him that he used to wipe his thumb clean after each squirt. After each bite of the jelly doughnut Albert took a sip of coffee: bite-wipe-sip, bite-wipe-sip, bite-wipe-sip.

Katherine was somewhat amused by Albert's awkwardness. She knew that jelly doughnuts were a bitch to eat, not the food of choice that a person of his supposed stature should select from a Corporate Pastry Tray. Jelly doughnuts were for the guys down in Shipping and girls over in Customer Service. Upper management and their minions did not eat jelly doughnuts. At $1500 dollars a day you would think that the guy would have enough sense to choose a croissant, or at least a Danish, and spare himself the embarrassment of looking like a gastronomic imbecile. But elegant eating was not the reason that Katherine had hired Albert. He was hired for another purpose and for that purpose he was doing just fine.

Albert, on the other hand, wasn't really trying to look proper; in fact, he cared not a twit. The stack of napkins was medicinal. He just hated the feeling of sticky goo on his fingers and wanted it gone as soon as it arrived. Clean hands made him feel better — cleanliness being next to godliness and all that.

Katherine sat in her chair and began to cut the bran muffin in two with a plastic knife that she had brought over with her from the pastry tray. The door to her office opened just a crack as she was completing her incision into her pastry. The intruding head of the Project Manager popped in through the newly created opening and greeted her hello.

Katherine liked her bran muffin a whole lot more than she liked the Project Manager. The bran muffin would leave behind a small amount of satisfaction when it was gone. The Project Manager would leave behind a headache. He always had before and she had no reason to believe that today would be any different.

The Project Manager asked permission to enter. His face contained a feigned smile. Katherine called this smile the "all hell could break lose at any moment, but rest assured, I am following the Project Plan" smile.

She hated that smile. She hated it so much that her first impulse was to surgically remove it from the Project Manager's face using the same plastic knife that she had used to cut the bran muffin.

But such grotesque behavior was beyond her capabilities. Katherine didn't like the sight of blood. Bloodletting was crude. It made her physically sick. Katherine was not crude; she was elegant. Thus, Katherine accommodated the Project Manager in her elegance.

The Project Manager entered Katherine's office followed by Ajita Orhtihawamein. Ajita was the new Technical Lead of the Sales System's Customer Transfer.

Life had been good to Ajita. Removing Rafael from the project had been a major decision for the Project Manager. Rafael was the only MidContinent employee on the Customer Transfer Module team. His removal had left a peculiar situation in a project that was turning out to be quite critical to MidContinent. With the removal of Rafael, MidContinent was out of the loop. The Customer Transfer Module was being made without any front line input, supervision or communication from a MidContinent employee. The only people left on the team after Rafael's departure were a group of contract consultants, except for Manfred the DBA, that is.

But he didn't really count. Manfred, as godlike as he was, was spread out over ten projects. He was beyond the mundane drudge of day-to-day software development. His concerns were on the Big Picture, and as ego-enhancing as his position was, his responsibilities were considerable. The ramifications of his errors, should he make them, which he almost never did, were substantial. Manfred was a poster boy for efficient time management. He showed up rarely, attended briefly, made limited commitments and got things done. Manfred was very good at being God.

Without MidContinent in the loop, the code was at risk. A band of mercenaries was making the software that would live and breathe in the bowels of the MidContinent digital infrastructure. When they were done, they would leave, binary Bedouins folding up their tents to move on the next digital settlement that needed their labor. Then, what would MidContinent do? Who would maintain the code? Who would add features? Who would fix bugs? Something had to be done. Darkies had taken the code hostage.

The Project Manager did an amazing thing that day: He solved a problem that was not in the Project Plan. The Project Manager knew that he had to get someone from MidContinent on the team as quickly as possible. However, the code was so far along that anybody coming to it new would need weeks to "get up to speed." A new MidContinent employee coming to the team would feel overwhelmed and entitled and thus try to dominate the development team. More than one project had come to a grinding halt while a self-centered, overconfident employee had tried to impose his cognitive and emotional will on the contract consultants around him. And the consultant couldn't do a thing about it, except to hold the employee in silent contempt.

At MidContinent consultants were stateless beings. Any MidContinent employee could kick around a consultant and the consultant took it. Like Christians in a coliseum full of Romans, they were trained to turn the other cheek, albeit for commercial, not spiritual reasons. Contract consultants had it drilled into their heads over and over again that, no matter what, any employee is always right and always the expert. Offending or even irking an employee could cause a tidal wave of resentment in which the consulting company that employed the offending consultant risked losing the contracts of all the consultants who were working at the particular engagement. It was not unheard of for ten consultants to be fired for the offense of one.

Bringing an employee into the team within the personnel infrastructure that now existed would slow down work on the project, if not stop it all together. The new employee would need day-to-day supervision, the type of which the Project Manger could not provide, because the Project Manager didn't know jack shit about the code. Besides, he did not have the time anyway. His job was to spend his time playing with and being played around by the Project Plan. Yet, the Project Manger had to have somebody in charge doing day-to-day supervision of the team. Otherwise it was only a matter of a short while before he lost control of the Customer Transfer Module forever.

All the members of project team were men, except for Ajita. There was no way in hell that a MidContinent employee would take day-to-day supervision from a contract employee who is a man. Testosterone would not permit it. So the Project Manager shot craps.

Since all the members of the Customer Transfer team had been together pretty much since the beginning, early on a Technical Lead wasn't needed. Somehow the team sort of knew what to do. Once in a while the Tech Lead for the entire system sat in on team meetings just to get a sense of what was going on. And until Rafael started to blow up in Q/A, that Tech Lead took care of interfacing between the team and the other coders and employees at MidContinent, leaving the Project Manger to deal with the higher-up mucky-mucks. But now Rafael was gone and things were getting bad. So, in an act of dumb genius, the Project Manager named

Ajita to be Acting Technical Lead of the Customer Transfer Module until the Mid-Continent employee became competent enough to assume the role.

The Project Manager asked the MidContinent employee to work with Ajita in order to learn the code. He told him that "between you and me, Ajita is more like an Administrative Assistant to help you deal with the other consultants than a Tech Lead. But, she has been here for a while and she knows the code. Once you Get Up to Speed, the Tech Lead job is yours."

Thus, the MidContinent employee was added to and contained within the team. Then something weird happened. Within the first two weeks that the new MidContinent employee was Getting Up to Speed, he actually began to *take* supervision from Ajita as did the other members of the team. What had started out as a sham to contain the Midwestern employee became a reality that actually made the team better.

Nobody knew what Ajita was doing, but whatever it was, she was doing it well. The daily code builds were getting bigger and better, more code was happening faster and the number of bugs reported on the Bug Sheet shrank. Things were looking up for the Customer Transfer Module of the Sales System.

Katherine took the plastic knife with which she had cut the bran muffin and spread the contents from the gold foil-wrapped package onto one of the cut halves. She took a sip of coffee followed by a bite of a half muffin.

She looked at the Project Manager who was sitting to her right. Ajita sat across from her at the small, round conference table. Albert Shulberg completed the circle to Katherine's left. Albert had, at Katherine's request, been attending all status meetings for all projects since his arrival at MidContinent a few weeks ago. It was part of his purpose.

The reason for the gathering was to review the weekly Project Status Report for the Customer Transfer Module of the Sales System. This was the first time that Ajita had been invited to attend. The format for the meeting was straightforward, right out of a Project Management textbook.

The Project Manager led the meeting. First there is the overall condition of the project (green = good, you have no headaches; yellow = watch out, if things keep going the way they're going you're going to have headaches; red = you're fucked). If the overall condition was green, the next agenda item was a line item discussion about what had been accomplished in the past week, what was planned for the next week and what the outstanding issues were.

Condition Green outstanding issues were typically matters such as the resolution of quarrels over vacation time, the need for additional personnel or the purchase of new tools and materials. If a Condition Yellow was in force, action items were defined that, once expedited, would hopefully bring the project into a state of

Condition Green. If the project was in Condition Red, the Project Manager was fired.

All eyes were on the Project Manager. He began by reporting that the project was "Green Light", that the project was moving along according to the current plan and that he had no impact statements to present. (An "impact statement" is a formal document presented to the Project Sponsor, in this case Katherine, which says, "You want me to do something that is not in the Project Plan and doing so will force me to incur costs that are not anticipated. Therefore, in order to proceed as you want me to, I will need to increase the project budget, both in terms of time and money. So I need your express written confirmation that you understand the impact of your request and I need you to approve additional funds for my budget. If you don't have them, then you need to go find them. And, if you can't fund what you want, then you can't have what you want. Sorry.")

After delivering the good news about the project status, the Project Manager then went on to talk about all the good things that they had accomplished that week, blah, blah, blah, blah, blah. As he was speaking, Ajita reached over under the table to her right and began to stroke Albert Shulberg's left thigh just as he was taking another bite of his jelly doughnut. Her touch caused him to bite down hard and squirt another gob of red jelly out onto his thumb from the pastry's center. As distressful as was the feel of sticky stuff on his thumb, Albert began to think that, overall, his day was looking up. Ajita continued to stroke his thigh. Albert could feel that he was getting hard. Then, just as the Project Manager was moving on to the part of the presentation that talked about the items that the team had planned to accomplish in the upcoming week, Ajita slid out of her chair and disappeared underneath the small, round conference table in Katherine Limeleaf's office.

Everyone at the table noticed her gesture. Katherine's eyes went wide for a moment. Albert moaned. A few moments later Albert's eye rolled up into his head as a big smile came to his face.

The Project Manager did not know what to do other than to keep doing what he was being paid to do: present the Project Status Report. He read on. His eyes never left the pages in front of him as he spoke, blah, blah, blah, blah, blah.

Albert started to writhe in his chair. He gripped the edge of the table. He was having an out-of-body experience. He was traveling in time and space to some backroom, in some strip club, in some major metropolitan area getting a blow job from one of the wonderful girls who offered the service as a sideline activity to her dancing career. Albert had been there, done that and "that" was wonderful!

Finally, Katherine could bear it no longer: she looked under the table. Ajita was on her knees, between Albert's legs with her head in his crotch.

Katherine tried to figure out the next step. What could she do? Instruct the Project Manager to instruct Ajita to get up off her knees at once? Instruct Albert to push Ajita away? She could not tell Ajita directly to get back to her seat at the table because she was a contract employee, under the supervision of the Project Manager. And if she did so, questions would come up. How did she get under the table in the first place? Who instructed her to get on her knees? Visions of endless litigation danced like sugar plum demons in Katherine's head.

Katherine got up out of her chair and went to her office door. She locked it. She had to contain the situation until she could figure out what to do next.

Ajita noticed the sound of Katherine's footsteps moving toward the door. Once Ajita heard the office door lock, she got off her knees and came out from underneath the table. She got up and walked behind Albert who was still writhing in his chair from her earlier attentions. She began to massage his shoulders.

Katherine stood by the locked door looking across the room directly at Ajita. They looked each other in the eyes. Ajita continued massaging Albert while looking into Katherine's distant eyes.

The Project Manager had seen Ajita emerge from underneath the table. Good! The worst was over. Things would get back to normal soon, he hoped. All he could do was continue his presentation of the Project Status Report, blah, blah, blah, blah, blah.

Ajita broke eye contact with Katherine for a moment. She whispered into Albert's ear that he should turn in his chair to face her. Albert's chair had no rollers on the bottom. It was the old fashioned type that needed a force of hands to be moved. Without getting up, Albert moved the chair around by holding onto its seat and jumping up and down in it, turning it a few degrees to the right with each jolt.

Finally Albert had the chair turned to Ajita. And, just as she had done with Rafael weeks earlier, she took Albert's exposed penis in her hand and mounted him.

The Project Manager could no longer ignore the events that were happening about him. He stopped reading the Status Report. He watched Ajita. He was mesmerized. As he watched, he too became erect. That he was hard was apparent to anybody who could see him; but no one could see him because he was seated with his lap hidden underneath the small, round conference table.

Katherine watched Ajita, too. Katherine was mesmerized also, more from fear than intrigue. The situation was out of her control. There was no one to call. There was nothing to do to stop that which she did not start, and to stop it would invite doom. She would not be able to explain what was happening before her. If discovered, blaming Ajita wouldn't fly. To the world at large Ajita Orhtihawamein was a contract consultant and an Indian one at that, demure, subservient, a foreigner from a land of servants. Nobody would believe that she had sexually engaged this guy on whim. The situation was out of Katherine's control. All that she could do was take it in.

Ajita changed positions. She moved off of Albert and turned so that he was in her from behind. She continued in this position for a while moving up and down on his lap, facing the Project Manager. Then Ajita got up off of Albert and walked over to the Project Manager. She motioned for him to stand up. He looked at her dumbfounded and gripped the edge of the table. Ajita took his hand from the table's edge and led him up and away from the tabletop. The bulge of his erection was in full view of all those gathered. Ajita unzipped his fly, exposed his penis, bent over and took it in her mouth. Albert walked up behind her, lifted her dress up over her protruding buttocks and put himself into her. She did not object.

The Project Manager closed his eyes. He was experiencing terror. He was experiencing ecstasy. And, for an effervescent moment, he was experiencing humor. He chuckled inside while he moaned outside. No Project Management course that he had ever taken had taught him how to manage an unexpected, maybe unwanted, blow job from a subordinate in the presence of a superior. This most definitely was a problem that was not in the Project Plan, if it was a problem at all. Managing this was beyond his competency. He could not sit on the outside looking in on this one. He was now a player in a game that was just not supposed to happen.

Within minutes, Ajita, Albert and Project Manager were a huddled mass of grunts and groans and sighs and thrusts. Ajita no longer looked at Katherine; her attentions were focused on the choreography in which she partook.

The dance went on for a while. A few minutes later it seemed as if Albert and the Project Manager achieved orgasm simultaneously.

Almost immediately the thrusting stopped. Ajita stood up, adjusted herself and went to the small conference table in Katherine Limeleaf's office. She picked up her belongings and then proceeded to the door where Katherine Limeleaf was standing guard. When she got to the door she turned to Katherine and said the following:

"I have found that there is no greater privilege than to give the clients exactly what they want."

Then she reached beyond Katherine, unlocked the door and left.

Katherine closed the door behind her.

Chapter 18: Connie Has Lunch

Connie took hold of the mirror in her makeup case and raised it to her face in order to see her reflection. She wanted to look as good as she could for Winkie. It was important to her, now that Rafael had gone off the deep end.

Usually Connie didn't give a rat's ass about her VidNetSex clients. She decided at the beginning of this whole business that the only thing she would let get involved in her online sex career was her image. Her body and mind were committed to Rafael. But since that thing at work happened, the guy had disappeared. Well, not really disappeared; they were still living together. But when he was home, all he did was plaster his face to his computer screen reading through line after line of arcane computer code and that online documentation stuff. All he did was code— code, code, code, code, code! Ever since he had been taken off that Customer Transfer thing he had been bitter and distant.

She remembered the day that he came home from work and sat in the kitchen and told her what had happened. She tried to be supportive. After all, she cared about the guy. But, as far as she was concerned, it was nothing more than a job. Jobs come and jobs go. However, for Rafael it was different.

She had never seen the guy like this before. She could still remember him, sitting at the kitchen table, finishing off a can of Diet-Pepsi, swearing that this would never, ever happen to him again, that his code would never suck again. He planned to do whatever it took to be the best programmer around, better than anybody. And then, poof!, he was gone into the machine.

Connie had no problems with guys going into the machine. It was good business for her. But Jesus!, Connie thought, at least the guys that plastered their faces to a screen with my image on it got a hard on. What was Rafael getting? All he did was code and read and read and code. For the life of her, she could not understand what this coding shit was all about. She was scared. Rafael was gone and it didn't look like he was coming back. Not even for a movie.

Then Connie became mad, really mad. She really liked the guy all right; but she had needs too, for chrissakes! She was a woman, a real woman. She needed attention, both physical and emotional. And if Rafael wasn't going to give it to her.... well, she knew how to take care of herself.

Why it was Winkie, she had no idea. Connie didn't even know who Winkie was. Well, that's not exactly true. Actually, she knew him at a very intimate level:

how he liked sweet talk, how he liked dirty talk, his favorite poses, clothes that got him horny, all that stuff. It was just that she had no idea what he looked like or sounded like in real life. For all she knew, he could have been sitting at the next table or watching her from the bar. He might even be the goddam waiter! But after weeks of abandonment by Rafael and a fluke chance that Winkie told her he lived near a small town in Iowa named Pleasant Lake — who would have thought? Connie made a bold move and suggested that they meet for lunch, at no charge. He agreed and then quickly logged out, a sure sign that she had gotten to him — whenever Winkie got overwhelmed, he logged out.

After the session with Winkie was over and as Connie was re-dressing herself for her next session of VidNetSex, the thought occurred to her that she should have her head examined for meeting a client in person, especially one so nearby. But she figured: What the hell?

Walt was taken aback and then intoxicated by Connie's suggestion. Never in a million years did he think that something like this would ever happen to him. It was just too good to be true. Walt had a lot of fantasies in life, but none had ever become reality. It was a little scary.

They decided to meet at a restaurant in a hotel downtown that catered mostly to business travelers. It was a nice enough environment, not ostentatious and very affordable. They scheduled the meeting for Wednesday at 11 a.m. Walt would be in the area for his monthly Rotary Meeting on the other side of town. The meeting ended at ten, thus giving him an hour to drive across town while stopping on the way to pick up some money at the cash machine.

Walt rarely kept more than twenty dollars in his pocket, but in this case he wanted to make sure that he had enough cash on hand to cover the cost of the entire meal. He wanted Connie to be able to order whatever she liked for lunch. The thought of not being able to pick up the tab and having to split the cost of the meal with her went against every gentlemanly sensibility he had. Yes, he could have paid by credit card; yet Walt's shame, as distant as it was, demanded that this meeting go undocumented.

Walt told Connie that he would be wearing standard business attire: a blue blazer, gray pants, black shoes and a gold-yellow silk tie with blue dots. Also, he planned to wear a matching solid gold-yellow handkerchief in the breast pocket of his blazer. She would be able to identify him by his apparel. Walt did not tell Connie his height, his weight, his hair color or his facial features.

There is only one word to describe how Walt felt the day of his meeting with Connie — horny, very horny — and it felt very good. He was so stimulated that morning that in order to eat his breakfast during the speaker presentation, he had to stand in the corner in the back of the Rotary Meeting, coffee cup in one hand, muffin in the other. During the meet-and-greet networking part of the gathering, he was like a captive animal, pacing back and forth across the room, trying to do his business, waiting for the moments to pass. He just couldn't sit down. He was just too horny.

And every time the middle-aged waitress came by to serve one of the seated attendees, he found himself watching her every move and gesture, wanting to pounce. Despite a little excess fat in her midriff, she looked hot. Her breasts were big, her makeup tastefully applied, and she smelled good. She looked like a woman who knew how to have fun. He would have done her in the coat check room, if he could have gotten away with it. Connie had done things for him, just for the asking (along with a few dollars on his credit card). Maybe the waitress would too. Maybe he should ask. Walt decided against it. He could not afford to get involved with the waitress now. He had to meet Connie at 11 a.m.

After the Rotary Meeting ended, Walt got in his car, drove to the bank, got some money and continued on to the hotel. During the drive from the bank to the hotel he had all sorts of fantasies about what he would do with Connie in real life. The best one was that he would stop at the hotel check-in desk, get a room and take Connie up to it immediately upon his arrival. No talking. He would just show her the hotel room key card and beckon her to accompany him. And then, once in the room, he would be fast and furious with her, much to her extreme satisfaction.

But first he had to get there. Walt drove his car into the underground garage, got a time-stamped admittance ticket from the automatic ticket machine, and parked the vehicle near the elevator that went to the main lobby. The time was 10:50 a.m. Walt would be on time. A gentleman does not keep a lady waiting, he thought to himself.

Before he entered the elevator, Walt took a well folded, solid gold-yellow handkerchief out of the inside pocket of his blazer and inserted it into the jacket's breast pocket. A gentleman always looks proper for a lady, he thought again. Then he pushed the elevator button.

The elevator came, he entered.

He took the elevator to the lobby, got out and went to an escalator that led to the restaurant entrance on the mezzanine level. Walt got on the cascading stairs and, once at the top of the escalator, got off. Then he stood still for a moment. His heart was pounding. Walt moved toward the restaurant, quickening his pace as he got closer to his destination. Within seconds he was in front of the restaurant.

He entered and went to the hostess podium. He looked beyond the hostess podium. He saw Connie looking into a small hand mirror. She was everything that he had hoped for in real life. She did not see him.

He stepped back out of her line of sight. He stood still. Seconds passed. And in those seconds Walt relived every session that he had had with Connie during those nights in his basement, at his home office underneath the stairs. He thought about how she undressed for him and posed for him. Sometimes she would masturbate for him. Sometimes she would just spend the time talking to him via online chat. The thing that stood out most in Walt's mind was that Connie had never said no to him. He could have his way with her. Anything he wanted, he could have, as best as she could deliver it from within the machine in which she lived.

But right here, right now, Connie lived in the real world. Her hair had fragrance and her skin had warmth and for all he knew, she might very well have bad breath. She was no longer an image. She was a real human being, right here, right now. And, if he proceeded into the dining room and sat down with her, she would be part of his real life. She would be out of the machine. He would not be able to log off and close the Web Page when it all became too much. She and he would be in the real world, over which he had little or no control.

Walt stood at the front of the restaurant for a while longer, away from the hostess podium, hidden from Connie. He tried to catch glimpses of her without being detected. His horniess was fading.

He walked back to the entrance of the restaurant. Walt knew what he had to do. He reached into the breast pocket of his blazer and removed the solid gold-yellow handkerchief and put it back into the inside pocket of the jacket. Then he turned around and walked out of the restaurant.

He returned to his car in the underground garage, got in, drove to the exit, gave his time stamped, machine issued admittance ticket to the real life attendant at the exit booth, paid and left.

Connie was getting impatient. It was 11:15 and still no Winkie. She could not stand the thought of being stood up. She was taking a big risk on this one, meeting a client for real and all. A no-show would just add insult to injury.

At that moment, Albert Shulberg, a.k.a. "BigDick6969," walked into the restaurant wearing his standard midweek business attire, blue blazer, gray pants, gold-yellow dotted tie with a solid gold-yellow handkerchief in the breast pocket of the blazer — who would have thought? Albert was nursing a very bad hangover and had slipped out of the office hoping to get some of the hair of the dog that bit him at the restaurant bar. He liked the bartender there. He made a good martini.

Connie saw him enter. She got up from her seat and waved him over. Connie looked good, real good. Albert, never one to let a good opportunity pass him by, went over to the table.

A short time later Albert and Connie were upstairs in Room 1103 of the business traveler hotel. Albert had learned a while ago that there were times when it was best to keep his mouth shut and pretend to be listening. Lunch with Connie was one of those times. She talked, he pretended to listened and within thirty minutes they were upstairs in Room 1103 doing the horizontal bop to their mutual satisfaction.

Walt, on the other hand, was not as clever. After leaving the restaurant, he drove back to MidContinent and sat in his car, which he parked at an isolated edge of one of the many very big parking lots that surrounded the main building. Walt just sat there, in his car, looking out over the steering wheel onto the flat, Midwestern landscape — miles of empty fields with dots of interspersed farmhouses. He watched as the clouds rolled about the blue sky to the end of the fields and then sank into the horizon. He listened to the intermittent car drive up behind him and then exit out to the interstate entrance a short distance away.

Walt reached over into the glove compartment of his car and took out a small pad of paper. He flipped through the book until he came to a blank page. He took a pen from his left hand shirt pocket and made a few scribbles. He tore the page from the pad, folded it and put it into the left-hand pocket of his shirt. He put the pad and pen down on the seat beside him.

Walt sat in the car for a while longer. Another car, a small red sedan, approached from behind and left the lot. Walt turned the ignition key in the steering column, started his car and followed the red car to the interstate.

The red car drove onto the on-ramp. Walt did not. He pulled his car over to the right, before the interstate entrance and got out. He walked up along the side of the on-ramp onto the highway.

Walt stood in the breakdown lane on the side of the interstate watching the various motor vehicles pass by. They moved quickly. Motorcycles sounded like a bumble bee; cars like a running horse; the big tractor-trailer trucks sounded like a stampede of bulls, and when they passed, the force of their wind created an invisible hand that pushed him back off the shoulder a little — whoosh!

He brought himself back to the roadside. His mind started to wander as he watched the traffic go by. He thought about Connie sitting in the restaurant. He imagined himself sitting at his workstation underneath the stairs leading into his basement, looking into his computer screen at her, held prisoner by her nice talk, her good looks and unquestioning obedience. Yet he desired more. He desired upstairs what he had downstairs. But now Walt knew that the cost of a life in which desires were fulfilled was more than he wanted to pay. Another tractor-trailer approached. Walt watched the giant truck as it got closer. He heard the clomp of its hoof-like tires, all eighteen of them, move toward him. The sound got louder. The ground shook a little. Then, just as the truck was about to pass by him, he stepped out in front of it.

Chapter 19: The Cruise to Hell

Rafael Martinez took hold of his seat cushion/life preserver and prayed like all hell that the plane did not blow up around him. The "in case of emergency" events described before takeoff by every flight attendant since the beginning of commercial aviation and ignored by every traveler during the same period (except children and panic-stricken first-time flyers) were happening to Rafael right now, right before his very eyes.

The main cabin was in pandemonium. Yellow oxygen masks were descending from overhead compartments; the emergency guide lights were illuminating the floor of the cabin aisle; flight attendants scurried up the illuminated aisles to the emergency exits trying to get the emergency doors open.

Rafael was sitting in the window seat by an emergency exit. A pretty, blonde, female flight attendant pushed him back in his seat. The force of her blow was surprising, given her size. She was small but she was all business. Her every move was completely focused on getting the emergency door open. Things were bad. The cabin had a slight odor of burnt electrical wiring. Smoke was creeping in.

This was incredible. What was supposed to be a routine takeoff wasn't. The plane hadn't taken off. It had just skidded into the water. And, seconds later, all 272,500 pounds of the aircraft, a Boeing 757-300, was floating in Boston Harbor five hundred yards from the end of the runway at Logan International Airport. Incredible. This was supposed to be a return flight from a code-and-cruise training session, not some eventual case study for the National Transportation Safety Board. Some perk this was.

It had all started when one of the Four Bothers and a Cousin had a Bright Idea. Things were bad at MidContinent. You had to be in political exile in Siberia not to know that cost overruns were rampant and the ERP implementation was significantly behind schedule. MidContinent needed all the help that it could get. And, StarTex was willing to help…for a price.

StarTex had a pile of coders in MidContinent and an inexhaustible supply of them on hand, should more be needed. MidContinent's tragic situation was good for StarTex's bottom line. All the StarTex's consultants were billing for time and materials, and, just as junkies need to keep shooting dope no matter how many times they are knocking on heavens door, MidContinent needed to keep coding. If they stopped, all that the company would have to show for its past effort was remnants of a system that didn't work. There would be no ERP; there would just be broken parts.

Thus, StarTex was making buckets of money on MidContinent's misery. Schedule delays meant that more coding time was required and more coding time turned into more billing hours, which turned into more revenue.

However, even the Four Brothers and a Cousin knew that when something seemed too good to be true, it wasn't. They knew that the gravy train was not going to run forever. They needed a plan to position themselves to get whatever follow-up business came up after the nightmare that was happening at MidContinent was over. Otherwise, the pile of developers that were billing at MidContinent would be exhumed and transformed from revenue sources into no-expense-paid trips back to India. StarTex's profits would be flying out of the country, literally.

So one of the Four Brothers and a Cousin came up with a Bright Idea: "Let's run some training classes for the MidContinent employees. The Human Resources Department will like this very much," he said in his best sub-continental, upper class English.

For the Human Resources Department at MidContinent Industries, training was the Holy Grail of software development: ship a developer off to a training class, sit him in front of a PC and a certified training professional for a week, supplement him with training materials and, *voila*, he will have all the knowledge and skill required to do the most delicate brain surgery on your most mission critical systems.

At least that is how the myth goes. The sad part is that HR just didn't get that the primary cause of most of the problems in software development is not lack of training; it's lack of thinking. Training is of limited benefit when it comes to solving the really big problems in software engineering. Training does not really teach you how to think; training teaches you how to behave, and you don't "behave up" a solution to a problem. You *think* up a solution to a problem. But, then again, it wasn't HR's mission to solve problems. Their mission was to *address* them.

But programmers liked training, mostly because it's a good vacation. More than one programmer has been recognized for his hard work and technical contributions by being sent to a weeklong training session delivered at a paradise-like destination — say a hotel in San Diego, California or a Convention Center in Orlando, Florida — to spend his days sitting in a dark, air conditioned room watching a talking head stand in front of a coliseum-sized screen, showing a set of PowerPoint slides on the latest high falutin' technology. It can be a grueling experience. Most times the room is too cold and the presentations are too boring. The only thing that keeps the programmer awake during the day is daydreaming of his plans for that night: sitting in a dark, smoke-filled room watching a pair of young, ripe breasts promenade down the runway to "dance-to-the-music" of KC and the Sunshine band singing,

Do a little dance.

Make a little love.

Get down tonight.

Get down tonight.

Get down, get down, get down, get down, get down, tonight baby!

"The timing for training cannot be better," said one of the Four Brothers and a Cousin, "MidContinent is in the process of purchasing a major upgrade to the ERP and those working on the customization of the package will need to be trained. The new version is Java-based, not the proprietary programming language of past versions. Most of the MidContinent staff working on the ERP does not know Java. They will need to learn it. We will provide the Java classes."

"Providing training classes will be a good marketing opportunity. We can focus the courses specifically on the needs of the ERP implementation. We will offer the courses offsite, free of charge, all expenses paid."

"At the moment, we have many Java developers on the bench, not billing. We will use one of them as a trainer."

"Our consultant will have a week alone with many key MidContinent developers. Just think of all the intelligence we will gather. This will position us for significant pull through. We will be very far ahead of our competition. We will make back our investment in no time. MidContinent is going to be in more trouble, not less. And, if we act wisely, the first call they make will be to us."

And so an action item was born: Create a custom, cost effective Java training program for the employees of the Information Technology Department of Mid-Continent Industries.

One of the other Four Brothers and a Cousin added to the idea. "Let's make the training really cool. Let's do it as a code-and-cruise." And so they did.

The code-and-cruise concept is simple. Rent some meeting rooms on a boat going somewhere. Put in some computers and a display screen. Throw in some curriculum and courseware and market the whole thing off as a learn-and-leisure event:

"While other companies offer you training in dull, dark classrooms, for the same price we'll take you on a sunny, fun-filled cruise where you'll learn the latest technology in our state-of-the-art onboard classrooms. Spend festive nights sitting at the captain's table, eating gourmet food from the 24-hour-a-day galley, and dancing into the early hours. Visit exciting ports of call."

Who could resist?

So the Four Brothers and a Cousin found a ship and put a deposit on a meeting room on an upper deck and a bunch of cheap cabins in the lower decks. They also rented some computers, networking equipment and a display projector. Then one of the Brothers pitched the offer to MidContinent.

HR hemmed and hawed a little, but not much. Things were pretty tense at MidContinent. The benefit of getting a little sea air into the lungs of a pile of stressed out programmers outweighed the risk of perceived impropriety in terms of procurement procedures, the cruise being free and all. Besides, those in the know at HR knew that Java was the next cool thing to be doing. So HR created a list of deserving programmers.

Much to his surprise, Rafael got to go on the cruise. Since being removed from the Customer Transfer team, Rafael had become obsessed with his redemption. His only thought was to become a premier coder and it was killing him. He was burning out. The guy needed some help and he needed to relax. He was stressing big time.

Despite his incompetence, Rafael was genuinely liked at MidContinent. Rafael was known as a guy who would "do anything for you." It was just that at times the things he did were not that good. So when the StarTex training opportunity came along, Marjorie, the HR Specialist assigned to keep an eye on Rafael and help him through his current difficulties, took it upon herself to make sure that Rafael was put on the attendee list for the training session. "He's such a good kid. All he needs is a little training and fresh air," thought Marjorie.

StarTex also included Ajita in the group, at their expense, of course. She was their insider. The Four Brothers and a Cousin wanted to use her to their full advantage. It was worth it to take her off billing for a little while.

Her ascent at MidContinent had not gone unnoticed. It was becoming common knowledge that Ajita got things done. Her team worked and her team's code worked. Try as they might, Q/A couldn't lay a hand on them. And, whereas other parts of the Sale System were significantly behind schedule, Customer Transfer was playing catch up. If the team kept going at the rate it was, they would be back on schedule within a month. And still nobody knew how she was doing it. Everybody was just chalking it up to Ajita's Coding Magic. So the Four Brothers and a Cousin figured, if she could get things done in the cubes, what could she do on the boat? It was a no-brainer. Ajita had to go.

Thus, three weeks later, Ajita, Rafael, Manfred the DBA and twenty other lucky software developers from throughout the various IT groups at MidContinent Industries were on their way to an all-expense-paid, seven-day code-and-cruise training session going from Boston, Massachusetts to the Island of Bermuda, six hundred and fifty miles off of the coast of North Carolina.

No Bon Voyage Party was planned. Manfred the DBA did, however, get good and drunk on the flight to Boston and threw up overboard when the ship left the dock that night. "What the hell," he figured. "It's a vacation."

And then the training began.

A significant change was to come about at MidContinent. The new version of the ERP, made by a top-tier manufacturer, was going to open source for customization, using a common language, Java. In the past, all customization was done in a proprietary programming language. Nobody else used the proprietary langauge and nobody at all liked it, not even the coders who were making a fortune as customization consultants. It was a pain in the ass to learn and even harder to get to work right. But if you wanted to customize the ERP, you needed to learn its language. (Sorta like the Catholic Church before Vatican II: Wanna talk to God? Then speak Latin.)

The only people who really liked this setup were the ERP manufacturers because the proprietary nature of the language bound programmers to the specific ERP, thus creating a dedicated, albeit captured, developer community. If a programmer wanted to program another ERP, he had to learn another language, which was a huge time investment. So they stuck with what they knew and made money.

However, the second-tier ERP companies chomping at the heels of the very few, top-tier proprietary ERP manufacturers, said, Hey, let's have our ERP's all speak a common, easy-to-learn, easy-to-use language.

And, just as Luther opened the door to God by making the Bible available in the vernacular so that anyone could read the Good Book, the second-tier ERP Manufacturers made their products work under a common language, allowing a broad cross section of programmers to code them.

Needless to say, if a lot of programmers could code the ERP, instead of a select few, the price of coding went down, way down. Customers liked this.

The second-tier companies began to win market share from the top-tier companies. So in order to keep market share, the top-tier proprietary ERP manufacturers jumped on the band wagon and made their products available in the same easy-to-learn, easy-to-use language. Pretty soon the whole world of ERP software developers was programming as one happy family talking directly to God in one common language. And this language was Java.

But you still had to *learn* the easy-to-learn and easy-to-use language, which was the objective of the StarTex cruise.

The curriculum was two sets of three-day sessions. The StarTex Talking Head Expert, a Java programmer named Sanjay, planned to deliver lectures on the first two days of the session followed on the third day by hands-on coding.

The floating classroom was configured like a lecture hall. Large tables were arranged like a U, seven seats to a side, with the open end facing a wall upon which hung a white projection screen. Inside the U was a small table upon which rested the Talking Head Expert's laptop. The laptop was plugged into a projector that displayed the contents of its screen onto the wall. The Talking Head Expert, Sanjay, sat at the table in the middle of the U and lectured while he typed out code examples. (The configuration looked like the bridge of the starship Enterprise, from the Next Generation episodes: Picard, Troi and Riker seated, Worf standing behind them, all in a protracted semi-circle surrounding Data manning the helm.)

Everyone attended the classes, even Manfred the DBA. Manfred had heard a lot about Java. He might as well learn it, he thought. Yeah, he lived and breathed SQL, the programming language common to all DBAs who would ever touch a database. But Manfred figured that one day he just might decide to unleash his programming power upon the general population, and knowing Java would be useful when working with the masses.

Manfred the DBA sat at the bottom of the U. Rafael and Ajita sat facing each other on opposite sides of the U. They had not seen one another since Rafael's departure from Customer Transfer. They were cordial to each and did not avoid contact when in class. During the coffee breaks, they engaged in geeky chit-chat: Rafael cracked jokes and Ajita laughed. There was a comfortable friendliness between them. But there was still no discussion whatsoever of that first meeting in the conference room when Ajita held Rafael close as Manfred watched. Both seemed to like it that way.

On the second day of training, the Talking Head Expert from StarTex had an exercise planned. The objective of the day was to learn to think like Java programmers. He said, "Language is made up of two parts, semantics and syntax. Syntax is how a language works. Semantics is what a language means. Today I want to spend time getting to the meaning of the programs which you will create. I do not want you to become overly concerned with having to learn the syntax of the programming language at this moment. Mastery of syntax will come over time. So instead of having you all program at separate machines and struggle on your own trying to get your programs to work properly, we will try a different approach."

"We will program together. You will not have to do any keyboard input. I will do it all. All you need to do is to call out an idea or a line of code that you think needs to be written and I will type it in my laptop for all to see. I'll be your 'coding slave.'" he said with in his best sub-continental, upper class English with a smile of self amusement on his face.

Manfred the DBA laughed out loud. He called out from his seat at the center of the U to the rest of the group, "Dude! You're a consultant. You're already our coding slave!"

No sooner had the words come from Manfred's mouth then Ajita and Rafael locked eyes. Things were now clear between them.

Ajita went to Rafael's cabin later that night. He was not surprised to see her. In fact, he was expecting her. The façade of cordiality was no longer needed. A new intimacy existed between them. The closeness was beyond words, beyond language. They were well beyond being friends. They were now conspirators. The mission was unmistakable. Plans needed to be made.

Ajita stayed late into the night with Rafael. They did not touch. They talked. Rafael cried a lot. So did Ajita.

The remainder of the cruise had its ups and downs. The ship made it to Bermuda without a hitch. The weather was nearly perfect and the shopping was fun, although a bit expensive.

On the way back to Boston, one of the programmers got food poisoning from a bad piece of shrimp and had to spend a day in his cabin, near the toilet. Another programmer made friends with a couple from Nashua, New Hampshire, who had a fifteen year old son in tow. The kid looked as if he was eleven. His forehead was full of zits. Yet, it turned out that the kid was a monster Java coder and a Gamer. His whole life centered on his Xbox, his computer and open source Java coding.

The programmer was a Gamer, too, and he spent the first three evenings of the cruise with the kid in the ship's video game arcade.

The programmer and the kid became friends. The programmer invited the kid to attend the second three-day Java session, suggesting that he might learn a thing or two.

It turned out that the kid knew more about Java than the Talking Head Expert and was not hesitant at all to taunt him at every chance. The kid was a ruthless bully. The minute the Talking Head Expert made a mistake — BAM! — the kid was all over him. If it wasn't so entertaining, it would have been cruel.

By the last day of the session, the Talking Head Expert was clearly shaken. His best sub-continental, upper class English was degrading. He muttered to himself in Hindi.

By now the kid was doing the teaching. All the Talking Head Expert could do was to stand at the bottom of the U and watch the kid do his thing.

The kid was disappointed when the boat docked in Boston. He did not want to leave the programmers. On board he was a player; on shore he would have to go back to being an undersize teenage boy trying to impress girls who were taller than him while trying to avoid jocks who wanted to knock his lights out.

Rafael thought about the kid as he grabbed his seat cushion. During the cruise many of the programmers joked about offering the kid a job. He would probably do better work than the average MidContinent coder and for less money, maybe even get to be a Tech Lead. Manfred joked that he would just buy the kid from his parents and give him to Rafael as a gift, make the kid his personal coding slave; that the kid could do all the work and Rafael could get all the credit.

Rafael was happy that the others let the idea go and that the kid went back to New Hampshire with his parents. He didn't like the idea of the kid floating around Boston Harbor in the middle of this mess. Things were no longer a joke.

The flight attendant asked Rafael to assist her in getting the emergency door open. Both took hold of the door's large red handle and gave a mighty pull up in unison. The door opened.

The water around the plane was as black as the night and tinged with red and yellow reflections from the lights of the emergency boats and helicopters that were beginning to surround the aircraft. The tops of the airplane's wings were visible; the bottom halves were submerged in water.

The flight attendant pulled a lever on top of the open hatch and the yellow inflatable slide exploded out from the emergency door, down beside the plane and into the water. The three other emergency doors were now open and their slides were extending out into the water too.

Passengers made their way to the doors. Each door was supervised by a flight attendant. The flight attendants coordinated the evacuation from the plane quickly and deliberately: "Next — jump! Next—jump! Next—jump! Don't worry sweetie — you'll be fine, just jump." Men, women and children slid down the slide and splashed into the water clutching the seat cushion/life preserver.

Police and fire boats scurried around the plane shining spotlights and picking up passengers from the harbor. More smoke was spewing out from the plane. Rafael was one of the last people to leave the plane.

Staying behind was not an act of conscious heroism. Rafael was terrified to go down the slide. He could not swim. He thought he was going to drown. Finally he had no choice. The cabin was becoming black with smoke. It was either suffocate by drowning or suffocate by smoke inhalation. Rafael chose the water.

Rafael went back in time. Going down the yellow escape slide was like being back in his kindergarten playground. He closed his eyes and jumped out of the emergency door clutching his seat cushion. Wheeeeeeee!

And then came the splash. Rafael felt the water surround him. It was cold. He opened his eyes. He could see the lights of the boats and the helicopters above him, but all around him the water was black. There was no boat nearby. He held his seat cushion for dear life. He tried to get it underneath his chest so that his head and shoulders were above water. He was struggling.

A police boat started to move toward him. He held the seat cushion tighter. The boat was near him. Rafael could hear its engines grow louder through the water. He was having trouble staying afloat. His shoes, jacket and trousers were saturated. The weight of the waterlogged clothing was pulling him down.

The police boat was next to him. Rafael felt hands grab hold of his jacket. They were trying to lift him into the boat. The seat cushion caught onto something on the side of the boat. It was stuck. Rafael would not let go of the cushion. He was too scared. The hands were having trouble getting him into the boat. He heard a voice, "Let go of the seat cushion! Let go of the seat cushion! For chissakes kid, let go!" The hands kept working and the voice kept shouting, "Let go, kid, let go!"

Rafael let go of the seat cushion. The hands lost their grip of Rafael's jacket. He was back in the water. He had no life preserver. He wanted to stay afloat. He wanted to keep his head above water. The sound of the boat engine was growing faint. Rafael had let go and now he was sinking.

Part 3: Emancipation

Chapter 20: Katherine Avoids Disaster

Katherine Limeleaf let go of the sugar cube. It fell into the coffee in her Mid-Continent coffee mug with a small plop. She stirred the sugar into the beige-colored coffee using a small silver teaspoon that she kept in the upper right hand drawer of her desk, next to the box that contained the sugar cubes. Katherine preferred sugar cubes to sugar packets. Although sugar packets were free for the taking at the many coffee stations situated throughout the MidContinent physical plant, Katherine found them cheap. Sugar packets may be hygienic and cost effective, but they were not elegant. Katherine preferred sugar cubes. She always kept a supply on hand in her desk. And she used small antique sugar tongs to serve herself her cube.

There was a knock at the door. She looked up.

"Come in," she called out.

The knob turned. The door opened. Ajita entered. Katherine stood.

"Sit down, please," said Katherine as she gestured to one of the two chairs in front of her desk.

Ajita sat down facing Katherine. Katherine's desk separated them.

"Would you like something to drink?" asked Katherine.

"Yes," answered Ajita. "Coffee will be fine, thank you."

Katherine picked up the phone handset and hit the number pad on the face of the console twice. Ajita could not tell which numbers she struck.

"Cindy, thank you for letting in my nine o'clock. Yes, that's a great idea," Katherine said, not at all surprised that Cindy had read her mind. Cindy was a model Admin.

Katherine looked up at Ajita, "How do you want it?"

"Black, thank you," answered Ajita.

"She says that she wants it black, if you can, Cindy. Thanks." Katherine placed the handset back on the telephone console.

Within seconds Cindy entered the office with a cup of coffee in a matching MidContinent mug in one hand and a coaster and napkin in the other. She placed the coaster on the desk in front of Ajita and then placed the mug on the coaster. She gave Ajita the napkin with a smile. Ajita thanked her. Cindy turned around and left the office as efficiently as she entered.

"Thank you for taking the time to meet with me," said Katherine.

"You are welcome," said Ajita.

Katherine sat back in her chair, picked up her coffee, took a sip and placed the mug back on her desk.

"OK Ajita, let me get directly to the point. What's the deal? Why did you do it?"

"Do what?" Ajita replied.

"Have sex with them?" asked Katherine.

"With whom?" Ajita asked in a sincere and polite manner.

Katherine spoke, "Albert and the Project Manager, right here in this office? I need to know, why did you do it?"

"Why?" asked Ajita.

"Yes, why?" Katherine responded.

Ajita waited a moment and then answered, "Because I believe that there is no greater honor than to give the client exactly what he or she wants."

"I see," said Katherine with an air of contemplation in her voice. "You know, you could have been fired."

"No, not really. I think that such risk was marginal. My analysis was that any risk incurred by firing me was greater for you. I am not unaware as to how each party is perceived by the world at large. The situation was in my favor. I am a foreign, female contract worker, you are a native-born, high-level executive, and the others were white, upper-middle class men. The perception would be that clearly you all had coerced me to do such things. You know how the American public loves a lurid sex scandal. The headlines would be bound to draw attention: 'Mid-Continent executives force foreign, contract technology worker into group sex orgy.' The risk was all yours. I am perceived to be powerless. You, Ms. Limeleaf, are anything but powerless. But please do not worry; my motivations were not acrimonious or malevolently self-serving. I will not spread false rumors. I genuinely want to do good. I want to serve my clients well," said Ajita

"Ajita, how is having sex in the middle of my office serving your clients well?"

"I was giving my clients — you, that gentleman Albert and the Project Manager — exactly what each of you wanted."

"You are telling me that I wanted an episode of sexual abandon in my office? This is a large corporation, not at brothel," said Katherine in a slightly incredulous manner.

"It is a simple matter of satisfying want, Ms Limeleaf. The sex was secondary. I satisfied everybody's want, even yours. It was obvious to me."

"Take Albert for instance. He had no real interest in the information being recited. All he wanted from that morning meeting was for nothing more than for his body to feel good. I could tell by his demeanor — the way he sat, the way he ate, the way he smelled. Albert is a man for whom one thing in life is important: abundant, almost distracting physical stimulation. You can tell by looking at him what his priorities are: to achieve orgasm and to achieve inebriation, preferably in that order. The man's mind is nothing but a tool to satisfy the cravings of his body. That is what he is all about. I simply gave the man what he wanted. It was apparent to me from the minute I walked into the room."

"The want of the Project Manager was a bit more obscure. It took me a while to figure it out. But, once I did, my duty was obvious. The Project Manager wanted 'in'; he wanted to participate in his world. He was tired of watching others make contributions to the world around him and having no other role than to define and defend that reality. His world, until that point, was nothing more than a photo that represented a possibility."

"The Project Manager was voyeur in the saddest sense of the world. He was no longer excited by what was going on around him. He was bored and he was void, not in the world and not out of it, a feeble scribe documenting the actions of others. My simple, erotic act brought him into the world."

"Please remember: at first he tried to ignore the episode, then all he could do was watch. I invited his participation. Yes, my invitation was unexpected. It was extreme, dramatic and it was dangerous. But it was very, very real. All that was required of him was that he believed the reality before him, take part in it and enjoy that which he found pleasurable."

"Your want was as simple as Albert's, Ms. Limeleaf. You wanted something to happen. I could tell by looking at you that you were bored and that you knew that the Status Meeting was a microcosmic symptom of the entire ERP implementation. You knew that everybody was going through the motions and nothing was happening. You knew that there was no information in the Status Report that would help the ERP get out of the quagmire that it is in. Something dramatic was required. I have discovered that there are few things in life more dramatic than a human orgasm."

"I wanted to demonstrate for you a solution to your problem: just do the unthinkable, be brave and serve the client. In this case, your client is all of MidContinent"

Katherine sat quietly for a moment. Then she said, "How are you running on time?"

"I am free until 11 a.m.," said Ajita.

Katherine reached over to her telephone, picked up the handset and tapped the console twice. "Hi, Cindy. Why yes, that is just what I was thinking." She looked up at Ajita, "Would you like something to eat?"

Ajita nodded yes.

"Yes, a tray of pastries with the coffee would be wonderful," Katherine said in the telephone's headset.

Cindy entered with the carafe, the cream and the pastries. Katherine thanked her as she put the food items on the small, round conference table in her office. Cindy turned around and left the office. Katherine got up out of the chair behind her desk and motioned for Ajita to join her at the small, round conference table..

An hour later, the pastry tray was empty. Ajita got up. Katherine thanked her for her time and accompanied Ajita to the door. Katherine opened it with her left hand. She shook Ajita's hand with her free right hand. Ajita left. Katherine closed the door behind her and returned to her desk to work.

Katherine took a legal-size manila file folder from her center desk drawer and opened it onto her desktop. She turned to the last page of the many pieces of paper in the folder. She picked up her fountain pen, applied her signature to the last page and dated it.

Cindy read Katherine's mind and came in with her notary stamp. Cindy was a Notary Public, a certification she picked up a few years ago in order to enhance her resume and make her more valuable as an executive level Administrative Assistant. She notarized the signature on the last page in the manila folder as being Katherine's. Then she took the folder and its contents down to the MidContinent Legal Department for verification and filing.

With a few strokes of her pen, Katherine Limeleaf had outsourced the entire workings of the MidContinent Information Technology Department to MidContinent's new strategic partner, StarTex Information Management Group, headquartered in Bangalore, India.

Not a single line of code would ever again be written again from within the company's walls. Every coder would be fired.

Two days later, Katherine named Albert Shulberg to be the new Chief Information Officer of MidContinent Industries, the position formerly held by the late Walter Vanderdale. Also, under a new reorganization plan, the Chief Information Officer would now report directly to the Chief Operating Officer, Katherine Limeleaf.

Chapter 21: Walt's Day

Walt's wife let go of the handful of dirt that she had been holding since the beginning of the ceremony. The dirt fell into Walt's open grave and landed like fairy dust on the coffin that held his remains. She then walked away. Others in the funeral party approached the grave and did the same.

After all the commemorative dirt had been distributed, the Reverend, a friend of the family for years, ended the event by reading some closing words from the Good Book.

The attendees left the grave site, returned to their cars and drove home. Walt's wife and three children, two grown, one still in her teens, were driven home in the black limousine that they had rented for the occasion. There was little talking in the back of the vehicle during the ride back.

The limousine drove down the interstate and then off into the housing development where Walt's wife and teenage daughter lived and Walt used to live. The car pulled into the cul-de-sac, in which their house was located, in the middle between two others of similar design. Two very official-looking cars, a blue Crown Victoria with big, black-wall tires and nondescript aluminum hubcaps and a black Crown Victoria with the same type of wheels, were parked in front of their house.

That these parked cars were in the cul-de-sac was very unusual. All the residents of the cul-de-sac parked their cars in the garages adjoining the houses. Only visitors parked in the cul-de-sac. And, to date no one who had visited the cul-de-sac had ever driven a blue or black Crown Vic with big, black-wall tires and nondescript aluminum hubcaps. These cars had law-enforcement written all over them.

The chauffeur got out of the limousine and walked to the back, passenger-side door of the vehicle and opened it. Almost in tandem the front-driver side and passenger-side doors of the blue Crown Vics opened. Walt's wife got out of the limousine. Two men in dark suits got out of the Crown Vic.

Walt's wife walked from the limousine up the flagstone path etched in her lawn to her front door. The two men in dark suits walked across the lawn toward her. All parties met at the front door.

The two men in the dark suits were taller than Walt's wife. She looked at them with eyes that were more in a state of grief than in a state of fear. She said nothing.

One of the men spoke up. "Ma'am, I am Agent Richard Stanton from the FBI and this is Carl Bergonan from the Securities and Exchange Commission. We have a warrant to search your residence for documents having to do with securities and tax fraud at MidContinent Industries. May we enter?" he said displaying the document in front of her.

Walt's wife's eyes grew wide, then relaxed. "Yes, you may," she replied.

Upon her reply the FBI agent waved back at the black Crown Victoria. The four doors of the sedan opened like two butterflies extending their wings sideways. Four men in dark suits exited the car, one from each door, and approached the house. One of the men in dark suits was Frank DiGrazia.

The men were surprisingly polite and tidy with their search, not the type of rough-and-tumble agents that you see on TV. The men said "please" when they needed assistance or permission and "thank you" when assistance and permission were given.

They showed some interest in documents that they found on MidContinent stationary on the upper floors of the house. The items that were of the most interest to them were the contents of the drawers in the workstation beneath the steps leading to the basement and the computer upon which it sat.

Frank DiGrazia was given the assignment of removing the computer from the workstation. Frank was one of the two IRS representatives in the group. They had been watching from afar for months. The stock fluctuation had been the tip off. Something was going on at MidContinent. Too much money had been moving around in too many weird ways for too long a time. The FBI noticed it, the SEC noticed it, and then the IRS noticed it.

The effect of the notoriety was a cursory, then criminal investigation into the financial innards of MidContinent. Part of that poking around was the Search Warrant that Frank was helping to execute.

Frank got down on his hands and knees and crawled underneath the workstation desk to the back of the computer on the lower left. He disconnected the mouse, keyboard, monitor and DSL cables. Then he crawled around to the front of the workstation and lifted the box out from behind the doors that hid it. He tagged the box as evidence and took it upstairs and into the blue Crown Victoria outside.

Another IRS agent went downstairs and collected all the papers in the workstation, put them in a number of large clear plastic envelopes, tagged them and then joined Frank outside by the blue Crown Vic. Their work was finished.

Upstairs in the house, the FBI and SEC guys continued to look through drawers and closets and shelves. They looked under chairs, cushions and rugs. They politely and neatly left no stone unturned and no crevice unchecked.

Then all but Agent Richard Stanton left. He stayed behind to thank Walt's wife for her cooperation and to say goodbye. Then he left, too.

After they were gone Walt's wife went into the recently searched, but neatly restored kitchen and took a glass of ice water from the automatic ice water dispenser on the door of her refrigerator. She drank the water slowly but with one raise of the glass. Her mouth was no longer dry. All of those strangers running through her house had made her thirsty. She wouldn't go in the kitchen while they were there. She wouldn't go anywhere in the house while they were there. She had stood in the corner of the living room, trying to be out of the way while they inspected every artifact of her life with Walt.

It was all beyond her. Walt was just Walt — in at nine, out by five Walt. And now these strangers just had come through her house and as polite and neat as they were, they had made his memory as messy as his death. There was too much mess around. Walt's body had been turned into hamburger when the tractor-trailer hit him. He was pulp, ugly mush, too destroyed for an open-casket viewing. And the note that he left behind was messy, all covered in blood, with the words, "I want to live in the real world," handwritten on the paper. And now there was this matter with the FBI, the SEC and the IRS. It was all too messy.

There was a bit of relief, however. Walt's wife was glad that he wasn't around to have to put up with this mess. While others were busy walking all over and through the remains of his life, Walt was resting in peace, deep down in the ground with the worms and the bugs. Some days, she thought, you're better off just being dead.

Chapter 22: Albert Has a Loss

Albert Shulberg, a.k.a. "BigDick6969," let go of his wallet. There was no more use in struggling. These guys were going to get his money, no matter what. They had a gun and a demonstrated ability to hit him in places where it hurt, which in this instance was Albert's left cheek bone and his jaw. He was bleeding from the mouth. He could taste his own blood. His face was swelling where he had been hit. This was a real mugging. It was obvious that if he didn't hand over his cash, they were going to keep hitting him. They might even shoot him. The easiest thing to do was to give up. No sense losing teeth over it.

Being mugged in the parking lot of MidContient Industries was a surprise and an embarrassment. This was Iowa, for chrissakes. Nobody did stuff like this. Yeah, you might have the occasional altercation between some of the third shift Mexican guys from Production over a gambling debt or something, but mugging the Chief Information Officer for MidContinent Industries right in front of his assigned space in the main parking lot was unimaginable. Was he wearing a sign on his back that said, "I am a defenseless, stupid fuck from the middle of somewhere, stuck out here in the middle of nowhere, and I have a little bit of money and plastic in my pocket and the last thing that I expect is to be robbed at gun point out here in God's fucking country?" Where the fuck was security anyway? They were supposed to make sure that shit like this didn't happen.

But, it *was* happening. So he took his hand off of his ass and let one of the assailants reach into his back trouser pocket, the one that contained the wallet that he was trying to protect. The thug took the wallet. His partner thug told Albert to turn his remaining pockets inside out. Albert obeyed. The contents of his pockets fell to the pavement — keys, business cards, a condom, old credit card receipts, some coins — mostly quarters and pennies — and cash in denominations of one-, five- and ten-dollar bills.

The wallet grabber dropped to his knees and collected the paper money. Once all the money was in hand, the other mugger gave Albert one last blow across the face that caused him to go sprawling across the hood of the parked car behind him. Then the robbers ran off across the dimly lit parking lot into the night.

Albert came out of his daze and stood up. He was a mess. He could see that his shirt was covered in blood. His face hurt.

Chapter 22: Albert Has a Loss

He brought his hand to his cheek. He felt the swelling and the presence of a thick liquid that he assumed to be his blood.

He had no idea how bad he looked. The parking lot was not illuminated well enough that he could see his reflection in the windshield or door windows of the car. All he could do was guess.

This CIO gig was going nowhere fast. At that moment, standing in the dark parking lot of MidContient Industries, covered in blood, face battered and relieved of his credit cards and pocket money, Albert Shulberg, a.k.a. "BigDick6969," regretted that he had ever accepted Katherine Limeleaf's offer to become the CIO of MidContinent Industries. Yeah, the money was good, $300,000 a year with company car, housing allowance and performance bonuses, and the stock options were better: 1,500,000 preferred shares of MidContinent Industries, which he had locked into at a dollar a share, and which were presently worth two dollars and six cents a share.

But everything else was a mess. There wasn't any information technology left at MidContinent to be chief of, seeing as how the whole shooting match had been shipped off to India. The FBI, SEC and IRS were all over MidContinent. And, as an officer of the corporation, albeit a new and completely ignorant officer of the corporation, he was spending most of his days being interviewed by one of the many humorless men in dark suits. Not to mention that by some coincidence that he did not consider to be very coincidental, his own tax returns were being audited by the IRS. Being mugged in the parking lot was just the icing on a very bad cake.

Albert wondered if it would have been better just to have remained a hired gun, doing his System Architect gig and then going home, if you can call an airplane home. But ever since that day in Katherine Limeleaf's office, with that woman Ajita, something had changed. Albert had watched a lot of women, had done a lot of women and had been done by just as many. So weird stuff, with weird women, in weird places were not new experiences for him. But despite the decadence of the situation, something about Ajita was real, more real than he had ever known — so real, in fact, that Albert wanted more.

Albert had tried to contact Ajita many times since the ménage-a-trois episode. He had emailed her, he had stopped by her desk, and he had tried to call her on her MidContinent number. All of his attempts were successful.

Ajita always replied. She was polite and she was professional, but, the scope of her replies never went outside of MidContinent. She refused Albert's requests that she join him for dinner, for lunch, or for breakfast, not for a movie, not for a cup of coffee.

One time he offered her $300 to fuck him, which he proposed to her in exactly those terms. Ajita refused politely and professionally. She said that accepting such an offer would constitute a significant conflict of interest for her. At the present time MidContinent was her one and only client. Such were the terms of her employment agreement with StarTex.

Yet, Albert kept trying and Ajita kept refusing to engage him in any activity that did not have direct relevance to MidContinent Industries.

So, when one day Katherine Limeleaf offered Albert the sweetheart deal to become CIO of MidContinent, he accepted the position. He was now an employee of MidContinent Industries. There was no conflict of interest in play. As an employee of MidContinent Industries, he was now Ajita's client; he was no longer a third party hired gun who got table scraps.

The move brought him closer to Ajita, true, but the move came with a price. Albert Shulberg, a.k.a. "BigDick6969," was now a model, a man with position but no mission, no raison d'être. Albert Shulberg, a.k.a. "BigDick6969," was being paid to sit in his office and look beautiful. He had no purpose other than to be on display and to be the object of desire by those around him. Whatever talent or expertise he had to offer his surrounding was of no value and no interest. All he had to do was to show up and be seen.

Occasionally he was called upon to participate in a conversation, mostly with a member of the FBI, SEC or IRS. All they wanted from him was that which he wanted from the dancers at the Sea Light lounge — attention, meaningful attention. That was it. No more. No less.

Albert bent over and collected the contents of his pockets that had been scattered about the parking lot. He picked up the keys, paper and coins that the muggers had left behind and put them back into his turned-in pockets. He was feeling a little bit stronger, not so beat up.

He walked over to his car, a red Cadillac. He took the electronic car key out of his pocket, punched the unlock button, opened the door and got in. He turned on the dome light inside the roof of the car. Then he reached up and turned the rear view mirror toward him and looked at his face in the mirror. It was a mess, all swollen, cut and bruised, covered with patches of dried blood.

"This is not the face of a model," he thought.

Then, he started his car, put it in gear, and drove it out of the parking lot onto the interstate beyond.

Chapter 23: Frank Looks for Evidence

Frank DiGrazia let go of his breath. He was almost through counting to ten. His heart rate was dropping. He could feel it. He took a breath in, six; a breath out, seven; in, eight; out, nine; in, ten and then out again. He was calm. The photo no longer disturbed him.

For the most part, counting to ten worked. Once in a while it didn't. Frank had the proverbial Italian temper — it came on fast, went white hot and then led him to break things, mostly things at home, but never at work. The IRS frowned upon such behavior. It wasn't professional. Frank was at work. It was important that he keep control of himself in the workplace.

Frank was spending the day in his temporary office in Iowa going over the data on Walt's computer. This Walt guy was a pervert. Most of the contents in his cache folder, the place on a computer where an internet browser stores temporary copies of things downloaded from the web, contained photographs of women in a variety of sexually provocative poses.

Some of the women displayed themselves in an alluring, but not lurid manner. Other photos showed women and couples in various forms of sexual foreplay and sexual intercourse. Some of the women were young, Playboy Bunny types. Others were older women, one-time porn queens who had had their day and were now trying to make ends meet working the only trade they knew. Some of the photos had women doing things with animals.

No big deal. Frank had seen it all before. This was not the first time he had to inspect a suspect's hard drive looking for evidence of the crime at hand.

So there he was, sifting through a pile of smut looking for something, anything that had to do with foul play at MidContinent Industries. Find a document, catalog it, find a document, catalog it, on and on and on. It was tedious work, just like he had been told it would be in cyber-school, the place where he had learned to do this stuff for the IRS. But, Hell, it beat interviewing creeps who had not paid their taxes. In a way, Frank was grateful for the tedium.

The day would not have been unusual if it had not been for the photo: a middle-aged woman, slightly plump, sitting naked on a bed, back against the headboard, legs spread, wearing only a red, lace brassiere. It was a hotel bed. Frank could tell from the background items — the mass-produced nightstand, the hotel-style phone with the little red light that blinks to tell you that you have a call waiting, the paintings that you have seen a hundred times before, in a hundred different hotel rooms. On the top of the nightstand next to the bed was a bottle of liquor, a few open beer bottles and a half filled glass.

There was no mistake. The woman in the photo was Miranda, his wife. The photo was quite clear, so clear, in fact, that Frank recognized the bra — he had bought it for her on Valentine's Day, three years ago.

The photo did not look recent. Miranda wore her hair shorter now and was about thirty pounds heavier. The hair style in the photo was about two years old. Yet, it really didn't matter when the photo was taken. The image was immortal and ubiquitous. It would be around forever, everywhere. It was now part of the Internet.

Frank was mad, but no longer furious. He took his rage and confusion and fear and sense of betrayal and stuffed it down inside himself, into that place where he stored all the other Miranda-on-booze incidents. This was just another entry into the well of resentment about which he had become too familiar. He was calmer now. He could move on and do what needed to be done. He had creeps to catch.

Frank continued to search and inventory the contents of Walt's machine well into the afternoon. Then he hit pay dirt: scanned images of purchase orders, eight of them that were made out to a company named "East Side Associates." The contact name was Albert Shulberg.

There was no federal tax identification number on the PO's. None of the PO's were for more than nine thousand dollars. A bank would not report the money, as long as no one deposit amount was over ten thousand dollars. Thus, unless they were subject to the scrutiny of an audit, the checks cut for these PO's would be invisible to the IRS. This was a gift. Frank had been going after Walt and he got Albert. Frank smelled that an indictment for income tax evasion was but a phone call away.

Frank finished off Walt's computer at about six in the evening. He recorded his findings and called his supervisor in Chicago to tell him the details of what he had found. The supervisor gave him an "atta-boy" and asked him to forward copies of the incriminating evidence by email. The supervisor said that he would start the ball rolling immediately for an audit of this guy, Albert Shulberg. If things panned out, and, given the significance of Frank's finding, there wasn't any reason why they shouldn't, a minor indictment would be handed down within thirty days. Albert Shulberg was toast.

The supervisor told Frank that his work in the Midwest was done, that it was time for him to go back to his base office in Rochester. He was no longer on loan to the boys in Iowa.

Frank was glad to hear the news. The Midwest stank. The place was a pit, a backwater. There was nothing to do and the people were yokels. A month had been enough; Frank wanted to go home.

Frank waited outside in front of the baggage claim area at the Greater Rochester International Airport for over an hour. He was waiting for Miranda to pick him up. They always met outside, in front of the baggage claim area. It would be a simple matter for her to drive up, for him to toss his luggage into the trunk of the car and for them to then drive home.

But Miranda never showed up.

Finally, Frank took a cab home.

Frank arrived at his house forty-five minutes later and forty-five dollars poorer. The driver helped him unload his bags and bring them to the front door.

Frank unlocked the door, pushed his bags inside and then followed them in behind. He walked up the three-step staircase to the living room level of his ranch-style house.

The living room had a fireplace at the far end with two sofas facing each other perpendicular to the fireplace. A coffee table sat between the sofas. A half empty bottle of liquor and a half empty glass sat on coasters on top of the coffee table.

Miranda was asleep on one of the sofas. She was snoring — heavy, heaving snores; pig-like snores; the snores that a drunk makes in a booze-sodden stupor.

Frank felt his heart start to race. He wanted to break something. His eyes went to the coffee table. They darted from the bottle of liquor to the glass. The glass looked good for throwing. WHAM — he could hear the sound of shattering glass against the wall. His eyes went back to the bottle. Grab the bottle by the neck, smack it against the coffee table, cut her throat with the jagged end.

But...no, throwing and breaking wouldn't work. He needed to calm down, way down. He started to count: "one..., two......, three........, four............, five.............."

On "six", he picked Miranda up off the sofa. Her bloated body lay prone over his extended arms. Years of boozing had made her heavy. Seven..., he moved away from the sofa and walked to the staircase like Frankenstein with a dead corpse. Eight..., he heaved Miranda over his shoulder as if she were a sack of potatoes. She grunted and then moaned a little. She was still asleep. She smelled like a sow sweating booze.

Nine..., he walked down the basement level of the house, into the Rec Room and opened the door that led to garage. Ten..., he calmly entered.

Frank walked over to Miranda's car and opened the passenger-side door with little difficulty, considering the fact that all one-hundred-and-seventy-five pounds of her drunken weight was sprawled over his shoulder.

Once the door was open, he laid Miranda on the front seat. She was still asleep. He closed the car door. Then he went over to the driver's side door, opened it and got in. He reached up over the steering wheel and took the car keys that were hidden in the sun visor overhead. Miranda and Frank always kept their car keys hidden in the sun visor when their cars were parked in the garage. That way they could use each other's car without having to go around the house searching for keys.

Frank started the car. He used the power controls to lower all the windows in the automobile. He got out of the car and checked the big garage doors to make sure that they were locked. Then, he went to the back of the garage, to the door that led into the house. He left the garage and closed the door behind him.

Frank returned upstairs to the living room. He took the bottle of liquor and the glass from the coffee table and brought them into the kitchen. He went to the kitchen sink and poured the contents of the liquor bottle down the drain. He listened to the sound of the liquid as it hit the stainless steel basin. When the bottle was empty, he tossed it into the trash container under the sink. Then he put the glass in the dishwasher.

Frank returned to the living room and put the coasters that protected the table top back into a drawer in a small side-table next to one of the sofas.

Once he was satisfied that the living room was clean enough, he went back downstairs to the Rec Room. He turned on the television. He channel surfed until he found a show that interested him. The odor of carbon monoxide seeped in through the bottom of the door that led to the garage. Frank continued to watch the television. The smell didn't bother him.

The bodies of Frank and Miranda DiGrazia were discovered six days later. Miranda's sister found them. She had been calling for three days, but all she had gotten was the answering machine. She and Miranda were supposed to have gone out for lunch. Nobody answering the phone for three days was unusual.

She drove over. She let herself in. The front door was unlocked. The kids were at summer camp. The television was on. The car had run out of gas. The smell of carbon monoxide was still in the air. Both bodies were blue, so blue, in fact, that it looked as if they had been made for each other.

Chapter 24: Albert Becomes Himself

Albert let go of Ajita. She moved back a little, put her lips to his forehead, and held them there for a few moments. Then she took them away and got up off of his lap.

"I have a question for you. Albert, have you ever had the experience of being wanted for who you are, not for what you do or for what you have?" she asked.

"What do you mean?" asked Albert. The look on his face gave the impression that she might as well had asked him if he could explain the fine points of sub-particle quantum physics or Kant's theory of the categorical imperative, both of which were subjects that he knew nothing about.

"Have you ever had the experience of a person wanting to be with you without you having to pay that person or to perform a service for that person?" asked Ajita.

"Is this why you invited me here, to sit on my lap and ask this me this stuff?" he said with a tinge of annoyance, "I was expecting more."

A few days earlier Ajita had sent him an email. She had information to share with him. Would he be interested in meeting with her to discuss it? He jumped on the opportunity faster than a mongoose on a cobra.

An early morning meeting was arranged in a small conference room. Albert was the first to arrive. He sat in one of the conference room chairs — high backed, leather bound, swivel style with comfortable arm rests. Ajita arrived five minutes later. She entered the room and without hesitation approached him directly. He rose to greet her. She pushed him back into the chair. Then she took his hands and pulled him forward toward her so that his lap was beyond the comfortable arm-rests. She spread her legs and sat across Albert's lap. She put her arms around Albert. He put her arms around her. His penis shot up like a Titan rocket on blast off. Fucking time, he thought.

He was wrong.

All she did was hold him.

Maybe all she needs is a little revving up, he thought. His hands ran up and down her back. They came to rest on her hips. He tried to move her back and forth across his lap. A steady embrace was her only response. Finally, Albert's erection dissipated. He was bored. He let go of her. She kissed his forehead.

She was standing in front of him now. Both she and Albert were fully clothed, nobody's private parts were exposed and no extreme impropriety was committed — not at all like last time.

"I was hoping to give you what you want, to feel love," said Ajita.

"Love is the last thing that I want to feel," he said. "You're sitting on my lap, Ajita! As far as I am concerned there is only one reason for you to be there and that reason is sex, s-e-x. Anything else is a waste of time, mine and yours. If you want more, then I suggest you take your efforts elsewhere. With me, what you see is what you get. It's pretty simple: I like getting fucked and I like getting fucked up. That's all the love that I need. Anything else that I do is just a means to that end. For me it's all about getting off."

"Does that apply to your work too?" she asked.

"Oh, I get off on my work, all right, as long as it pays. For me the work that I do is about what I make. If I weren't doing technology, I'd be selling Ferraris. The money is just as good and the clientele is similar, if not better."

"It's all about the money and the people and the things that it brings you?" asked Ajita.

"Yes it is," said Albert

"Well, then, just give me some money and I will let you have sex with me. And it will be even better than the last time," replied Ajita

"How much?"

"One-hundred-and-twenty-five thousand dollars."

"What!!!!!" Albert said as his eyes went wide.

"Yes," said Ajita, "give me one-hundred-and-twenty-five thousand dollars and I will have sex with you."

"And what will you do with this money?" he asked.

"I will take the money and travel around the world and organize all software developers and computer programmers into the International Guild of Software Developers."

"The what!.....?" His eyes went wider.

Ajita waited a moment until Albert's demeanor returned to a more calm state. Then, she continued. "Have you ever read Plato?" she asked

"No."

"What a pity. You seem better educated. I read him while I was in college, in a required philosophy class. Isn't philosophy a required subject in college here in the U.S.?" she asked.

"Not for electrical engineering students," said Albert

"You are an electrical engineer?" she asked

"Yep," said Albert. "Bachelor's in EE, Masters in Computer Science."

"I see. And you have not read Plato. Have your read Aristotle or Aquinas?" she asked.

"No," answered Albert again.

Ajita continued. "I like reading Plato. He makes me think. I like the Dialogues best. The Dialogues are the discussions that Socrates had with his students. Plato recorded them in dialog form, hence the name of the book. I particularly like the Meno. I liked it so much that I memorized portions of it. It was like memorizing Shakespeare. Have you read any Shakespeare, Albert?"

"Not since high school," he replied.

"What a pity. I had a professor in college who told me that everything that I need to know about life can be found in Shakespeare and Plato. I think that you might like the Meno, Albert. Many topics are covered in it — virtue, competence, temperance, justice, many, many topics. My favorite part is when Socrates is inquiring about virtue and how it is learned: by practice or by teaching. He uses an analogy. He asks Anytus, one of the participants in the conversation, this question, if he thinks the best way to make his friend Meno a good physician is to send him to the physicians? Anytus answers, yes. Then Socrates responds:

'When we say that we should be right in sending him to the physicians if we wanted him to be a physician, do we mean that we should be right in sending him to those who profess the art, rather than to those who do not.'"

"Do you know what I like about this part, Albert?"

"No," he responded.

"I like the idea of professions taking responsibility for their own. In Socrates' world, the physicians make physicians. This is how I think that coding should work: if you want to learn to code, you go to the coders. I think it is best if professionals run their profession."

"What does this have to do with my one-hundred-and-twenty-five G's?" Albert asked. He was beginning to get annoyed.

"Albert, the code is not working. Modern software development is fraught with neglect, waste, incompetence, misunderstanding, dishonesty and misguidance. And the sad part is that, for the most part, we, the programmers and the software developers, the people who make and maintain the code, are the ones who are making it this way. We think that it is the poorly designed systems, the folly of the corporations or the absurd demands of end users and customers that are responsible for our condition. But it is not.

"The current condition is of our own making. We think of ourselves as victims, gilded slaves, bought and sold on the auction blocks of technical recruiters, beholden to insane systems that are out of our control. We think that we have little

Coding Slave

power over the system's authority; that it does with us as it wishes; that when it needs us, it treats us well for as long as we are healthy and knowledgeable. We fear that should our knowledge lapse or our brain wither, we will be set aside. Should there not be enough work for us, we will be let go. Should we complain, we will be fired. We see ourselves as slaves, coding slaves. But it is not the system or the corporation that enslaves us."

"You see Albert, *we* are the authority. *We* are the people who live in the code, live with the code and control the code. Those who want things from the code go through us. We are the masters and yet we behave like the slaves. We depend on others to educate us, to find us work, to guarantee our competence, to keep us smart, and, in the extreme, to care for us in our old age. We are fragmented and unorganized. We have no loyalty. We go it alone. Just give us a monitor and a keyboard and we are quite happy to be left to ourselves and our thoughts. We are a profession of solipsists. And then we wonder why the systems we make do not work to specification."

"Albert, we do not work to specification. We are disparate systems that cannot be integrated. It is time that we grew up as a profession. It's time to integrate. Just as the physicians take care of their own and the plumbers take care of their own, so should we, the software developers, take care of our own. And to do this, we must organize."

"I want to create an International Guild of Software Developers. We will use the framework of the guilds and early trade unions. We will be what unions where meant to be before they became partners of the corporations and a haven that protects the lazy and incompetent."

"To be a software developer you will be with software developers. You will become an apprentice, then a journeyman, and then finally a master. We will provide employment, benefits, social programs, health care, education, and retirement pensions. We will coordinate compensation. We will guarantee quality. We will stand as one voice, one international voice. No longer will our profession pit national against national, in which the nation with the lowest standard of living and the brightest developers are sent work at the lowest possible rate. Just as the corporation is becoming transnational, so will our profession."

"Have you ever heard the term 'curry-head,' Albert?" she asked.

"No," he said

"I am a 'curry-head,' Albert, an Indian software developer. That is what some of the American developers here call me, Albert — a curry-head. I do not blame them. The American developers are angry because corporations like to hire foreigners like me. I will work for a wage below the national average. I will work until the job is done, no matter how long it takes, no matter what needs to be done, no matter what time of day or night. I will do anything to please my client. And this makes the American developer resentful. They look to the corporation for loyalty, sustenance and for justice. They feel that the corporation is neglecting them."

"Looking to the corporation for such things is unwise. The developers will do better to look to each other for sustenance and justice. The corporation cares about one thing, making the most money that it can on the least possible investment. Such is the nature of the corporation. The corporation is not good, it is not bad. It just is. It is counterproductive to expect the corporation to act any other way. The corporation is working to specification."

"And we software developers, our nature is to code. Coding is what we do. Coding is what we care about. It is senseless to ask the corporation to care about the code. The corporation cares only for the profits that the code brings them. The code is our responsibility. We are the coders. We know best. It is our responsibility to make ourselves and our code better."

"I think that the best way to care for the code is to organize. Send us those who want to code. We will make the coders. Coding and virtue are learned by practice. Such things cannot be taught," said Ajita

"You are talking union. Unions are not very popular in this country," said Albert.

"Actually, I am talking more of a guild, an organized cooperative that promotes the well being and competence of its members," said Ajita

"And I want to help you do this, why?" asked Albert.

"Because it is good and it is right and you will have the opportunity to have me in a way that no man has ever had before, and you will have a tax deductible donation that you can use to help make some of your current problems with the IRS go away," said Ajita with authority.

A moment passed. Albert was silent. He turned his high back, leather bound, swivel style chair with comfortable armrests into the conference table. He took his wallet out of the back of his pants. The wallet was new, a replacement for the one that had been stolen from him in the parking lot weeks before.

He opened his wallet and took a folded personal check out from the billfold. The check was blank. Albert always kept one blank check in his wallet. He never knew when he would need to write one.

He placed the check before him on the conference table. He took a ballpoint pen from his front shirt pocket. He fiddled with the pen for a while, tapping it on the surface of the conference table. Then he muttered to himself, "What the hell."

Albert filled out the check, folded it in two and gave it to Ajita. She accepted it. She moved toward him.

He put his hands up to keep her away. Then he got up and went to the door of the conference room. He opened the door to leave. As he was about to exit the room, he turned to her and said, "Ajita?"

"Yes Albert?" she said.

"You owe me one."

Then Albert Shulberg, a.k.a. "BigDick6969," left the room and closed the door behind him. After the door closed Ajita unfolded the check to examine it. The check was made out for the amount of two hundred and fifty thousand dollars, half the sale price of his condo. In the memo line on the lower left hand side of the check Albert had written: "Take a friend".

Chapter 25: Rafael at the Fair

Rafael let go of the thought. It was driving him crazy. It was the arrays. They got him every time. It was the second inning, two runs behind, the count — no balls, two strikes, men on first and third with two outs. Rafael's job was to make the pitcher act. The pitcher's action was not random; it was intentional, based on the situation before him and the possibilities that the situation offered. There were many possibilities, yet only one outcome. That's how it is programming arrays. You organize all the facts into similar groups, throw them up in the air and then, when they hit the ground, you sift through them. Based on what you find, you act. The human mind does this without thinking. Software is not so lucky. It has to be programmed.

Rafael was doing a side project, contract, code for hire. His piece was the pitcher code. He didn't really need the money. The startup cash from Albert had led to bigger and better things. The Guild was taking off and Rafael was reaping the benefits of its existence. But he still had to code, mostly out of habitual compulsion and marginally out of the fear of losing it by not using it.

Rafael was not alone in his fear. Anybody who codes for a living has it. The pace at which new technology makes its way into the mainstream of everyday software development is fast and furious. It seems as if not a day passes without a new acronym, coding product or technique becoming the darling of the weekly IT magazines. Columnists from coast to coast, continent to continent, tout the product as a must have, despite the fact that the columnist has not written a piece of code in the last five years nor experienced firsthand the frustration and agony of actually having to get the coding toy to work productively.

That the technology really does anything really innovative is of marginal interest. In the world of software development there are two things never to be underestimated: new and cool. If the industry deems it new and cool, then the developer is expected to embrace it; otherwise, the developer is destined to become a mass of flesh and blood filled with outdated knowledge, old and somewhat useful, but mostly in the way. The new stuff is the cool stuff and those who do not know how to do the cool stuff are destined to third shift, climate controlled rooms without windows, maintaining legacy mainframe code, spit out to old dot matrix printers that rat-a-tat necessary but arcane reports on very wide paper with alternating green and white rows. Or they are fired. Such is the world of the knowledge worker.

Coding Slave

Rafael got the job from a consortium of dentists from New Jersey. The dentists really liked baseball and they really liked computer gaming. They thought that they could steal a piece of market share, have some fun and make some money. So they put their money where their interests were and sent the project out for bid through the Guild. Rafael made a bid and much to his satisfaction got the job. He had to code. That it was gaming code was an added plus. Rafael was a gamer at heart. That his code, the pitcher code, had degraded into the chore of programming array logic was inevitable.

After all, what is a baseball game but a collection of arrays? A team is an array of nine players. A game is an array of nine innings. An inning is an array of three outs. An out is an array of pitches and so forth and so on. And in that inevitability Rafael went bonkers. He hated array programming. It hurt his head.

The pitcher was throwing strikes only, no balls, ever. The pitcher had thrown balls and strikes at one time; but something had happened about a week back that had changed the pitcher's behavior. The pitcher had lost the ability to throw balls. Rafael had no idea why. That's how the big ones always showed up, unexpectedly and just when it hurts most. This was a big bug and had to be fixed. The code was supposed to ship next week. The sponsor was going berserk.

Rafael emulated another scenario: bottom of the ninth, no outs, two strikes, the bases are loaded and the winning run is on third. So many arrays, so many situations. The more he thought, the more lost he became, the more elusive was the solution to the problem before him. Yet he felt no pain, or joy, for that matter. Actually, he felt very little other than moments of cognitive frustration. He was anesthetized, as if he was on dope. The code owned him. And he wasn't even sitting at a computer. It was all in his head.

Rafael took the code with him. The night before he had been sitting alone, in the dark, in front of a keyboard and computer monitor trying to get the code to work. Today he was walking the midway at the fair with the code occupying every cell in his brain.

Rafael no longer needed a computer to code. Rafael's code went way beyond The Box. It lived inside of him. Despite the noise, smells and activities going on about him, Rafael heard none of it, smelled none of it, saw none of it. It was just his mind and the code that lived in it.

But Ajita saw it all, she heard it all, she smelled it all. Ajita liked the smell of the food court: the fragrance of fresh, golden brown French Fries cooked in clear, clean oil; deep fried corn dogs on a stick; the sweet, smoky aroma of barbecued ribs. The smells made her nose dance.

Yet, the only thing that she was interested in eating was the cotton candy. She liked pulling little wads of the sweet steel wool-like substance off of the cone and putting them in her mouth. Everything about cotton candy was fun: the ridiculous color, the way the candy sat like an old lady's wig on the cone, the sticky residue it left on your fingers.

In fact, everything about the Our Lady of Perpetual Devotion Summer Fair was fun: the kiddie rides, the stage shows produced by the local dance schools, the bake sales, the concession stands, the games of chance — it was all fun, the most fun that a person could have on a Sunday afternoon in Pleasant Lake, Iowa.

She was glad that she and Rafael had decided to go to the fair, but she wished that Rafael would come back to the fair. Rafael was lost in the code. She knew all about that place. It was the Land of Pure Abstraction.

Anything was possible in the Land of Pure Abstraction as long as you could keep the logic right. But the minute you violated the logic, everything collapsed. The logic violation might show up as a little speck of irregular behavior, a little annoyance, and then, like a tooth in the process decay, it turns into an excruciating pain that takes over your whole head, your whole consciousness.

You have two choices only: Fix it or get it out of your head. However, each time you try to fix it you run the risk of making things worse, causing greater infection rather than effective remedy: fix the code here, you break it there, or someplace else that you don't even know about.

Coding is a risky affair. There is always the possibility of killing the code, making it lifeless and unusable; death caused by an initial flaw that was addressed with a regimen of ineffective fixes that left the code more wounded than cured, its demise now only a matter of time.

Rafael could not get the problem out of his head. He had to fix it. He had talked to Ajita about the pitcher problem a while back. The first sign of trouble was the pitcher throwing strikes in the third inning only. Nobody noticed it at first, not even the guys in Q/A. But as time went on it seemed strange that there were never any balls thrown in the third inning. After running two hundred games it was statistically improbable, but not impossible, that the pitcher would never throw a ball in the third inning.

The Q/A people brought the issue to Rafael's attention. He looked into it. He found the problem, so he thought. He made a fix. The pitcher threw balls in the third inning for a week. Then the problem started again, only worse: The pitcher started throwing strikes only in both the third *and* seventh inning. He made another fix. The pitcher behaved properly in the third inning, but the seventh inning problem was still there, and the pitcher was now throwing balls only in the second inning.

The more he fixed the code, the worse it became, and the worse it became, the angrier Rafael got. The emotional numbness that results from continuous, compulsive coding was wearing off. He was mad at the pitcher for not doing what it was supposed to do. He was mad at himself for being such a stupid programmer. He was mad at the project sponsor for bringing this thing into his life — the world did not need another computer baseball game, he thought. They were suckering him, taking advantage of his good nature and superior skills. Fatigue was setting in. Rafael was getting paranoid.

The Guild was supposed to make this insanity go away, he thought. The promise of the Guild was "Better Code From Better Living." This Guild stuff was bullshit. The insanity would never end. The voices in Rafael's mind raged so loud that thinking was becoming impossible.

Ajita knew that Rafael would lapse into self-pity, possibly paranoia. He always did when the code fought back. She knew also that his ego would prevail. Rafael was from the breed of programmer that believed in conquering The Box. The anger, fear, resentment and self-doubt were but side trips to the inevitable result, bringing the code to life. Ajita knew that for a woman, making life was inherent in her being. For a man it was distant work. And, Rafael knew how to bring code to life, as flawed as that life may be.

Rafael hated those flaws. He thought the flaws were of his doing, a sign of his fallibility.

Ajita, on the other hand, knew that all life is flawed. The flaws did not bother her.

Ajita knew also that for men like Rafael, the Guild would have little or no impact upon the humanity of their lives. Ajita knew that no matter how humane the industry became, no matter how justly wealth was distributed, no matter how efficiently projects were managed, Rafael would be enslaved until he could let the code be. His code was his prison.

Ajita stopped Rafael in front of the portable Ferris Wheel, the type that sits on the back of flatbed trailer and is transported to and from state and county fairs throughout the Midwest. The portable Ferris Wheel was not big, but it was not so small that children did not laugh and scream as it ascended up toward the sky. A set of very big loudspeakers sat at the base of the portable Ferris Wheel. The sound of child-like happiness mixed well with the heavy bass of the speakers.

Ajita turned to Rafael. She pulled a wad of cotton candy from the main mass of the blue treat.

"Open your mouth, please," she said.

Rafael obeyed.

She tossed the wad into his mouth.

"Will you taste it, will you *really* taste it?" she asked

He complied with her request. He was coming to. The voices were subsiding. The code was moving aside.

A song by the Eagles blared from the loudspeakers. It was so loud that Rafael could not help but hear it.

"So often times it happens,

That we live our lives in chains,

And we never even know we have the key."

And in that moment, Rafael knew the next, best thing to do.

"I want to get something to eat," he said.

Chapter 26: Charlemagne's Scribes

Ajita let go of the armrest. Flying was getting hard for her now. She was spending too much time in the air, going from city to city delivering speeches, sometimes two speeches a day, sometimes five cities a week. She was beginning to feel like a politician.

On the other hand, Raphael didn't mind the time in the air so much; it was the takeoff and landing that terrified him. That he ever survived Boston was still a surprise to him. If that cop in the boat had not jumped into the water after him, he would still be at the bottom of the harbor sharing underwater real estate with abandoned stolen cars and contaminated fish.

The flight attendant announced over the intercom that they were about to land, that it was time to stow all electronic devices, but that cell phones could be used once the plane landed safely.

Rafael grabbed the armrest. He hated this part.

The plane landed without incident. Ajita and Rafael took down their rolling suitcases, the box-like, fit-in-the-overhead-compartment-size pieces of luggage with extending handle and wisely-placed wheels that you use to roll through airplanes and airports.

They deplaned down the ramp to the arrival gate.

A blast of air conditioning hit them as they entered the terminal. The A/C made them both shiver slightly.

They made their way through the terminal to ground transportation. A tall black man in a black suit with black necktie and a white shirt was standing by the terminal exit. He held a sign in his hand with the word, "Gates" written on it in large black marker letters.

"Gates" was their current travel name. Ajita had stopped using her name a while ago. Today she was "Gates." In the past she had been Wang, Ellison, Kapor, Jobs, Noorda, Kahn, and Barksdale. One time she had even been Watson.

The Four Brothers and a Cousin were after her. Hence, the use of an alias when traveling. Ever since she had left StarTex they had been ruthless in the lengths they would go to harass her.

One time they found her hotel reservation and delivered seventy-five pizzas to her room. Another time they found her car service reservation and changed the destination hotel. The driver picked her up at the airport and took her to a hotel that was fifty miles from the one that she was booked into. It was her first time to that particular city. Ajita had no idea where she was. Traffic was horrible. It took over two hours to straighten things out and get her to where she was supposed to be. She almost missed the speaking engagement.

Ajita had messed up everything for StarTex. They were going broke. The Guild was growing and Ajita was becoming famous, almost infamous. The backlash was significant. The only notoriety that StarTex had now was that of being known as the consulting company that Ajita Orhtihawamein *used* to work for, the company that recruited her, exploited her and enslaved her. The Four Brothers and a Cousin had discovered that there was indeed such a thing as bad publicity and they were its ongoing victims.

Other than the MidContinent contract, which was a five-year deal, the Four Brothers and Cousin couldn't sell a programmer anymore than Jack the Ripper could get a date with Lily Langtry. The entire industry was afraid of unionization and it viewed anything that had the hint of StarTex on it as the first stop on the excruciating road to collective bargaining. Thus, the only solace that the Four Brothers and a Cousin found in their descent was the semi-sweet taste of two-bit revenge.

Rafael approached the driver.

"We're the Gates party. Are you parked nearby?" he asked.

"Ootside, sur" said the driver. There was a deep, rolling, French-Caribbean accent to his English.

The driver took the rolling suitcase from Ajita as well as the shoulder bag that she was carrying. Rafael kept his baggage. All three of them walked outside to the driver's automobile, a black Lincoln Town Car, the suitcases rolling behind them.

The driver opened the car's trunk, retracted the handle into Ajita's rolling suitcase and stowed her luggage. Then he asked Rafael for his bags, retracted his handle and stowed his luggage too.

The driver closed the trunk, walked up to the curbside rear passenger door and opened it for Ajita and Rafael. They got in. He closed the door. Then he went to the front of the car and got in.

"What hotel are we going to?" asked Rafael.

"Zee Hoolton on Northlake, sur," said the driver.

"Yes, that's what it says on our itinerary," Rafael said, making sure that the Four Brothers and Cousin were not pulling a fast one. "But please wait once we get there. I want you to take us on to the Convention Center after we check in."

"Yoos, sur," said the driver

A bellhop greeted the car as it pulled up in front of the hotel. He had a plush red, brass railed luggage cart.

The driver got out and opened the door for Ajita and Rafael. They exited the car. The bellhop was loading their luggage from the car's trunk onto the cart. The driver had auto-opened the trunk before getting out. The bellhop met Ajita and Rafael at the hotel entrance as they were about to go through the revolving doors.

"Shall I take these up to your room?" asked the bellhop.

"Yes, please do," said Rafael. "We are the Gates party. We will be going on to the Convention Center right after we register."

"Very well, Mr. Gates, I'll take these up directly."

Rafael gave the bellhop five bucks. Good hotel, Rafael thought to himself; Albert had made a good recommendation. He said it was the best one that you could find for the money in the Magic Kingdom.

Ajita and Rafael proceeded to the Main Desk and checked in. Then they returned to the Town Car. The driver took them to the Convention Center. They arrived twenty minutes before Ajita was scheduled to go on. Rafael tipped the driver well.

Ajita stopped outside the Convention Center to smoke a cigarette. What had started out as a lark was now a habit. Public speaking was still hard for her. Cigarette smoking brought her the calmness and the confidence that she needed in order to get on stage.

It was getting better though. When she first started doing this, she had to go to the women's room to throw up. Now, a cigarette was all it took.

Ajita found a quiet spot outside by a palm tree away from the other smokers. She lit up a new cigarette, smoked it and then disposed of its remains in a large, sand-filled ashtray situated nearby the building entrance.

She entered the Convention Center and proceeded on to the main auditorium. It was full.

Ajita was the Tuesday morning keynote speaker at the annual TechOne Conference. TechOne was the third largest gathering of software developers within the US. The conference was big, not as big as Comdex — the be-all and end-all of computer technology expositions — but big nonetheless.

Comdex was becoming irrelevant now, going into bankruptcy, coming out of bankruptcy and losing more exhibitors and attendees every year. And the people that did come were more tech-tourists than tech-heads. TechOne, on the other hand, had a well-defined attendee base: people who created code, supported code or sold code for a living. These were hardcore tech-geeks. TechOne was becoming known within the various circles of software development as the place to be and be seen, sort of like the Oscars for the tech world.

TechOne ran from Monday to Thursday. The keynote session with the most status was Wednesday morning's. The real Gates was scheduled to appear at that one. The Monday morning session was a dog. Nobody ever went because they were all too busy registering, getting their conference badge, conference literature and commemorative briefcase with the conference logo embossed on the side. The briefcase would be brought back home and shown off at work to the envy of other programmers who did not get to go. In the choice between getting the briefcase and attending the first keynote, the briefcase won every time. Thus, in terms of the reality of a four-day conference, Tuesday was the kick-off keynote and it was all Ajita's.

There were about eleven thousand people in the audience, mostly men. Each member of the audience held a Votometer™ in his hand. Rafael had designed the Votometer™, a small, disposable wireless device about the size of an electronic key for an automobile. It was round and black about two-and-a-half-inches in diameter. It fit well into the user's palm.

The Votometer™ allowed an audience member to register a vote to a question that Ajita planned to ask during her speech. The face of the Votometer™ had two buttons, a green one and a red one. Pressing the green button registered a yes vote, the red button one a no vote. When an audience member pressed a button on the Votometer™, the device sent that audience member's vote to a server backstage via wireless transmission. The server tallied all the votes reported by the audience and stored the results in a database, which was then projected onto a coliseum-size display hung from the back of the stage for all to see.

It's show time.

Ajita enters the auditorium. It's dark. Rafael is already backstage. Ajita goes to join him. She approaches the stage entrance area. A security guard asks to see her conference badge.

Color determines the status and privilege of a conference badge. A regular attendee's badge is white; an organizer's badge is blue; a vendor's badge is red. Ajita's is a gold speaker's badge. She shows it to the guard. He lets her pass.

She is greeted by a sound technician. He attaches a small lapel microphone to the collar of her blouse. He wants to hang the powerpak-transmission unit on her back, from her belt, in order to be hidden from view. But Ajita has no belt. She is wearing a plain, formless, brown corduroy jumper over her beige blouse. The dress has no waist or fashion. But, the dress has two big pockets on its front.

The sound technician gives up. He gives Ajita the powerpak-transmission unit. She takes it and puts it in one of the front pockets, the right one. A wire runs up across her front, from the right, front pocket to the lapel microphone on the collar of her blouse. Ajita looks a little funny.

The sound technician tells her to not forget to switch the button "On" before starting to speak.

Multi-colored spotlights illuminate the empty, theatrically designed stage. The stage is big enough to support an opera. Reggae music plays loudly from the stack of oversized sound system speakers situated on both sides of the stage and suspended from the rafters throughout the auditorium in Rock Concert fashion.

"Get up, stand up, stand up for your rights.

Get up, stand up, don't give up the fight."

A single spotlight goes white. A Master of Ceremonies appears on the stage. He is dressed in standard Trade Show marketing attire: denim shirt with conference logo over his left breast pocket, khaki pants, penny loafers and a million dollar smile. The main speaker podium is positioned left-center at the front of the stage, far enough away from the center to not distract from the main event, but close enough to be noticeable when attention is required. He approaches it. The music from the speakers dies down. The light shines on him. He speaks.

"Welcome to the Tuesday keynote session. I hope that everybody is enjoying the conference."

He gets a slight response. "Before I introduce our speaker, I want to go over some conference administrivia."

His role is both to entertain and coordinate, to keep attention and to provide information.

He continues, looking down onto the podium, reading from his notes. "First, please be advised that the Credit Card Security breakout session in Meeting Room B20 at 4 p.m. today has been cancelled. Also, Data Server Lockdown breakout session scheduled for 9 a.m. tomorrow morning in Meeting Room C11 has been moved to Meeting Room C13.

"The Vendor Booths in the Exhibition Hall will be open from 1 p.m. to 8 p.m.. The sponsor for tonight's After Hours Buffet is NeuroSoft. The buffet is open to all conference attendees. Beer is free. There is a cash bar for hard liquor. You will need your conference badge to get in."

The MC continues. "OK, now that that's out of the way, let's move on."

He pauses. The audience becomes quieter.

He resumes. "Introducing this morning's keynote speaker is not an easy task. What can you say about her? This lady is changing the way that software is made in this country and throughout the world. Over the last year she has appeared on 60 Minutes and Nightline and has been featured on the cover of Wired Magazine. InformationWeek described her in a recent article as 'one of the twenty most important people to watch in the world of commercial software technology.' Time Magazine has called her the Scourge of Modern Software Development. And given all that has been said about her, I still cannot pronounce her last name, nor can most of us, for that matter."

He smiles. The audience laughs.

"All I can tell you is that what she is doing is important and she deserves our complete attention. It is my privilege to introduce to you, Ajita!"

The audience applauds.

Ajita comes on stage. The applause grows louder. She walks to center stage. The applause continues. She raises her hands to quiet the crowd. The applause stops, slowly. She is a little lady, dressed in a formless, brown, corduroy jumper without style or fashion, in the middle of a very big stage, with nothing, not even a podium to protect her. She is completely vulnerable.

She smiles.

She waits.

She speaks, "Greetings!"

The audience cheers.

"Good morning, my dear colleagues! It is an honor to be here today and to speak to you. Before I start the main part of my talk, I want to get to know you all a little better. In order to do this, I am going to ask you some questions. This will take only a few minutes. Your answers will provide important information that will be very relevant to the matters that we will discuss here this morning."

"After I ask you a question, please answer it using the Votometer™ that you were given when you came into the auditorium this morning. Please remember, green for yes, red for no."

"First, let's run a test. Here is the first question: Do you understand that pressing the green button indicates a yes vote? OK, vote now."

The dull click-click of thousands of buttons pressing simultaneously fills the auditorium, sounding like a field full of crickets on a summer night.

A few moments pass. The coliseum size screen behind Ajita displays the following:

Do you understand that pressing the green button indicates a yes vote?

Yes: 10,938

No: 12

"Ah, I see that a few of you have trouble mastering new technology," says Ajita smiling.

The audience giggles lightly.

"Great. Now, that we know that the machines work, for the most part, let's get down to business."

"Here is the first question: Do you labor in an environment where the primary source of light is fluorescent?"

The sound of button pressing fills the air again.

The coliseum size screen lights up:

1. Do you labor in an environment where the primary source of light is fluorescent?

Yes: 10,185

No: 98

"Hmmm…," says Ajita. "Let's try another one. Are you overweight due to lack of exercise and movement?"

2. Are you overweight due to lack of exercise and movement?

Yes: 9,942

No: 910

Ajita continues to ask questions and the audience continues to answer.

3. Does your behind hurt from sitting in a chair all day?

Yes: 9,159

No: 894

4. Do you talk about yourself and the others with whom you work as "Resources"?

Yes: 7,103

No: 3,412

5. Are you forced to create a lame system, about which you haven't any input on requirements or design, that will be associated with you forever?

Yes: 9,005

No: 1,476

6. Have you avoided speaking to a client or end user in the last 5 years?

Yes: 8,040

No: 2,078

7. Do you find yourself writing code that has been written 1000 times before, just to provide a trace amount of intellectual stimulation?

Yes: 8,324

No: 1,777

8. Do you wear jeans to work on Friday only?

Yes: 9,597

No: 1,014

9. Do you have frequent fantasies about intimate human contact (physical and otherwise) within your work environment, yet in reality have little or none at all?

Yes: 10,451

No: 54

10. Do you work in a cube that others have made for you?

Yes: 10,976

No: 25

11. Are you afraid of or resentful about your supervisor?

Yes: 9,006

No: 1,127

12. Do you spend more time writing code you hate than with your loved ones?

Yes: 10,489

No: 389

13. Do you find yourself thinking that you'll get it right on the next version?

Yes: 10,740

No: 218

14. Do you find yourself fearing a new technology because you don't have the time or desire to learn it?

Yes: 8,482

No: 2,147

15. Do you have more than $1000 in credit card debt?

Yes: 10,568

No: 304

16. Are you dissatisfied with your sex life?

Yes: 10,224

No: 438

17. Do you find yourself fearing that if you go to a meeting and say what's really on your mind, you'll get into trouble?

Yes: 10,684

No: 23

18. Are you afraid of losing your possessions?

Yes: 9,853

No: 984

19. Have you ever had to change plans in order to work overtime?

Yes: 10,874

No: 235

20. Do you find Dilbert funny, but know in your heart that it's really much, much worse?

Yes: 10,417

No: 267

"Hmmm… Looks as if we have a problem, does it not?" Ajita asks the audience, "and I don't think it is a technology problem."

She smiles. The audience laughs.

"I have another question," she says, "How many of you think that in terms of the history of mankind, Information Management and Information Technology are fairly recent phenomena?"

How many of you think that in terms of the history of mankind, Information Management and Information Technology are fairly recent phenomena?

Yes: 8,472

No: 2,620

An intent silence descends on the crowd. She has their attention.

"My dear colleagues, I have some news for you. Information Technology has been around for a long while, since time immemorial, even before the time when that person in China figured out that he could send a data packet cross-country by writing a message on a piece of paper and then running it up and down that physical transport mechanism we now call The Great Wall.

Information Management is a timeless as mankind. Using computers just happens to be where we are at now."

She pauses. She looks across the audience.

She continues "And, for as long as there has been Information Management, there have been people who are in it and people who are out of it. The ones who are in it rule the world and the ones who aren't…. well, they do other things."

"My dear colleagues, we are the people who are 'in it.'"

Ajita stops for a moment. Someone heckles, "Yes!" from the back of the room, "Yes, we are in it!"

The audience laughs briefly.

A photo appears on the coliseum-size display. It looks like a painting of a medieval king.

"Let's take a look at Charlemagne. I am sure that you remember Charlemagne," she smiles to herself. She knows that most of the people in the auditorium had heard of the name, but had no idea who he was. "Charlemagne was emperor of practically all of what we know today as Europe. He lived from 742 to 814 A.D.

Chapter 26: Charlemagne's Scribes

His empire included France, Switzerland, Belgium, and the Netherlands, as well as half of present-day Italy and Germany, and parts of Austria and Spain. Charlemagne was a very powerful man. And do you know what, my colleagues?" The audience is listening closely.

"Charlemagne was illiterate! He could not read or write, not a word…well, maybe a word here and there, but not much, certainly not with any competency. He used scribes to document his information and he used messengers to deliver it. He was completely dependent on these people to run his empire. They were his technology. Charlemagne used the technology of his day to do what he had to do. You can think," she continues, with tongue in cheek, "of his whole technological framework as a bio-robotic word processor/email system with voice recognition features, very advanced for its time." The audience chuckles.

"Dear colleagues, Charlemagne, with all of his supposed political greatness, with all his supposed military power, with all of his supposed wisdom… without his technology, he was nothing. Outside of his castle he was just another one of the majority of men in the world who could not read or write."

"The scribes and messengers ruled Charlemagne's world. Just think what would have happened if the scribe wrote down, 'Invade Paris' instead of 'Invade Vienna'. Charlemagne most likely would never have known until it was too late. Data packets took a long time to transport in those days," Ajita says with a smile. The audience laughs.

Ajita continues "Just as it is today, the technology worker of that day ruled his world. And, just as it is today, the technology worker never knew it."

"I am sure that some of you, dear colleagues, think that I am exaggerating our role and the degree of our impact on the world at large. But, think about it, please. The President of the United States can push all the buttons on the console of any Star Wars machine of his choosing, as hard as his mighty fingers will allow, but if the poor coder at Raytheon or Lockheed Martin who wrote the software for the missile tracking system was distracted in Love-Chat the night he was supposed to be programming the ShootTheThingDown function, the President might well find himself annihilating a 747 full of tourists on their way to see Shamu, instead of an evil intercontinental ballistic missile on its way to Toledo, Ohio."

The audience laughs, but the laugh has an element of concern mixed with trepidation.

"My friends, we have been obsessed with managing information since the beginning to time, since the Chinese started using the abacus and Croesus minted money. Mankind likes to keep track of things. Always has. Sometime we go to extremes. The Nazis *really* liked to keep track of things. In fact, the Nazis were so obsessed with numbering that their IT Department, although they never actually called it that back then, kept track of all the Jews that they had rounded up. At the Auschwitz Concentration Camp they tattooed a serial number on the forearm of each one, sort of like a very perverse asset management system. Every Jew, whether destined for life or death, had a number inscribed on his or her forearm. Those numbers did not appear by magic. Some distant professional predecessor of a modern IT worker did the deed. One of us, dear colleagues, did this deed."

Ajita pauses. A morose silence comes over the audience. The awareness of atrocity makes the room sad. Things are getting more serious.

She continues, "Now, please do not misunderstand me. I do not mean to imply that we IT workers descend from and are agents of fascist tyranny or relish behaving inhumanely. As individuals we tend to be good men and women."

"Yet, in today's world, now more than ever, it really does come down to the bits and bytes of information, what we call the code — those who create it, those who can control it, those who understand it and those who do not. Those who code rule the world and those who do not, well... they do other things, such as pretend to rule the world."

"And, my dear colleagues, we, the people in this room here today, we are members of that group that controls the bits and bytes of information, the code, if you will. And this information, now more than ever, not only defines our world, the world in which we live, it *is* our world. We make the code. Thus, *we make the world.*"

"But, as you see from our little informal, real time, survey, today things do not look bright. The world in which we live leaves a bit to be desired. We are building a world we do not want and a world we do not like.

A stunned silence descends on the room.

"We have abdicated our responsibilities. We have become nothing more than slave laborers building modern-day pyramids glorifying the vanity of pharaohs, instead of the greatness of mankind. We isolate ourselves in stall-like cubicles away from sunlight and make code that has marginal personal value. We are lonely, angry and scared. We sit alone looking to our code for companionship and meaning, when what we really desire is the warmth and closeness of another human being. And still we code alone."

"Our code is fragmented and disjointed, and then we wonder why the world is fragmented and disjointed; we wonder why we are still isolated from one another."

"In order to make ourselves feel better in our isolation, we medicate ourselves with credit card debt that we cannot pay, oversized automobiles that we cannot afford and large houses to which we give more love than we give our children. The family orthodontist and the family therapist hold us hostage."

"We know a lot and we understand little. We want more when we need less. And still the fact remains: *we rule the world.* But, sadly, we allow others to pretend to do it for us."

"But that was then and this is now."

She pauses again.

She is taking hold of the room.

"The time for pretending is over. It is time to take responsibility and to be accountable for this world, because, dear colleagues, this is the world that we have made. Just as Charlemagne's world ran on his scribe's code, our world runs on our code. We are the coders. We rule the world."

"I ask you, right here, right now, is this the world that you want? Is this the world that you want to serve?"

The auditorium is silent.

Ajita smiled; her voice was kind, "Silence means yes."

A few seconds pass. Then a single voice, way in the back of the hall yells, "No!" The sound reverberates throughout the rafters.

"Ah, a lone voice in the desert." Ajita says. She smiles again. "Maybe it will help if I ask the question another way. But, first, I need some more information. Please turn on the house lights. I want to see you, dear colleagues, each and everyone of you."

The overhead lights illuminate the entire auditorium. The hall now looks like the scene of a political convention.

Ajita asks, "Please raise your hand if you have children."

Most of the people in the hall raise their hands.

Ajita continues, "Now repeat after me, this is the world that I want to leave to my children."

The audience remains silent. Ajita waits. She hears nothing.

"We are making progress, I see," she says jokingly. Her smile continues.

Finally a voice yells out, "Go for it Ajita! We're with you!"

Ajita looks out into the audience. "Thank you."

"Dear colleagues, everybody in this room has a choice today, a choice between freedom and slavery. It is about time — who owns our time and what we will do with our time. The free man and the slave share the same time. The only difference is that the time of the free man his and her own; the slave's time belongs to another."

"Mankind has made great strides. There are more healthy people on this planet than there have ever been. There are more literate people than there have ever been. There is more technology. We have men in space and robots on Mars. Children have cell phones."

"And yet, we toil just as much as we ever have, if not more. For most of us, our time is not our own. Our time belongs to another, still. This is a sad fact."

Ajita pauses for a moment. The lights dim. The room goes dark.

Ajita continues, "Yet there is hope because we can seize the moment."

She pauses again. She brings her hands together, palm to palm, in a praying gesture. Then she raises her fingertips to her lips. Then she lowers her hands and presents her palms to the audience.

She continues "Yes, there is hope. Now is the moment to make a change. Now is the moment to take back our time. Now is the moment to make the world that which we want to leave to our children. We have the power; we have the knowledge; we have the right; we have the responsibility. All that we need to do is to get our code, the code within each of us and all of us working right. *Once we work right, the world will work right.* Now is the moment of our emancipation!"

Ajita continued to speak for another thirty minutes. There was no longer any need to use the Votometer™. The audience knew what the story was.

The International Guild of Software Developers increased its rolls by fourteen thousand more members the week that Ajita gave her keynote in the Magic Kingdom. Within a month of the talk, ten medium-size companies, each employing over five thousand employees as well as four municipal governments running cities with populations of over a million people had contracted with the Guild to implement a comprehensive ERP to run their enterprise. The ERP in question was created and maintained by the Guild. It was the same one that the Guild used for its own operations.

Ajita and Rafael had written the first line of code for the ERP that night on the boat on the way to Bermuda. The code had left their hands long ago, but it was still part of their soul.

Both Ajita and Rafael had understood during the cruise that they were servants to a system that they did not like and could not control. That the current system was the MidContinent ERP was circumstantial. Ajita had been indentured to other out-of-control systems in the past and there would be other out-of-control systems in the future. Rafael knew he was to share a similar fate unless something changed. Both knew that large scale, enterprise wide software systems were necessary. The world had become so big and so unified that the only real way to hold it together was with and through a comprehensive piece of software that had the ability to coordinate and explain everything. Yet, on that night, on that boat, Ajita and Rafael understood that the MidContinent ERP and systems like it would never work.

There were many theories as to why the software would not work — too many incompetent coders, poor specifications, poor project plans, unrealistic demands made by management, the list went on and on. Ajita and Rafael had a better understanding about the ongoing failure. It was about imposed systems.

Ajita and Rafael knew that imposed systems — dictatorships — are doomed to fail over the long term. Systems of the people, by the people, for the people, work better than systems that are imposed *on* the people. Ajita and Rafael understood that the reason that the MidContinent ERP was blowing up was because it was not designed to serve the people who used it. The system was designed to serve itself only.

Ajita and Rafael knew that the world needed an ERP that met the needs of the people that used it, made by the people that used it and for the people that used it. Ajita and Rafael understood on that night, on that boat, that their course of action, that the purpose of the rest of their lives, was to organize every coder in the world in order to make a comprehensive software system that worked well enough to make a world in which all coders wanted to live. They also knew that the system they made needed to work for themselves first, because if they could not make an ERP that served the needs of their organization, the code could never meet the needs of any other organization.

And so Ajita and Rafael went about creating that ERP, and every waking moment of every waking day of their lives from that time forward was a day spent making that ERP better. As a result, the primary purpose of the Guild became to make that ERP, which was its one and only product, better. They had the knowledge. They had the talent. They had the desire. They had seen all the horror shows. Now it was time to make paradise.

The Guild named the ERP *Justice*.

Justice handled all Guild activity: education, compensation, payroll, health care benefits, employment assignment and, of course, membership voting. It seemed as if the members were forever voting on something. *Justice* handled it with ease.

No Guild member was ever without work. When a member's contract expired or if his job was eliminated, the ERP used its state-of-the-art logic and data-mining capabilities to provide the Guild member with a new assignment that met the exact skills and interests of the member.

A member could work as much or as little as he or she liked. The highest paid software developer was never paid more than seven times the rate of the lowest developer. Pay rate for a job was calculated using a formula that accounted for member competency, status, and job complexity. This formula was reviewed every six months and subject to four-fifths membership approval. Voting took place over the Internet and via cell phones using *Justice*.

Any software developer was free to join the Guild. In fact, joining the Guild made you a software developer. In order to assure quality, the Guild used a competency hierarchy developed in the Middle Ages and adopted by twentieth century skilled trade unions: Apprentice, Journeyman and Master.

There were no dues for membership. The Guild supported itself by taking a 1% service charge from each member's pay, which it seemed just about every member was happy to pay. The Guild had its own bank, which provided all financial services for its members: twenty-four-hour banking, credit, financial planning and affordable insurance of every make and model.

The Guild also provided education in all relevant technologies. In order to move from one competency status to another — from Apprentice, to Journeyman to Master — a member had to be Board Certified. All members were certified by a board of five Guild members, in person, over a period which took days. Written tests were only a component of the certification process. Exhaustive personal interviews were the key determinant of competency.

A Journeyman's Board was made up of three Journeyman and two Masters. A Master's board was made of one Journeyman and four Masters. For the Master's board, two of the Masters had to have practiced software development for over twenty years.

This framework for the Certification process was created and approved using *Justice*.

And every day the ERP got better.

Six months after her talk in the Magic Kingdom, Ajita collapsed in the Kiev Airport due to exhaustion. It was her first time to Europe. She had been invited to give a speech there. The Ukraine was rapidly becoming a center for European software development. Rafael was with her. The speech was cancelled. Riots broke out.

Ajita returned to Pleasant Lake to get some rest. She liked the Midwest in the summer. The doctor told her that she was to take a three-month vacation. He also told her to quit smoking. She did. She got a cat. Two months later she was pregnant. Rafael asked her to marry him. She refused.

Two weeks later he asked her again. She refused again.

He said that it was important that the child be legitimate. Ajita replied that the child could be nothing but legitimate. All human life was legitimate.

A week later Rafael bought her a ring. She would not accept it. Throughout the week he pouted.

Finally Ajita asked, "Rafael, what is it that you want from marrying me?"

Rafael responded, "I want the world to know that we are together. I want you to be my wife."

Ajita replied, "Do you want to be bound to me, forever? And me to you, forever?"

"Yes," responded Rafael.

Ajita thought about his answer for a moment and then responded.

"Rafael, now that I am free, why would I want to be otherwise? At last, our time is our own. This is the world that we wanted to build. Is this not true?" she asked.

"Yes, it's true," he answered.

Then, without saying a word, she took his face into her hands and tenderly kissed him on the lips as she kissed no other man on the face of the Earth. After a few moments passed, she let him go. There was nothing more to say. All that was needed was the silence of the moment and the love that connected them in it.

Epilogue: Katherine Takes a Swim

Katherine Limeleaf put her signature to the five year lease on three thousand square feet of office space in the San Fernando Valley without hesitation. Limeleaf Associates needed an office on the West Coast and this spot was perfect. Who could ask for more? The location was about a half hour from the technical community in Los Angeles and right in the center of the Adult Film industry. Katherine knew that this location would provide the type of continuous training that her consultants required.

The idea was a no-brainer. Katherine got it from Ajita.

"Too bad she decided to go off with that kid Rafael and do Guild organizing," she thought. "She could have made a fortune working for me."

Katherine had seen the writing on the wall: give the clients exactly what they want and they will pay any price for it. Anyway things were going to pieces at Mid-Continent. Even the Justice Department was getting in on the act. Katherine knew that she was not at that great of a risk. Most of the hanky panky had started well before she got to MidContinent.

Turns out that the company was cooking the books. The late Walt Vanderdale as well as the now indicted CEO and CFO were in on it. In a way, it was funny. If it had not been for the ERP implementation, their activities would have gone undiscovered for years; but once the customization started and people took a close look at the financial systems, all sorts of irregularities came to light.

"It's time to get out," Katherine thought to herself. "I'm working much too hard. Comprehensive consulting services are the way to go."

Ajita was onto something. Let the guys come and the code gets better. So Katherine decided to take the idea for a ride. She talked to Albert about it. He was almost perfect for this venture. You had to be brain dead not to know that the guy cared only about two things in life: getting off and getting laid. Also, he was good at code, in its many convolutions and manifestations. He had no other interests. His simplicity in this regard was his virtue and his downfall. Despite his tendency toward debauchery, he could bring some serious technical competence to the table. So she ran the idea by him.

"Albert, I know I brought you on board to run technology here, and I'm sorry that I pulled the rug out from under you — well, a little sorry anyway — but I need to tell you, I am getting out of MidContinent. It's no secret that the company is in turmoil. I'm going to go and I want to take you with me. I have a sweetheart deal for you."

"What do you think about doing an IT consulting company that gave the client *everything* it wants? Do you remember Ajita, the woman from that day in my office with the Project Manager? What do you think that you could do with a company full of Ajitas?" asked Katherine.

And then the lights went off in Albert's hung-over head. So Albert talked to his girlfriend, Connie about it.

"You'd be selling sex and code, huh?" said Connie

"Actually *we'd* be selling professional information technology services. That sex might be involved is ancillary." said Albert.

"And *we're* not breaking the law?" she asked.

"Ajita never solicited sex. She just took it. In fact, when I offered her money, she refused. We're selling professional information technology services. The sex is a feature, not the focus of our offering. We will never negotiate with a client for or around sex." said Albert.

Connie asked another question. "And these men and women are going to be able to code?"

"Yes," he replied

Her questioning continued. "Where are you going to find these people?"

"That's where you come in. That fact is that if a person is half bright and has a good sense of abstraction, the coding can be taught. That's easy. It's the giving the clients 'exactly what they want', part that's hard. Only a very special person can do this. Ajita was that type of person. She always seemed to know exactly what the clients wanted. You could be this type of person, if you decide that this sort of work has something to offer you."

"My gut says that you could find these sort of people quite easily too. You have a nose for it. We do not need many — maybe twenty or thirty, from anywhere in the world. You find them and I will teach them the technology. I am a good teacher, you know that. You have learned a lot of technology in the time that we've been together. The other stuff — the full service stuff; that is your domain," said Albert.

"Yes, I am this 'type' of person. And yes, I have learned a lot about code from you. But don't flatter yourself. I learned a lot more from being with Rafael and sitting in front of that WebCam. But you are right, there are a lot of men and women out there who can and will do this type of work. What sort of money are we talking about?" asked Connie.

"If the code works, at $1500 a day for 200 billable days a year, that's three hundred thousand gross per employee. The client pays all additional expenses.

Twenty billing employees make six million a year. You do the math. The company takes a third, two million gross. Keep in mind that in the third year we'll have better clients and our consultants will be worth a lot more in terms of daily billing rate, say $2500 to $3000."

"You'd be looking at around seven hundred and fifty thousand a year in your pocket, gross, not to mention stock options,'" said Albert. "The trick is that the code has to work."

"And you're sure this is not breaking the law?" she asked.

"If we do it right, it is all quite legal," he said.

"And how will we find these clients?" asked Connie

"That's Katherine's job. She knows a lot of people."

So that's how it started. Katherine, Albert and Connie took a seven-hundred-square-foot office on the twelfth floor of a building near Grand Central Station in New York City. They had three cell phones with voice mail, a T1 line, a static IP address and a bunch of computers in every size, shape and form. The website looked like something that an accountant would make.

Within a year Limeleaf Associates had an office manager and thirty-three consultants billing. Sales came in at a little under four million dollars, gross. In the second year, with the same size staff, sales topped seven million. Katherine spent most of her time selling; Albert went to a lot of technology conferences and strip bars; Connie was spending every other month in Asia doing recruiting, dividing her time between Korea and the People's Republic. Asian consultants were in very high demand.

When it came time to open the West Coast office, Katherine informed Albert and Connie that she was going to move out there to oversee operations. The office manager was put in charge of New York.

Katherine bought a house on Sunset Boulevard in Brentwood. The house was moderately big, with a swimming pool and a large garden that required the attention of a full-time gardener.

Katherine developed an interest in talking birds. She bought a red-and-blue Macaw. She had the gardener build a medium-size house for it in the garden by the pool. The medium-size bird house had a front door through which the bird could come out and sit on a perch. Katherine had a trainer teach the bird to talk.

Everyday before she went into the pool for her daily swim she stopped by the medium size bird house and opened its door. The red-and-blue Macaw always came out — he never had to be coaxed — and while Katherine swam under the warm Southern California sunshine, gliding effortlessly through the clear, chlorine treated water of her very expensive swimming pool, the bird walked back and forth on its perch squawking in a parrot-like cadence:

"Katherine wins,
Katherine's won.
Katherine wins,
Katherine's won."
...over and over and over again.

Appendices

Appendix A: The Meno

380 BC
MENO
by Plato
translated by Benjamin Jowett

PERSONS OF THE DIALOGUE:
MENO;
SOCRATES;
A SLAVE OF MENO;
ANYTUS.

[Meno] Can you tell me, Socrates, whether virtue is acquired by teaching or by practice; or if neither by teaching nor practice, then whether it comes to man by nature, or in what other way?

[Socrates] O Meno, there was a time when the Thessalians were famous among the other Hellenes only for their riches and their riding; but now, if I am not mistaken, they are equally famous for their wisdom, especially at Larisa, which is the native city of your friend Aristippus. And this is Gorgias' doing; for when he came there, the flower of the Aleuadae, among them your admirer Aristippus, and the other chiefs of the Thessalians, fell in love with his wisdom. And he has taught you the habit of answering questions in a grand and bold style, which becomes those who know, and is the style in which he himself answers all comers; and any Hellene who likes may ask him anything. How different is our lot! my dear Meno. Here at Athens there is a dearth of the commodity, and all wisdom seems to have emigrated from us to you. I am certain that if you were to ask any Athenian whether virtue was natural or acquired, he would laugh in your face, and say: "Stranger, you have far too good an opinion of me, if you think that I can answer your question. For I literally do not know what virtue is, and much less whether it is acquired by teaching or not." And I myself, Meno, living as I do in this region of poverty, am as poor as the rest of the world; and I confess with shame that I know literally nothing about virtue; and when I do not know the "quid" of anything how can I know the "quale"? How, if I knew nothing at all of Meno, could I tell if he was fair, or the opposite of fair; rich and noble, or the reverse of rich and noble? Do you think that I could?

[Men.] No, Indeed. But are you in earnest, Socrates, in saying that you do not know what virtue is? And am I to carry back this report of you to Thessaly?

[Soc.] Not only that, my dear boy, but you may say further that I have never known of any one else who did, in my judgment.

[Men.] Then you have never met Gorgias when he was at Athens?

[Soc.] Yes, I have.

[Men.] And did you not think that he knew?

[Soc.] I have not a good memory, Meno, and therefore I cannot now tell what I thought of him at the time. And I dare say that he did know, and that you know what he said: please, therefore, to remind me of what he said; or, if you would rather, tell me your own view; for I suspect that you and he think much alike.

[Men.] Very true.

[Soc.] Then as he is not here, never mind him, and do you tell me: By the gods, Meno, be generous, and tell me what you say that virtue is; for I shall be truly delighted to find that I have been mistaken, and that you and Gorgias do really have this knowledge; although I have been just saying that I have never found anybody who had.

[Men.] There will be no difficulty, Socrates, in answering your question. Let us take first the virtue of a man — he should know how to administer the state, and in the administration of it to benefit his friends and harm his enemies; and he must also be careful not to suffer harm himself. A woman's virtue, if you wish to know about that, may also be easily described: her duty is to order her house, and keep what is indoors, and obey her husband. Every age, every condition of life, young or old, male or female, bond or free, has a different virtue: there are virtues numberless, and no lack of definitions of them; for virtue is relative to the actions and ages of each of us in all that we do. And the same may be said of vice, Socrates.

[Soc.] How fortunate I am, Meno! When I ask you for one virtue, you present me with a swarm of them, which are in your keeping. Suppose that I carry on the figure of the swarm, and ask of you, What is the nature of the bee? and you answer that there are many kinds of bees, and I reply: But do bees differ as bees, because there are many and different kinds of them; or are they not rather to be distinguished by some other quality, as for example beauty, size, or shape? How would you answer me?

[Men.] I should answer that bees do not differ from one another, as bees.

[Soc.] And if I went on to say: That is what I desire to know, Meno; tell me what is the quality in which they do not differ, but are all alike, Would you be able to answer?

[Men.] I should.

[Soc.] And so of the virtues, however many and different they may be, they have all a common nature which makes them virtues; and on this he who would answer the question, "What is virtue?" would do well to have his eye fixed: Do you understand?

[Men.] I am beginning to understand; but I do not as yet take hold of the question as I could wish.

[Soc.] When you say, Meno, that there is one virtue of a man, another of a woman, another of a child, and so on, does this apply only to virtue, or would you say the same of health, and size, and strength? Or is the nature of health always the same, whether in man or woman?

[Men.] I should say that health is the same, both in man and woman.

[Soc.] And is not this true of size and strength? If a woman is strong, she will be strong by reason of the same form and of the same strength subsisting in her which there is in the man. I mean to say that strength, as strength, whether of man or woman, is the same. Is there any difference?

[Men.] I think not.

[Soc.] And will not virtue, as virtue, be the same, whether in a child or in a grown-up person, in a woman or in a man?

[Men.] I cannot help feeling, Socrates, that this case is different from the others.

[Soc.] But why? Were you not saying that the virtue of a man was to order a state, and the virtue of a woman was to order a house?

[Men.] I did say so.

[Soc.] And can either house or state or anything be well ordered without temperance and without justice?

[Men.] Certainly not.

[Soc.] Then they who order a state or a house temperately or justly order them with temperance and justice?

[Men.] Certainly.

[Soc.] Then both men and women, if they are to be good men and women, must have the same virtues of temperance and justice?

[Men.] True.

[Soc.] And can either a young man or an elder one be good, if they are intemperate and unjust?

[Men.] They cannot.

[Soc.] They must be temperate and just?

[Men.] Yes.

[Soc.] Then all men are good in the same way, and by participation in the same virtues?

[Men.] Such is the inference.

[Soc.] And they surely would not have been good in the same way, unless their virtue had been the same?

[Men.] They would not.

[Soc.] Then now that the sameness of all virtue has been proven, try and remember what you and Gorgias say that virtue is.

[Men.] Will you have one definition of them all?

[Soc.] That is what I am seeking.

[Men.] If you want to have one definition of them all, I know not what to say, but that virtue is the power of governing mankind.

[Soc.] And does this definition of virtue include all virtue? Is virtue the same in a child and in a slave, Meno? Can the child govern his father, or the slave his master; and would he who governed be any longer a slave?

[Men.] I think not, Socrates.

[Soc.] No, indeed; there would be small reason in that. Yet once more, fair friend; according to you, virtue is "the power of governing"; but do you not add "justly and not unjustly"?

[Men.] Yes, Socrates; I agree there; for justice is virtue.

[Soc.] Would you say "virtue," Meno, or "a virtue"?

[Men.] What do you mean?

[Soc.] I mean as I might say about anything; that a round, for example, is "a figure" and not simply "figure," and I should adopt this mode of speaking, because there are other figures.

[Men.] Quite right; and that is just what I am saying about virtue — that there are other virtues as well as justice.

[Soc.] What are they? Tell me the names of them, as I would tell you the names of the other figures if you asked me.

[Men.] Courage and temperance and wisdom and magnanimity are virtues; and there are many others.

[Soc.] Yes, Meno; and again we are in the same case: in searching after one virtue we have found many, though not in the same way as before; but we have been unable to find the common virtue which runs through them all.

[Men.] Why, Socrates, even now I am not able to follow you in the attempt to get at one common notion of virtue as of other things.

[Soc.] No wonder; but I will try to get nearer if I can, for you know that all things have a common notion. Suppose now that someone asked you the question which I asked before: Meno, he would say, what is figure? And if you answered "roundness," he would reply to you, in my way of speaking, by asking whether you would say that roundness is "figure" or "a figure"; and you would answer "a figure."

[Men.] Certainly.

[Soc.] And for this reason-that there are other figures?

[Men.] Yes.

[Soc.] And if he proceeded to ask, What other figures are there? you would have told him.

[Men.] I should.

[Soc.] And if he similarly asked what colour is, and you answered whiteness, and the questioner rejoined, Would you say that whiteness is colour or a colour? you would reply, A colour, because there are other colours as well.

[Men.] I should.

[Soc.] And if he had said, Tell me what they are? — you would have told him of other colours which are colours just as much as whiteness.

[Men.] Yes.

[Soc.] And suppose that he were to pursue the matter in my way, he would say: Ever and anon we are landed in particulars, but this is not what I want; tell me then, since you call them by a common name, and say that they are all figures, even when opposed to one another, what is that common nature which you designate as figure — which contains straight as well as round, and is no more one than the other — that would be your mode of speaking?

[Men.] Yes.

[Soc.] And in speaking thus, you do not mean to say that the round is round any more than straight, or the straight any more straight than round?

[Men.] Certainly not.

[Soc.] You only assert that the round figure is not more a figure than the straight, or the straight than the round?

[Men.] Very true.

[Soc.] To what then do we give the name of figure? Try and answer. Suppose that when a person asked you this question either about figure or colour, you were to reply, Man, I do not understand what you want, or know what you are saying; he would look rather astonished and say: Do you not understand that I am looking for the "simile in multis"? And then he might put the question in another form: Mono, he might say, what is that "simile in multis" which you call figure, and which includes not only round and straight figures, but all? Could you not answer that question, Meno? I wish that you would try; the attempt will be good practice with a view to the answer about virtue.

[Men.] I would rather that you should answer, Socrates.

[Soc.] Shall I indulge you?

[Men.] By all means.

[Soc.] And then you will tell me about virtue?

[Men.] I will.

[Soc.] Then I must do my best, for there is a prize to be won.

[Men.] Certainly.

[Soc.] Well, I will try and explain to you what figure is. What do you say to this answer?-Figure is the only thing which always follows colour. Will you be satisfied with it, as I am sure that I should be, if you would let me have a similar definition of virtue?

[Men.] But, Socrates, it is such a simple answer.

[Soc.] Why simple?

[Men.] Because, according to you, figure is that which always follows colour.

([Soc.] Granted.

[Men.] But if a person were to say that he does not know what colour is, any more than what figure is — what sort of answer would you have given him?

[Soc.] I should have told him the truth. And if he were a philosopher of the eristic and antagonistic sort, I should say to him: You have my answer, and if I am wrong, your business is to take up the argument and refute me. But if we were friends, and were talking as you and I are now, I should reply in a milder strain and more in the dialectician's vein; that is to say, I should not only speak the truth, but I should make use of premises which the person interrogated would be willing to admit. And this is the way in which I shall endeavour to approach you. You will acknowledge, will you not, that there is such a thing as an end, or termination, or extremity? — all which words use in the same sense, although I am aware that Prodicus might draw distinctions about them: but still you, I am sure, would speak of a thing as ended or terminated — that is all which I am saying — not anything very difficult.

[Men.] Yes, I should; and I believe that I understand your meaning.

[Soc.] And you would speak of a surface and also of a solid, as for example in geometry.

[Men.] Yes.

[Soc.] Well then, you are now in a condition to understand my definition of figure. I define figure to be that in which the solid ends; or, more concisely, the limit of solid.

[Men.] And now, Socrates, what is colour?

[Soc.] You are outrageous, Meno, in thus plaguing a poor old man to give you an answer, when you will not take the trouble of remembering what is Gorgias' definition of virtue.

[Men.] When you have told me what I ask, I will tell you, Socrates.

[Soc.] A man who was blindfolded has only to hear you talking, and he would know that you are a fair creature and have still many lovers.

[Men.] Why do you think so?

[Soc.] Why, because you always speak in imperatives: like all beauties when they are in their prime, you are tyrannical; and also, as I suspect, you have found out that I have weakness for the fair, and therefore to humour you I must answer.

[Men.] Please do.

[Soc.] Would you like me to answer you after the manner of Gorgias, which is familiar to you?

[Men.] I should like nothing better.

[Soc.] Do not he and you and Empedocles say that there are certain effluences of existence?

[Men.] Certainly.

[Soc.] And passages into which and through which the effluences pass?

[Men.] Exactly.

[Soc.] And some of the effluences fit into the passages, and some of them are too small or too large?

[Men.] True.

[Soc.] And there is such a thing as sight?

[Men.] Yes.

[Soc.] And now, as Pindar says, "read my meaning" colour is an effluence of form, commensurate with sight, and palpable to sense.

[Men.] That, Socrates, appears to me to be an admirable answer.

[Soc.] Why, yes, because it happens to be one which you have been in the habit of hearing: and your wit will have discovered, I suspect, that you may explain in the same way the nature of sound and smell, and of many other similar phenomena.

[Men.] Quite true.

[Soc.] The answer, Meno, was in the orthodox solemn vein, and therefore was more acceptable to you than the other answer about figure.

[Men.] Yes.

[Soc.] And yet, O son of Alexidemus, I cannot help thinking that the other was the better; and I am sure that you would be of the same opinion, if you would only stay and be initiated, and were not compelled, as you said yesterday, to go away before the mysteries.

[Men.] But I will stay, Socrates, if you will give me many such answers.

[Soc.] Well then, for my own sake as well as for yours, I will do my very best; but I am afraid that I shall not be able to give you very many as good: and now, in your turn, you are to fulfil your promise, and tell me what virtue is in the universal; and do not make a singular into a plural, as the facetious say of those who break a thing, but deliver virtue to me whole and sound, and not broken into a number of pieces: I have given you the pattern.

[Men.] Well then, Socrates, virtue, as I take it, is when he, who desires the honourable, is able to provide it for himself; so the poet says, and I say too —

Virtue is the desire of things honourable and the power of attaining them.

[Soc.] And does he who desires the honourable also desire the good?

[Men.] Certainly.

[Soc.] Then are there some who desire the evil and others who desire the good? Do not all men, my dear sir, desire good?

[Men.] I think not.

[Soc.] There are some who desire evil?

[Men.] Yes.

[Soc.] Do you mean that they think the evils which they desire, to be good; or do they know that they are evil and yet desire them?

[Men.] Both, I think.

[Soc.] And do you really imagine, Meno, that a man knows evils to be evils and desires them notwithstanding?

[Men.] Certainly I do.

[Soc.] And desire is of possession?

[Men.] Yes, of possession.

[Soc.] And does he think that the evils will do good to him who possesses them, or does he know that they will do him harm?

[Men.] There are some who think that the evils will do them good, and others who know that they will do them harm.

[Soc.] And, in your opinion, do those who think that they will do them good know that they are evils?

[Men.] Certainly not.

[Soc.] Is it not obvious that those who are ignorant of their nature do not desire them; but they desire what they suppose to be goods although they are really evils; and if they are mistaken and suppose the evils to be good they really desire goods?

[Men.] Yes, in that case.

[Soc.] Well, and do those who, as you say, desire evils, and think that evils are hurtful to the possessor of them, know that they will be hurt by them?

[Men.] They must know it.

[Soc.] And must they not suppose that those who are hurt are miserable in proportion to the hurt which is inflicted upon them?

[Men.] How can it be otherwise?

[Soc.] But are not the miserable ill-fated?

[Men.] Yes, indeed.

[Soc.] And does anyone desire to be miserable and ill-fated?

[Men.] I should say not, Socrates.

[Soc.] But if there is no one who desires to be miserable, there is no one, Meno, who desires evil; for what is misery but the desire and possession of evil?

[Men.] That appears to be the truth, Socrates, and I admit that nobody desires evil.

[Soc.] And yet, were you not saying just now that virtue is the desire and power of attaining good?

[Men.] Yes, I did say so.

[Soc.] But if this be affirmed, then the desire of good is common to all, and one man is no better than another in that respect?

[Men.] True.

[Soc.] And if one man is not better than another in desiring good, he must be better in the power of attaining it?

[Men.] Exactly.

[Soc.] Then, according to your definition, virtue would appear to be the power of attaining good?

[Men.] I entirely approve, Socrates, of the manner in which you now view this matter.

[Soc.] Then let us see whether what you say is true from another point of view; for very likely you may be right: — You affirm virtue to be the power of attaining goods?

[Men.] Yes.

[Soc.] And the goods which mean are such as health and wealth and the possession of gold and silver, and having office and honour in the state — those are what you would call goods?

[Men.] Yes, I should include all those.

[Soc.] Then, according to Meno, who is the hereditary friend of the great king, virtue is the power of getting silver and gold; and would you add that they must be gained piously, justly, or do you deem this to be of no consequence? And is any mode of acquisition, even if unjust and dishonest, equally to be deemed virtue?

[Men.] Not virtue, Socrates, but vice.

[Soc.] Then justice or temperance or holiness, or some other part of virtue, as would appear, must accompany the acquisition, and without them the mere acquisition of good will not be virtue.

[Men.] Why, how can there be virtue without these?

[Soc.] And the non-acquisition of gold and silver in a dishonest manner for oneself or another, or in other words the want of them, may be equally virtue?

[Men.] True.

[Soc.] Then the acquisition of such goods is no more virtue than the non-acquisition and want of them, but whatever is accompanied by justice or honesty is virtue, and whatever is devoid of justice is vice.

[Men.] It cannot be otherwise, in my judgment.

[Soc.] And were we not saying just now that justice, temperance, and the like, were each of them a part of virtue?

[Men.] Yes.

[Soc.] And so, Meno, this is the way in which you mock me.

[Men.] Why do you say that, Socrates?

[Soc.] Why, because I asked you to deliver virtue into my hands whole and unbroken, and I gave you a pattern according to which you were to frame your answer; and you have forgotten already, and tell me that virtue is the power of attaining good justly, or with justice; and justice you acknowledge to be a part of virtue.

[Men.] Yes.

[Soc.] Then it follows from your own admissions, that virtue is doing what you do with a part of virtue; for justice and the like are said by you to be parts of virtue.

[Men.] What of that?

[Soc.] What of that! Why, did not I ask you to tell me the nature of virtue as a whole? And you are very far from telling me this; but declare every action to be virtue which is done with a part of virtue; as though you had told me and I must already know the whole of virtue, and this too when frittered away into little pieces. And, therefore, my dear, I fear that I must begin again and repeat the same question: What is virtue? for otherwise, I can only say, that every action done with a part of virtue is virtue; what else is the meaning of saying that every action done with justice is virtue? Ought I not to ask the question over again; for can anyone who does not know virtue know a part of virtue?

[Men.] No; I do not say that he can.

[Soc.] Do you remember how, in the example of figure, we rejected any answer given in terms which were as yet unexplained or unadmitted?

[Men.] Yes, Socrates; and we were quite right in doing so.

[Soc.] But then, my friend, do not suppose that we can explain to anyone the nature of virtue as a whole through some unexplained portion of virtue, or anything at all in that fashion; we should only have to ask over again the old question, What is virtue? Am I not right?

[Men.] I believe that you are.

[Soc.] Then begin again, and answer me, What, according to you and your friend Gorgias, is the definition of virtue?

[Men.] O Socrates, I used to be told, before I knew you, that you were always doubting yourself and making others doubt; and now you are casting your spells over me, and I am simply getting bewitched and enchanted, and am at my wits' end. And if I may venture to make a jest upon you, you seem to me both in your appearance and in your power over others to be very like the flat torpedo fish, who torpifies those who come near him and touch him, as you have now torpified me, I think. For my soul and my tongue are really torpid, and I do not know how to answer you; and though I have been delivered of an infinite variety of speeches about virtue before now, and to many persons — and very good ones they were, as I thought — at this moment I cannot even say what virtue is. And I think that you are very wise in not voyaging and going away from home, for if you did in other places as you do in Athens, you would be cast into prison as a magician.

[Soc.] You are a rogue, Meno, and had all but caught me.

[Men.] What do you mean, Socrates?

[Soc.] I can tell why you made a simile about me.

[Men.] Why?

[Soc.] In order that I might make another simile about you. For I know that all pretty young gentlemen like to have pretty similes made about them — as well they may — but I shall not return the compliment. As to my being a torpedo, if the torpedo is torpid as well as the cause of torpidity in others, then indeed I am a torpedo, but not otherwise; for I perplex others, not because I am clear, but because I am utterly perplexed myself. And now I know not what virtue is, and you seem to be in the same case, although you did once perhaps know before you touched me. However, I have no objection to join with you in the enquiry.

[Men.] And how will you enquire, Socrates, into that which you do not know? What will you put forth as the subject of enquiry? And if you find what you want, how will you ever know that this is the thing which you did not know?

[Soc.] I know, Meno, what you mean; but just see what a tiresome dispute you are introducing. You argue that man cannot enquire either about that which he knows, or about that which he does not know; for if he knows, he has no need to enquire; and if not, he cannot; for he does not know the very subject about which he is to enquire.

[Men.] Well, Socrates, and is not the argument sound?

[Soc.] I think not.

[Men.] Why not?

[Soc.] I will tell you why: I have heard from certain wise men and women who spoke of things divine that —

[Men.] What did they say?

[Soc.] They spoke of a glorious truth, as I conceive.

[Men.] What was it? And who were they?

[Soc.] Some of them were priests and priestesses, who had studied how they might be able to give a reason of their profession: there have been poets also, who spoke of these things by inspiration, like Pindar, and many others who were inspired. And they say — mark, now, and see whether their words are true — they say that the soul of man is immortal, and at one time has an end, which is termed dying, and at another time is born again, but is never destroyed. And the moral is that a man ought to live always in perfect holiness. "For in the ninth year Persephone sends the souls of those from whom she has received the penalty of ancient crime back again from beneath into the light of the sun above, and these are they who become noble kings and mighty men and great in wisdom and are called saintly heroes in after ages." The soul, then, as being immortal, and having been born again many times, rand having seen all things that exist, whether in this world or in the world below, has knowledge of them all; and it is no wonder that she should be able to call to remembrance all that she ever knew about virtue, and about everything; for as all nature is akin, and the soul has learned all things; there is no difficulty in her eliciting, or, as men say, learning, out of a single recollection — all the rest, if a man is strenuous and does not faint; for all enquiry and all learning is but recollection. And therefore we ought not to listen to this sophistical argument about the impossibility of enquiry: for it will make us idle; and is sweet only to the sluggard; but the other saying will make us active and inquisitive. In that confiding, I will gladly enquire with you into the nature of virtue.

[Men.] Yes, Socrates; but what do you mean by saying that we do not learn, and that what we call learning is only a process of recollection? Can you teach me how this is?

[Soc.] I told you, Meno, just now that you were a rogue, and now you ask whether I can teach you, when I am saying that there is no teaching, but only recollection; and thus you imagine that you will involve me in a contradiction.

[Men.] Indeed, Socrates, I protest that I had no such intention. I only asked the question from habit; but if you can prove to me that what you say is true, I wish that you would.

[Soc.] It will be no easy matter, but I will try to please you to the utmost of my power. Suppose that you call one of your numerous attendants, that I may demonstrate on him.

[Men.] Certainly. Come hither, boy.

[Soc.] He is Greek, and speaks Greek, does he not?

[Men.] Yes, indeed; he was born in the house.

[Soc.] Attend now to the questions which I ask him, and observe whether he learns of me or only remembers.

[Men.] I will.

[Soc.] Tell me, boy, do you know that a figure like this is a square?

[Boy] I do.

[Soc.] And you know that a square figure has these four lines equal?

[Boy] Certainly.

[Soc.] And these lines which I have drawn through the middle of the square are also equal?

[Boy] Yes.

[Soc.] A square may be of any size?

[Boy] Certainly.

[Soc.] And if one side of the figure be of two feet, and the other side be of two feet, how much will the whole be? Let me explain: if in one direction the space was of two feet, and in other direction of one foot, the whole would be of two feet taken once?

[Boy] Yes.

[Soc.] But since this side is also of two feet, there are twice two feet?

[Boy] There are.

[Soc.] Then the square is of twice two feet?

[Boy] Yes.

[Soc.] And how many are twice two feet? Count and tell me.

[Boy] Four, Socrates.

[Soc.] And might there not be another square twice as large as this, and having like this the lines equal?

[Boy] Yes.

[Soc.] And of how many feet will that be?

[Boy] Of eight feet.

[Soc.] And now try and tell me the length of the line which forms the side of that double square: this is two feet-what will that be?

[Boy] Clearly, Socrates, it will be double.

[Soc.] Do you observe, Meno, that I am not teaching the boy anything, but only asking him questions; and now he fancies that he knows how long a line is necessary in order to produce a figure of eight square feet; does he not?

[Men.] Yes.

[Soc.] And does he really know?

[Men.] Certainly not.

[Soc.] He only guesses that because the square is double, the line is double.

[Men.] True.

[Soc.] Observe him while he recalls the steps in regular order. (To the Boy.) Tell me, boy, do you assert that a double space comes from a double line? Remember that I am not speaking of an oblong, but of a figure equal every way, and twice the size of this — that is to say of eight feet; and I want to know whether you still say that a double square comes from double line?

[Boy] Yes.

[Soc.] But does not this line become doubled if we add another such line here?

[Boy] Certainly.

[Soc.] And four such lines will make a space containing eight feet?

[Boy] Yes.

[Soc.] Let us describe such a figure: Would you not say that this is the figure of eight feet?

[Boy] Yes.

[Soc.] And are there not these four divisions in the figure, each of which is equal to the figure of four feet?

[Boy] True.

[Soc.] And is not that four times four?

[Boy] Certainly.

[Soc.] And four times is not double?

[Boy] No, indeed.

[Soc.] But how much?

[Boy] Four times as much.

[Soc.] Therefore the double line, boy, has given a space, not twice, but four times as much.

[Boy] True.

[Soc.] Four times four are sixteen — are they not?

[Boy] Yes.

[Soc.] What line would give you a space of eight feet, as this gives one of sixteen feet; — do you see?

[Boy] Yes.

[Soc.] And the space of four feet is made from this half line?

[Boy] Yes.

[Soc.] Good; and is not a space of eight feet twice the size of this, and half the size of the other?

[Boy] Certainly.

[Soc.] Such a space, then, will be made out of a line greater than this one, and less than that one?

[Boy] Yes; I think so.

[Soc.] Very good; I like to hear you say what you think. And now tell me, is not this a line of two feet and that of four?

[Boy] Yes.

[Soc.] Then the line which forms the side of eight feet ought to be more than this line of two feet, and less than the other of four feet?

[Boy] It ought.

[Soc.] Try and see if you can tell me how much it will be.

[Boy] Three feet.

[Soc.] Then if we add a half to this line of two, that will be the line of three. Here are two and there is one; and on the other side, here are two also and there is one: and that makes the figure of which you speak?

[Boy] Yes.

[Soc.] But if there are three feet this way and three feet that way, the whole space will be three times three feet?

[Boy] That is evident.

[Soc.] And how much are three times three feet?

[Boy] Nine.

[Soc.] And how much is the double of four?

[Boy] Eight.

[Soc.] Then the figure of eight is not made out of a line of three?

[Boy] No.

[Soc.] But from what line? — tell me exactly; and if you would rather not reckon, try and show me the line.

[Boy] Indeed, Socrates, I do not know.

Coding Slave

[Soc.] Do you see, Meno, what advances he has made in his power of recollection? He did not know at first, and he does not know now, what is the side of a figure of eight feet: but then he thought that he knew, and answered confidently as if he knew, and had no difficulty; now he has a difficulty, and neither knows nor fancies that he knows.

[Men.] True.

[Soc.] Is he not better off in knowing his ignorance?

[Men.] I think that he is.

[Soc.] If we have made him doubt, and given him the "torpedo's shock," have we done him any harm?

[Men.] I think not.

[Soc.] We have certainly, as would seem, assisted him in some degree to the discovery of the truth; and now he will wish to remedy his ignorance, but then he would have been ready to tell all the world again and again that the double space should have a double side.

[Men.] True.

[Soc.] But do you suppose that he would ever have enquired into or learned what he fancied that he knew, though he was really ignorant of it, until he had fallen into perplexity under the idea that he did not know, and had desired to know?

[Men.] I think not, Socrates.

[Soc.] Then he was the better for the torpedo's touch?

[Men.] I think so.

[Soc.] Mark now the farther development. I shall only ask him, and not teach him, and he shall share the enquiry with me: and do you watch and see if you find me telling or explaining anything to him, instead of eliciting his opinion. Tell me, boy, is not this a square of four feet which I have drawn?

[Boy] Yes.

[Soc.] And now I add another square equal to the former one?

[Boy] Yes.

[Soc.] And a third, which is equal to either of them?

[Boy] Yes.

[Soc.] Suppose that we fill up the vacant corner?

[Boy] Very good.

[Soc.] Here, then, there are four equal spaces?

[Boy] Yes.

[Soc.] And how many times larger is this space than this other?

[Boy] Four times.

- 161 -

[Soc.] But it ought to have been twice only, as you will remember.

[Boy] True.

[Soc.] And does not this line, reaching from corner to corner, bisect each of these spaces?

[Boy] Yes.

[Soc.] And are there not here four equal lines which contain this space?

[Boy] There are.

[Soc.] Look and see how much this space is.

[Boy] I do not understand.

[Soc.] Has not each interior line cut off half of the four spaces?

[Boy] Yes.

[Soc.] And how many spaces are there in this section?

[Boy] Four.

[Soc.] And how many in this?

[Boy] Two.

[Soc.] And four is how many times two?

[Boy] Twice.

[Soc.] And this space is of how many feet?

[Boy] Of eight feet.

[Soc.] And from what line do you get this figure?

[Boy] From this.

[Soc.] That is, from the line which extends from corner to corner of the figure of four feet?

[Boy] Yes.

[Soc.] And that is the line which the learned call the diagonal. And if this is the proper name, then you, Meno's slave, are prepared to affirm that the double space is the square of the diagonal?

[Boy] Certainly, Socrates.

[Soc.] What do you say of him, Meno? Were not all these answers given out of his own head?

[Men.] Yes, they were all his own.

[Soc.] And yet, as we were just now saying, he did not know?

[Men.] True.

[Soc.] But still he had in him those notions of his — had he not?

[Men.] Yes.

Coding Slave

[Soc.] Then he who does not know may still have true notions of that which he does not know?

[Men.] He has.

[Soc.] And at present these notions have just been stirred up in him, as in a dream; but if he were frequently asked the same questions, in different forms, he would know as well as any one at last?

[Men.] I dare say.

[Soc.] Without anyone teaching him, he will recover his knowledge for himself, if he is only asked questions?

[Men.] Yes.

[Soc.] And this spontaneous recovery of knowledge in him is recollection?

[Men.] True.

[Soc.] And this knowledge which he now has must he not either have acquired or always possessed?

[Men.] Yes.

[Soc.] But if he always possessed this knowledge he would always have known; or if he has acquired the knowledge he could not have acquired it in this life, unless he has been taught geometry; for he may be made to do the same with all geometry and every other branch of knowledge. Now, has any one ever taught him all this? You must know about him, if, as you say, he was born and bred in your house.

[Men.] And I am certain that no one ever did teach him.

[Soc.] And yet he has the knowledge?

[Men.] The fact, Socrates, is undeniable.

[Soc.] But if he did not acquire the knowledge in this life, then he must have had and learned it at some other time?

[Men.] Clearly he must.

[Soc.] Which must have been the time when he was not a man?

[Men.] Yes.

[Soc.] And if there have been always true thoughts in him, both at the time when he was and was not a man, which only need to be awakened into knowledge by putting questions to him, his soul must have always possessed this knowledge, for he always either was or was not a man?

[Men.] Obviously.

[Soc.] And if the truth of all things always existed in the soul, then the soul is immortal. Wherefore be of good cheer, and try to recollect what you do not know, or rather what you do not remember.

[Men.] I feel, somehow, that I like what you are saying.

[Soc.] And I, Meno, like what I am saying. Some things I have said of which I am not altogether confident. But that we shall be better and braver and less helpless if we think that we ought to enquire, than we should have been if we indulged in the idle fancy that there was no knowing and no use in seeking to know what we do not know; — that is a theme upon which I am ready to fight, in word and deed, to the utmost of my power.

[Men.] There again, Socrates, your words seem to me excellent.

[Soc.] Then, as we are agreed that a man should enquire about that which he does not know, shall you and I make an effort to enquire together into the nature of virtue?

[Men.] By all means, Socrates. And yet I would much rather return to my original question, Whether in seeking to acquire virtue we should regard it as a thing to be taught, or as a gift of nature, or as coming to men in some other way?

[Soc.] Had I the command of you as well as of myself, Meno, I would not have enquired whether virtue is given by instruction or not, until we had first ascertained "what it is." But as you think only of controlling me who am your slave, and never of controlling yourself, — such being your notion of freedom, I must yield to you, for you are irresistible. And therefore I have now to enquire into the qualities of a thing of which I do not as yet know the nature. At any rate, will you condescend a little, and allow the question "Whether virtue is given by instruction, or in any other way," to be argued upon hypothesis? As the geometrician, when he is asked whether a certain triangle is capable of being inscribed in a certain circle, will reply: "I cannot tell you as yet; but I will offer a hypothesis which may assist us in forming a conclusion: If the figure be such that when you have produced a given side of it, the given area of the triangle falls short by an area corresponding to the part produced, then one consequence follows, and if this is impossible then some other; and therefore I wish to assume a hypothesis before I tell you whether this triangle is capable of being inscribed in the circle": — that is a geometrical hypothesis. And we too, as we know not the nature and qualities of virtue, must ask, whether virtue is or not taught, under a hypothesis: as thus, if virtue is of such a class of mental goods, will it be taught or not? Let the first hypothesis be that virtue is or is not knowledge, — in that case will it be taught or not? or, as we were just now saying, remembered"? For there is no use in disputing about the name. But is virtue taught or not? or rather, does not everyone see that knowledge alone is taught?

[Men.] I agree.

[Soc.] Then if virtue is knowledge, virtue will be taught?

[Men.] Certainly.

[Soc.] Then now we have made a quick end of this question: if virtue is of such a nature, it will be taught; and if not, not?

[Men.] Certainly.

[Soc.] The next question is, whether virtue is knowledge or of another species?

[Men.] Yes, that appears to be the question which comes next in order.

[Soc.] Do we not say that virtue is a good? This is a hypothesis which is not set aside.

[Men.] Certainly.

[Soc.] Now, if there be any sort of good which is distinct from knowledge, virtue may be that good; but if knowledge embraces all good, then we shall be right in thinking that virtue is knowledge?

[Men.] True.

[Soc.] And virtue makes us good?

[Men.] Yes.

[Soc.] And if we are good, then we are profitable; for all good things are profitable?

[Men.] Yes.

[Soc.] Then virtue is profitable?

[Men.] That is the only inference.

[Soc.] Then now let us see what are the things which severally profit us. Health and strength, and beauty and wealth — these, and the like of these, we call profitable?

[Men.] True.

[Soc.] And yet these things may also sometimes do us harm: would you not think so?

[Men.] Yes.

[Soc.] And what is the guiding principle which makes them profitable or the reverse? Are they not profitable when they are rightly used, and hurtful when they are not rightly used?

[Men.] Certainly.

[Soc.] Next, let us consider the goods of the soul: they are temperance, justice, courage, quickness of apprehension, memory, magnanimity, and the like?

[Men.] Surely.

[Soc.] And such of these as are not knowledge, but of another sort, are sometimes profitable and sometimes hurtful; as, for example, courage wanting prudence, which is only a sort of confidence? When a man has no sense he is harmed by courage, but when he has sense he is profited?

[Men.] True.

[Soc.] And the same may be said of temperance and quickness of apprehension; whatever things are learned or done with sense are profitable, but when done without sense they are hurtful?

[Men.] Very true.

[Soc.] And in general, all that the soul attempts or endures, when under the guidance of wisdom, ends in happiness; but when she is under the guidance of folly, in the opposite?

[Men.] That appears to be true.

[Soc.] If then virtue is a quality of the soul, and is admitted to be profitable, it must be wisdom or prudence, since none of the things of the soul are either profitable or hurtful in themselves, but they are all made profitable or hurtful by the addition of wisdom or of folly; and therefore if virtue is profitable, virtue must be a sort of wisdom or prudence?

[Men.] I quite agree.

[Soc.] And the other goods, such as wealth and the like, of which we were just now saying that they are sometimes good and sometimes evil, do not they also become profitable or hurtful, accordingly as the soul guides and uses them rightly or wrongly; just as the things of the soul herself are benefited when under the guidance of wisdom and harmed by folly?

[Men.] True.

[Soc.] And the wise soul guides them rightly, and the foolish soul wrongly.

[Men.] Yes.

[Soc.] And is not this universally true of human nature? All other things hang upon the soul, and the things of the soul herself hang upon wisdom, if they are to be good; and so wisdom is inferred to be that which profits — and virtue, as we say, is profitable?

[Men.] Certainly.

[Soc.] And thus we arrive at the conclusion that virtue is either wholly or partly wisdom?

[Men.] I think that what you are saying, Socrates, is very true.

[Soc.] But if this is true, then the good are not by nature good?

[Men.] I think not.

[Soc.] If they had been, there would assuredly have been discerners of characters among us who would have known our future great men; and on their showing we should have adopted them, and when we had got them, we should have kept them in the citadel out of the way of harm, and set a stamp upon them far rather than upon a piece of gold, in order that no one might tamper with them; and when they grew up they would have been useful to the state?

[Men.] Yes, Socrates, that would have been the right way.

[Soc.] But if the good are not by nature good, are they made good by instruction?

[Men.] There appears to be no other alternative, Socrates. On the supposition that virtue is knowledge, there can be no doubt that virtue is taught.

[Soc.] Yes, indeed; but what if the supposition is erroneous?

[Men.] I certainly thought just now that we were right.

[Soc.] Yes, Meno; but a principle which has any soundness should stand firm not only just now, but always.

[Men.] Well; and why are you so slow of heart to believe that knowledge is virtue?

[Soc.] I will try and tell you why, Meno. I do not retract the assertion that if virtue is knowledge it may be taught; but I fear that I have some reason in doubting whether virtue is knowledge: for consider now and say whether virtue, and not only virtue but anything that is taught, must not have teachers and disciples?

[Men.] Surely.

[Soc.] And conversely, may not the art of which neither teachers nor disciples exist be assumed to be incapable of being taught?

[Men.] True; but do you think that there are no teachers of virtue?

[Soc.] I have certainly often enquired whether there were any, and taken great pains to find them, and have never succeeded; and many have assisted me in the search, and they were the persons whom I thought the most likely to know. Here at the moment when he is wanted we fortunately have sitting by us Anytus, the very person of whom we should make enquiry; to him then let us repair. In the first place, he is the son of a wealthy and wise father, Anthemion, who acquired his wealth, not by accident or gift, like Ismenias the Theban (who has recently made himself as rich as Polycrates), but by his own skill and industry, and who is a well-conditioned, modest man, not insolent, or over-bearing, or annoying; moreover, this son of his has received a good education, as the Athenian people certainly appear to think, for they choose him to fill the highest offices. And these are the sort of men from whom you are likely to learn whether there are any teachers of virtue, and who they are. Please, Anytus, to help me and your friend Meno in answering our question, Who are the teachers? Consider the matter thus: If we wanted Meno to be a good physician, to whom should we send him? Should we not send him to the physicians?

[Any.] Certainly.

[Soc.] Or if we wanted him to be a good cobbler, should we not send him to the cobblers?

[Any.] Yes.

[Soc.] And so forth?

[Any.] Yes.

[Soc.] Let me trouble you with one more question. When we say that we should be right in sending him to the physicians if we wanted him to be a physician, do we mean that we should be right in sending him to those who profess the art, rather than to those who do not, and to those who demand payment for teaching the art, and profess to teach it to anyone who will come and learn? And if these were our reasons, should we not be right in sending him?

[Any.] Yes.

[Soc.] And might not the same be said of flute-playing, and of the other arts? Would a man who wanted to make another a flute-player refuse to send him to those who profess to teach the art for money, and be plaguing other persons to give him instruction, who are not professed teachers and who never had a single disciple in that branch of knowledge which he wishes him to acquire — would not such conduct be the height of folly?

[Any.] Yes, by Zeus, and of ignorance, too.

[Soc.] Very good. And now you are in a position to advise with me about my friend Meno. He has been telling me, Anytus, that he desires to attain that kind of wisdom and virtue by which men order the state or the house, and honour their parents, and know when to receive and when to send away citizens and strangers, as a good man should. Now, to whom should he go in order that he may learn this virtue? Does not the previous argument imply clearly that we should send him to those who profess and avouch that they are the common teachers of all Hellas, and are ready to impart instruction to any one who likes, at a fixed price?

[Any.] Whom do you mean, Socrates?

[Soc.] You surely know, do you not, Anytus, that these are the people whom mankind call Sophists?

[Any.] By Heracles, Socrates, forbear! I only hope that no friend or kinsman or acquaintance of mine, whether citizen or stranger, will ever be so mad as to allow himself to be corrupted by them; for they are a manifest pest and corrupting influences to those who have to do with them.

[Soc.] What, Anytus? Of all the people who profess that they know how to do men good, do you mean to say that these are the only ones who not only do them no good, but positively corrupt those who are entrusted to them, and in return for this disservice have the face to demand money? Indeed, I cannot believe you; for I know of a single man, Protagoras, who made more out of his craft than the illustrious Pheidias, who created such noble works, or any ten other statuaries. How could thata mender of old shoes, or patcher up of clothes, who made the shoes or clothes worse than he received them, could not have remained thirty days undetected, and would very soon have starved; whereas during more than forty years, Protagoras was corrupting all Hellas, and sending his disciples from him worse than he received them, and he was never found out. For, if I am not mistaken, he was about seventy years old at his death, forty of which were spent in the practice of his profession; and during all that time he had a good reputation, which to this day he retains: and not only Protagoras, but many others are well spoken of; some who lived before him, and others who are still living. Now, when you say that they deceived and corrupted the youth, are they to be supposed to have corrupted them consciously or unconsciously? Can those who were deemed by many to be the wisest men of Hellas have been out of their minds?

[Any.] Out of their minds! No, Socrates; the young men who gave their money to them were out of their minds, and their relations and guardians who entrusted their youth to the care of these men were still more out of their minds, and most of all, the cities who allowed them to come in, and did not drive them out, citizen and stranger alike.

[Soc.] Has any of the Sophists wronged you, Anytus? What makes you so angry with them?

[Any.] No, indeed, neither I nor any of my belongings has ever had, nor would I suffer them to have, anything to do with them.

[Soc.] Then you are entirely unacquainted with them?

[Any.] And I have no wish to be acquainted.

[Soc.] Then, my dear friend, how can you know whether a thing is good or bad of which you are wholly ignorant?

[Any.] Quite well; I am sure that I know what manner of men these are, whether I am acquainted with them or not.

[Soc.] You must be a diviner, Anytus, for I really cannot make out, judging from your own words, how, if you are not acquainted with them, you know about them. But I am not enquiring of you who are the teachers who will corrupt Meno (let them be, if you please, the Sophists); I only ask you to tell him who there is in this great city who will teach him how to become eminent in the virtues which I was just, now describing. He is the friend of your family, and you will oblige him.

[Any.] Why do you not tell him yourself?

[Soc.] I have told him whom I supposed to be the teachers of these things; but I learn from you that I am utterly at fault, and I dare say that you are right. And now I wish that you, on your part, would tell me to whom among the Athenians he should go. Whom would you name? Any. Why single out individuals? Any Athenian gentleman, taken at random, if he will mind him, will do far more, good to him than the Sophists.

[Soc.] And did those gentlemen grow of themselves; and without having been taught by anyone, were they nevertheless able to teach others that which they had never learned themselves?

[Any.] I imagine that they learned of the previous generation of gentlemen. Have there not been many good men in this city?

[Soc.] Yes, certainly, Anytus; and many good statesmen also there always have been and there are still, in the city of Athens. But the question is whether they were also good teachers of their own virtue; — not whether there are, or have been, good men in this part of the world, but whether virtue can be taught, is the question which we have been discussing. Now, do we mean to say that the good men our own and of other times knew how to impart to others that virtue which they had themselves; or is virtue a thing incapable of being communicated or imparted by one man to another? That is the question which I and Meno have been arguing. Look at the matter in your own way: Would you not admit that Themistocles was a good man?

[Any.] Certainly; no man better.

[Soc.] And must not he then have been a good teacher, if any man ever was a good teacher, of his own virtue?

[Any.] Yes certainly, — if he wanted to be so.

[Soc.] But would he not have wanted? He would, at any rate, have desired to make his own son a good man and a gentleman; he could not have been jealous of him, or have intentionally abstained from imparting to him his own virtue. Did you never hear that he made his son Cleophantus a famous horseman; and had him taught to stand upright on horseback and hurl a javelin, and to do many other marvellous things; and in anything which could be learned from a master he was well trained? Have you not heard from our elders of him?

[Any.] I have.

[Soc.] Then no one could say that his son showed any want of capacity?

[Any.] Very likely not.

[Soc.] But did any one, old or young, ever say in your hearing that Cleophantus, son of Themistocles, was a wise or good man, as his father was?

[Any.] I have certainly never heard any one say so.

[Soc.] And if virtue could have been taught, would his father Themistocles have sought to train him in these minor accomplishments, and allowed him who, as you must remember, was his own son, to be no better than his neighbours in those qualities in which he himself excelled?

[Any.] Indeed, indeed, I think not.

[Soc.] Here was a teacher of virtue whom you admit to be among the best men of the past. Let us take another, — Aristides, the son of Lysimachus: would you not acknowledge that he was a good man?

[Any.] To be sure I should.

[Soc.] And did not he train his son Lysimachus better than any other Athenian in all that could be done for him by the help of masters? But what has been the result? Is he a bit better than any other mortal? He is an acquaintance of yours, and you see what he is like. There is Pericles, again, magnificent in his wisdom; and he, as you are aware, had two sons, Paralus and Xanthippus.

[Any.] I know.

[Soc.] And you know, also, that he taught them to be unrivalled horsemen, and had them trained in music and gymnastics and all sorts of arts — in these respects they were on a level with the best — and had he no wish to make good men of them? Nay, he must have wished it. But virtue, as I suspect, could not be taught. And that you may not suppose the incompetent teachers to be only the meaner sort of Athenians and few in number, remember again that Thucydides had two sons, Melesias and Stephanus, whom, besides giving them a good education in other things, he trained in wrestling, and they were the best wrestlers in Athens: one of them he committed to the care of Xanthias, and the other of Eudorus, who had the reputation of being the most celebrated wrestlers of that day. Do you remember them?

[Any.] I have heard of them.

[Soc.] Now, can there be a doubt that Thucydides, whose children were taught things for which he had to spend money, would have taught them to be good men, which would have cost him nothing, if virtue could have been taught? Will you reply that he was a mean man, and had not many friends among the Athenians and allies? Nay, but he was of a great family, and a man of influence at Athens and in all Hellas, and, if virtue could have been taught, he would have found out some Athenian or foreigner who would have made good men of his sons, if he could not himself spare the time from cares of state. Once more, I suspect, friend Anytus, that virtue is not a thing which can be taught.

[Any.] Socrates, I think that you are too ready to speak evil of men: and, if you will take my advice, I would recommend you to be careful. Perhaps there is no city in which it is not easier to do men harm than to do them good, and this is certainly the case at Athens, as I believe that you know.

[Soc.] O Meno, think that Anytus is in a rage. And he may well be in a rage, for he thinks, in the first place, that I am defaming these gentlemen; and in the second place, he is of opinion that he is one of them himself. But some day he will know what is the meaning of defamation, and if he ever does, he will forgive me. Meanwhile I will return to you, Meno; for I suppose that there are gentlemen in your region, too?

[Men.] Certainly there are.

[Soc.] And are they willing to teach the young? and do they profess to be teachers? and do they agree that virtue is taught?

[Men.] No indeed, Socrates, they are anything but agreed; you may hear them saying at one time that virtue can be taught, and then again the reverse.

[Soc.] Can we call those teachers who do not acknowledge the possibility of their own vocation?

[Men.] I think not, Socrates.

[Soc.] And what do you think of these Sophists, who are the only professors? Do they seem to you to be teachers of virtue?

[Men.] I often wonder, Socrates, that Gorgias is never heard promising to teach virtue: and when he hears others promising he only laughs at them; but he thinks that men should be taught to speak.

[Soc.] Then do you not think that the Sophists are teachers?

[Men.] I cannot tell you, Socrates; like the rest of the world, I am in doubt, and sometimes I think that they are teachers and sometimes not.

[Soc.] And are you aware that not you only and other politicians have doubts whether virtue can be taught or not, but that Theognis the poet says the very same thing?

[Men.] Where does he say so?

[Soc.] In these elegiac verses:

Eat and drink and sit with the mighty, and make yourself agreeable to them; for from the good you will learn what is good, but if you mix with the bad you will lose the intelligence which you already have.

Do you observe that here he seems to imply that virtue can be taught?

[Men.] Clearly.

[Soc.] But in some other verses he shifts about and says:

If understanding could be created and put into a man, then they [who were able to perform this feat] would have obtained great rewards.

And again:

Never would a bad son have sprung from a good sire, for he would have heard the voice of instruction; but not by teaching will you ever make a bad man into a good one.

And this, as you may remark, is a contradiction of the other.

[Men.] Clearly.

[Soc.] And is there anything else of which the professors are affirmed not only not to be teachers of others, but to be ignorant themselves, and bad at the knowledge of that which they are professing to teach? or is there anything about which even the acknowledged "gentlemen" are sometimes saying that "this thing can be taught," and sometimes the opposite? Can you say that they are teachers in any true sense whose ideas are in such confusion?

[Men.] I should say, certainly not.

[Soc.] But if neither the Sophists nor the gentlemen are teachers, clearly there can be no other teachers?

[Men.] No.

[Soc.] And if there are no teachers, neither are there disciples?

[Men.] Agreed.

[Soc.] And we have admitted that a thing cannot be taught of which there are neither teachers nor disciples?

[Men.] We have.

[Soc.] And there are no teachers of virtue to be found anywhere?

[Men.] There are not.

[Soc.] And if there are no teachers, neither are there scholars?

[Men.] That, I think, is true.

[Soc.] Then virtue cannot be taught?

[Men.] Not if we are right in our view. But I cannot believe, Socrates, that there are no good men: And if there are, how did they come into existence?

[Soc.] I am afraid, Meno, that you and I are not good for much, and that Gorgias has been as poor an educator of you as Prodicus has been of me. Certainly we shall have to look to ourselves, and try to find some one who will help in some way or other to improve us. This I say because I observe that in the previous discussion none of us remarked that right and good action is possible to man under other guidance than that of knowledge (*episteme*); and indeed if this be denied, there is no seeing how there can be any good men at all.

[Men.] How do you mean, Socrates?

[Soc.] I mean that good men are necessarily useful or profitable. Were we not right in admitting this? It must be so.

[Men.] Yes.

[Soc.] And in supposing that they will be useful only if they are true guides to us of action — there we were also right?

[Men.] Yes.

[Soc.] But when we said that a man cannot be a good guide unless he have knowledge (*phrhonesis*) this we were wrong.

[Men.] What do you mean by the word "right"?

[Soc.] I will explain. If a man knew the way to Larisa, or anywhere else, and went to the place and led others thither, would he not be a right and good guide?

[Men.] Certainly.

[Soc.] And a person who had a right opinion about the way, but had never been and did not know, might be a good guide also, might he not?

[Men.] Certainly.

[Soc.] And while he has true opinion about that which the other knows, he will be just as good a guide if he thinks the truth, as he who knows the truth?

[Men.] Exactly.

[Soc.] Then true opinion is as good a guide to correct action as knowledge; and that was the point which we omitted in our speculation about the nature of virtue, when we said that knowledge only is the guide of right action; whereas there is also right opinion.

[Men.] True.

[Soc.] Then right opinion is not less useful than knowledge?

[Men.] The difference, Socrates, is only that he who has knowledge will always be right; but he who has right opinion will sometimes be right, and sometimes not.

[Soc.] What do you mean? Can he be wrong who has right opinion, so long as he has right opinion?

[Men.] I admit the cogency of your argument, and therefore, Socrates, I wonder that knowledge should be preferred to right opinion — or why they should ever differ.

[Soc.] And shall I explain this wonder to you?

[Men.] Do tell me.

[Soc.] You would not wonder if you had ever observed the images of Daedalus; but perhaps you have not got them in your country?

[Men.] What have they to do with the question?

[Soc.] Because they require to be fastened in order to keep them, and if they are not fastened they will play truant and run away.

[Men.] Well, what of that?

[Soc.] I mean to say that they are not very valuable possessions if they are at liberty, for they will walk off like runaway slaves; but when fastened, they are of great value, for they are really beautiful works of art. Now this is an illustration of the nature of true opinions: while they abide with us they are beautiful and fruitful, but they run away out of the human soul, and do not remain long, and therefore they are not of much value until they are fastened by the tie of the cause; and this fastening of them, friend Meno, is recollection, as you and I have agreed to call it. But when they are bound, in the first place, they have the nature of knowledge; and, in the second place, they are abiding. And this is why knowledge is more honourable and excellent than true opinion, because fastened by a chain.

[Men.] What you are saying, Socrates, seems to be very like the truth.

[Soc.] I too speak rather in ignorance; I only conjecture. And yet that knowledge differs from true opinion is no matter of conjecture with me. There are not many things which I profess to know, but this is most certainly one of them.

[Men.] Yes, Socrates; and you are quite right in saying so.

[Soc.] And am I not also right in saying that true opinion leading the way perfects action quite as well as knowledge?

[Men.] There again, Socrates, I think you are right.

[Soc.] Then right opinion is not a whit inferior to knowledge, or less useful in action; nor is the man who has right opinion inferior to him who has knowledge?

[Men.] True.

[Soc.] And surely the good man has been acknowledged by us to be useful?

[Men.] Yes.

[Soc.] Seeing then that men become good and useful to states, not only because they have knowledge, but because they have right opinion, and that neither knowledge nor right opinion is given to man by nature or acquired by him — do you imagine either of them to be given by nature?

[Men.] Not I.

[Soc.] Then if they are not given by nature, neither are the good by nature good?

[Men.] Certainly not.

[Soc.] And nature being excluded, then came the question whether virtue is acquired by teaching?

[Men.] Yes.

[Soc.] If virtue was wisdom [or knowledge], then, as we thought, it was taught?

[Men.] Yes.

[Soc.] And if it was taught, it was wisdom?

[Men.] Certainly.

[Soc.] And if there were teachers, it might be taught; and if there were no teachers, not?

[Men.] True.

[Soc.] But surely we acknowledged that there were no teachers of virtue?

[Men.] Yes.

[Soc.] Then we acknowledged that it was not taught, and was not wisdom?

[Men.] Certainly.

[Soc.] And yet we admitted that it was a good?

[Men.] Yes.

[Soc.] And the right guide is useful and good?

[Men.] Certainly.

[Soc.] And the only right guides are knowledge and true opinion — these are the guides of man; for things which happen by chance are not under the guidance of man: but the guides of man are true opinion and knowledge.

[Men.] I think so, too.

[Soc.] But if virtue is not taught, neither is virtue knowledge.

[Men.] Clearly not.

[Soc.] Then of two good and useful things, one, which is knowledge, has been set aside, and cannot be supposed to be our guide in political life.

[Men.] I think not.

[Soc.] And therefore not by any wisdom, and not because they were wise, did Themistocles and those others of whom Anytus spoke govern states. This was the reason why they were unable to make others like themselves — because their virtue was not grounded on knowledge.

[Men.] That is probably true, Socrates.

[Soc.] But if not by knowledge, the only alternative which remains is that statesmen must have guided states by right opinion, which is in politics what divination is in religion; for diviners and also prophets say many things truly, but they know not what they say.

[Men.] So I believe.

[Soc.] And may we not, Meno, truly call those men "divine" who, having no understanding, yet succeed in many a grand deed and word?

[Men.] Certainly.

[Soc.] Then we shall also be right in calling divine those whom we were just now speaking of as diviners and prophets, including the whole tribe of poets. Yes, and statesmen above all may be said to be divine and illumined, being inspired and possessed of God, in which condition they say many grand things, not knowing what they say.

[Men.] Yes.

[Soc.] And the women, too, Meno, call good men divine — do they not? and the Spartans, when they praise a good man, say "that he is a divine man."

[Men.] And I think, Socrates, that they are right; although very likely our friend Anytus may take offence at the word.

[Soc.] I do not care; as for Anytus, there will be another opportunity of talking with him. To sum up our enquiry — the result seems to be, if we are at all right in our view, that virtue is neither natural nor acquired, but an instinct given by God to the virtuous. Nor is the instinct accompanied by reason, unless there may be supposed to be among statesmen some one who is capable of educating statesmen. And if there be such an one, he may be said to be among the living what Homer says that Tiresias was among the dead, "he alone has understanding; but the rest are flitting shades"; and he and his virtue in like manner will be a reality among shadows.

[Men.] That is excellent, Socrates.

[Soc.] Then, Meno, the conclusion is that virtue comes to the virtuous by the gift of God. But we shall never know the certain truth until, before asking how virtue is given, we enquire into the actual nature of virtue. I fear that I must go away, but do you, now that you are persuaded yourself, persuade our friend Anytus. And do not let him be so exasperated; if you can conciliate him, you will have done good service to the Athenian people.

Appendix B: Glossary

A

Action item: Something that you do, usually the result of a condition or situation determined in a business meeting. For example, condition: the inventory is too high; action item: tell the guys in inventory to buy less stuff; owner: Ralph. (See: Action item owner.)

Action item owner: The person or persons responsible for executing an action item.

ADA: A programming language named after Ada Byron, a.k.a, Lady Lovelace, nineteenth century mathematician and daughter of the poet, Lord Byron. Ada Byron was a friend, confident and colleague of Charles Babbage. She helped him refine and enhance his ideas for the Analytic Engine, a theoretical predecessor to the modern computer.

Admin: see Administrative Assistant

Administrative Assistant: a secretary without secretarial skills. The ability to type, take shorthand, answer the phone and handle correspondence are not part of the Administrative Assistant's job description. Such functions are now left to computers. Administrative Assistants do things such as book meeting rooms, organize the collection of money for funerals and golf outings, and protect the political wellbeing of the department within the organization. (The position of secretary still exists, but only for high-level executives, and is now called "Executive Secretary".)

Administrivia: The trivial facts and procedures that are a vital part of the day-to-day functioning of an organization.

American Dream: Making something from nothing by the force of sheer desire and a willingness to work hard, thus reaping the rewards of one's labor: a house, car, kids and status within the community.

Amiga: A personal computer of considerable power and engineering prowess, with significant market share circa 1984. That was then. This is now. In 2003 the remnants of the company are being run by a handful of guys in Washington State.

Ariel: A character from the play, *The Tempest* by William Shakespeare; a spirit of the air who does the bidding of Prospero.

Asset management system: A software system that keeps track of the physical property of a company or organization.

Atari: A company that makes computer games, hardware and software.

Atta-boy: A compliment; a gesture of recognition for work well done.

B

Barksdale, Jim: Partner of the now defunct venture capital firm Barksdale Group, former President and CEO of Netscape Communication, former CEO of ATT Wireless, former COO of McCaw, former CIO of Federal Express.

BASIC: (an acronym for **B**eginner's **A**ll-purpose **S**ymbolic **I**nstruction **C**ode) an early computer programming language that was the precursor to one of the most popular programming languages on the planet, Visual Basic.

Beer shits: a diarrheic bowel movement in which the stool has very, very large water content due to the dehydration of the body, usually due to a hangover.

Berlitz: A commercial language training school and product line geared to teaching a foreign language quickly, usually to business executives.

Bismarck, Otto von (1815-1898): considered one of the most significant political figures of modern Germany. As Prussia's president minister and than imperial chancellor of from 1862 to 1890 is credited with being the person that transformed Germany from a collection of semi-independent principalities into an imperial German nation-state.

Box: a slang term for the personal computer excluding monitor, keyboard, mouse and other peripherals.

Breakout session: A smaller technical lecture that is part of an overall larger technical conference. A breakout session usually focuses on the details of one topic.

Burn rate: The rate at which a company or organization uses money.

C

C++: A computer programming language; the object-oriented extension of the computer language, C.

Categorical imperative: A philosophical concept introduced by Emmanuel Kant that describes ethical actions that are done solely due to the logic of the action's definition. The best-known example is the Golden Rule.

Channel surf: To continuously go from one television channel to another using a remote control to switch channels.

COBOL: Common Business Oriented Language is a widely-used high-level programming language for business applications. The program is mainframe-based and was used to write early payroll and accounting applications.

Comdex: The Computer Distributor Exposition — the largest exposition held in the United States for the computer industry. The exposition takes place every November in Las Vegas, Nevada. Over the years the show has suffered setbacks and lost popularity among exhibitors. At one point the company that produces the show filed for bankruptcy.

Comments: text that appears in code as notes that explain what the code is doing so that other developers who need to make changes will know exactly what is going on without having to spend a lot of time trying to figure things out. Well-written code is usually well-commented.

Contract consultants: another term for a contract computer programmer.

Cooking the books: slang for falsifying financial records.

Corporate State: A circumstance in which one or many private commercial corporations are the organizational agent and primary governing force of the body politic.

Crown Victoria: A big sedan made by the Ford Motor Company.

Corn Dog: A hot dog that is encased in corn bread batter and deep fried, usually served on a stick.

Cotton candy: A very sweet candy of threaded sugar that is tinted with food coloring and twirled onto a stick.

Cul-de-sac: A street that ends in a circular dead end that has houses situated around the outer edge of the circular termination.

Custom software development: Making software that is intended for use by a limited number of users. Usually such software is made to meet a specific need or address a specific business process of a company or enterprise.

Cozumel: A city in Mexico known for its vacation resort facilities.

D

Data-mining: The practice of retrieving, sorting, and analyzing large amounts of data from very, very, very, very big databases and groups of databases.

Daily Build: The code that is collected from the many programmers working on a software project and compiled into a single application. The daily build reflects that current state of a piece of software under development.

Database Administrator (DBA): The man or woman in charge of the design and wellbeing of (a) database(s).

Developer Community: The programmers, developers and support personnel who specialize in a particular software product or technology.

Disposable pastry tissue: a light piece of paper used for the hygienic handling of pastry products.

Dog: A slang term that describes something that is not worthwhile, without value, a mistake. *syn*: Lemon

Dog-and-pony show: a slang term for a product demonstration.

DSL: Digital Subscriber Line is a technology for delivering high-bandwidth information from the Internet over ordinary copper telephone lines.

E

eBay: The most popular auction site on the Internet.

Ellison, Larry: CEO of Oracle, the second largest software manufacturer in the United States.

End User: The person who uses a computer to do work that does not involve programming, fixing, maintaining or upgrading a computer or computer system. Also known as "user scum" and "the fucking end user".

Engagement: A period of contractual employment.

Entity Relationship Diagram: See ERD

ERD: Entity Relationship Diagram, the diagram that provides a DBA with a detailed abstract description of a database.

ERP: Enterprise Resource Planning, the software that controls very, very, very, very big companies.

F

Federal Tax Form 1099: A tax form that is statement of earnings which a corporation issues to a consultant or short-term contractor, and for which taxes have not been withheld.

Ferrari: A very fast, very expensive automobile, manufactured in Italy and sold throughout the world.

Former Soviet Union: The old Soviet Union until its collapse in 1990.

Franklin Planner: A big, complex loose-leaf bound book/calendar/diary that busy business people use to keep tack of of their activities, current, recent and projected. Owning and carrying a Franklin Planner is a sign of being a professional. Some companies will not allow an employee to buy Franklin Planners using company money unless that employee's position is classified by the Human Resources department as "professional" as opposed to "clerical", "general" or "administrative".

G

Gamer: A person for whom a significant portion of life involves playing computer games, planning to play computer games or creating computer games.

Gates, Bill: Chairman and Chief Software Architect of Microsoft Corporation. Former CEO.

Gravy train: A situation or series of events in which the requirement to do work is minimal, everything is easy, benefits are good and profits are large.

H

H1 Visa: A visa that allows a foreign technical worker to live and work in the USA.

HR Specialist: A non-management employee who works in the Human Resource Department of a corporation. Usually an HR Specialist is charged with implementing human resource policy and procedures and assuring that such policy and procedures are followed within the company. Sort of like the hall monitor in High School.

I

Intergenerational bric-a-brac: crap and novelties of inconsequence that are passed on from mother, father, uncle or aunt to son, daughter, niece or nephew.

Isaac, the son of Abraham: according to the Bible, Isaac was the only promised son of Abraham. Abraham was ordered by God to offer Isaac in sacrifice atop a mountain in the land of Moriah. Abraham attempted to do as instructed, but God interceded before the sacrifice was made. God commended Abraham on his faithfulness and obedience and as a reward made his offspring the Chosen People.

Abraham had another son, older than Isaac, born of a handmaiden. His name was Ishmael. Islam has great respect for Ishmael as an example of devotion and obedience on the part of a son to the father, regardless of the degree of favor by which the son is held by the father. Some believe that it was actually Ishmael who was to be sacrificed, but this assertion has been the subject of heated debate for centuries among people who know about this stuff. On the whole, there are many in the Muslim world that believe that the neglect of Ishmael in favor of Isaac is just another example of the white guy taking all the credit.

IT: Information Technology

J

Jack the Ripper: A serial killer, still unidentified, who terrorized the White Chapel area of East London in the 1880's. His modus operandi was to mutilate street prostitutes with a knife.

Java: A very popular object-oriented programming language, with ever-growing appeal, created by Jim Gosling at Sun Microsystems. Java is an interpreted language, which means that an intermediary technology is used to "translate" the executing code in order to make it understandable to the operating system on which it is being run. The intermediary technology, the interpreter, is called the Java Virtual Machine [q.v.]. In theory, one can write

Java code on a computer running the Unix operating system and have that same code run as intended on a computer running the Windows operating system. In practice, however, having the same code run properly in multiple environments has proven to be difficult.

Java Virtual Machine: The translation technology that interprets Java code to run on a specific operating system.

Jobs, Steve: One of the founders and current CEO of Apple Computer and Pixar. John Scully, former President of PepsiCo USA was CEO for a while, as was Gil Amelio. The company fared miserably under their stewardship. Now it's just Steve.

K

Kahn, Philippe: Founder of the software company Borland International. Borland made its name early in the DOS era by publishing a high-quality, low-cost compiler for the programming language Pascal. For a while in the 1980s, Borland enjoyed enormous success by making programming language tools and productivity applications such as Quattro Pro, a strong competitor to both Lotus 1-2-3 and Microsoft Excel. As its fortunes dwindled in the 1990s, Kahn caused controversy by using Borland funds to support his extravagant executive lifestyle (for example, maintaining a company jet) while the company was not profitable. Khan stepped down from the CEO position in 1995. After Khan left, Borland was headed by numerous CEOs of marginal talent throughout the 1990s who were never able to bring the company back to its former glory.

Kapor, Mitch: Co-founder of the software development company Lotus Development. Lotus created the spreadsheet program Lotus 1-2-3, at one time the largest-selling piece of software in the world. Lotus 1-2-3 was designed from its inception to run under Microsoft's DOS operating system on the IBM personal computer. Many in the computer industry think that the proliferation of Lotus 1-2-3 was the main reason that the IBM PC and IBM compatible PCs became the de facto standard for personal computing in business. Under Kapor's less visionary successor, Lotus resisted developing 1-2-3 for Windows, the operating platform pushed by its arch-competitor in applications Microsoft, and instead sank large amounts of time and R&D capital into developing a version of 1-2-3 that ran on IBM's new, ill-faring OS/2 as well as on the obsolescent DOS. Microsoft Excel became the market leader in desktop spreadsheet programs in tandem with the success of Microsoft Windows 3.1, for which Excel was the compelling application -- people would buy a Windows machine just to run Excel, as formerly they had bought DOS machines in order to run 1-2-3. Lotus Development was acquired by IBM in 1995.

Appendix B: Glossary

Keynote session: The most important speech of the day at a software development conference. Presenting a keynote speech is a great honor bestowed upon very important people. Typically keynote sessions set the tone for a conference and are used to discuss topics of general interest to the industry and make important product or industry announcements.

Knowledge transfer: the act of teaching or training. The term is used often in IT consulting.

L

Labor Fulfillment: The practice of providing contract employees to fill labor shortages.

LAN: Local Area Network, a group of interconnected computers usually connected within a floor, building or group of buildings that allows an enterprise to share data, printing services and Internet access.

Lily Langtry (1853-1925): A New Jersey-born actress of great beauty who enjoyed great acclaim in England. Eventually she became the mistress of King Edward VII. She made her first stage appearance in England in 1881.

Linux: Linux is a robust and highly reliable operating system used to power Internet servers and mission critical commercial enterprise servers. Linux was created by Linus Torvalds of Helsinki, Finland at the age of 22, when he was in college. Linux is free for the downloading. Go figure.

Lockheed Martin: A very big corporate conglomerate, the result of merging Lockheed and Martin–Marietta, two very big corporate conglomerates focused primarily on defense and aerospace products. Lockheed Martin makes the Voyager space exploration satellite, the F-117 Nighthawk stealth fighter, the U-2 Reconnaissance Aircraft and the Titan rocket, to name a few of the more well-known products. There are many, many others. Lockheed Martin also runs the Saudi Joint Air Operations School, which trains pilots and officers of the Saudi Royal Air Force.

M

Meet and Greet: a slang term for an introductory meeting and sales presentation.

Metternich, Clemens Wenzel Nepomuk Lothar, Fürst von (1773–1859): Austrian statesman, Austrian Foreign Minister and arch-conservative, considered to be the arbiter of Europe following the fall of Napoleon. Metternich was known for his use of censorship, espionage, secret police and imprisonment for political purposes.

Mucky-mucks: a slang term for very important people.

N

National Transportation Safety Board (NTSB): an independent Federal agency charged by Congress with investigating every civil aviation accident in the United States and significant accidents in the other modes of transportation — railroad, highway, marine and pipeline — and issuing safety recommendations aimed at preventing future accidents. When an airplane blows up, the NTSB has to figure out what happened and whom to hold accountable.

Netscape: The company that created the first Internet browser available to the general computer user. The Netscape Navigator browser is widely credited for the explosive growth of the Internet. The Netscape Navigator browser first appeared in 1994 and by some accounts soon controlled more than 80% of the browser market. By the year 2002 the company had been acquired by AOL and Navigator had a less than commanding presence in the Internet browser market that was dominated by Microsoft's product, Internet Explorer.

No-brainer: An easy decision; the logical decision, a decision that one does not need to think about a great deal.

Noorda, Ray: Former CEO of Novell. Novell is a Utah-based company that pioneered computer networking and, for a while in the late 1980s and early 1990s, made the dominant operating system for computer networks, NetWare. Eventually NetWare lost ground to Microsoft's Windows NT, which eventually grew into the Windows Server product line. Noorda retired from Novell in 1994, started a technology company Caldera as well as an investment company, Canopy Group. The Canopy group has funded various initiatives based on the Linux operating system and is a major stockholder in the SCO Group. The SCO Group is accusing Linux developers of stealing Unix software the company bought from Novell. This accusation is in turn the thrust of a major lawsuit, the result of which will have repercussion throughout the software industry. In essence, SCO is alleging that it owns the rights to Linux, the most respected and widely-used Open Source operating system in the world today. Companies such as IBM and Novell support the Linux Operating system.

North Pole: 1. 0 degrees longitude, 0 degrees latitude. 2. The place where Santa Claus lives.

O

Offline: the state or condition of not having access to the Internet or a local area network. Typically a user is "offline" if he or she cannot get email or surf the Internet.

Oliver Twist: A novel by Charles Dickens about a small boy who is adopted by street criminals and almost becomes one.

On the Bench: 1. (baseball) Where a player sits when he has not been chosen to be one of the nine players in his team's starting lineup for a given game, or when he has been replaced in a game by a teammate whom the coach hopes will be more effective. Not in the game. 2. (Slang) A term indicating that a consultant is not engaged and is not billing for his or her time. When a consultant is "on the bench," the time of that employee is considered expense. When a consultant is billing, that time is considered income.

Online documentation: The help manuals and other support documentation that are available to the user in digital format from within the software program being used. (Another term for online documentation is "online help.")

Open Source: The practice of creating software and making the source code (the code that the programmer creates, as text) available to other developers for them to improve and redistribute. Open Source development has become a powerful initiative — almost a techno-political movement worldwide — allowing for the creation of significant pieces of software, most notably Linux. See, Linux.

OSHA: Occupational Health and Safety Administration, a division of the federal (national) government

Outsourcing: The act of assigning work and commercial duties previously done by employees to independent vendors and off-site contractors.

P

Pay dirt: slang for a profitable event or situation.

P and L: A Profit and Loss statement. A Profit and Loss statement is a report of an organization's financial health at a given point in time. It is usual in a large corporation for upper level managers to be responsible and accountable for producing a favorable P and L for the group, department or division he or she governs. Otherwise, that manager's job is at risk.

Physical transport mechanism: The part of network architecture that moves the actual bits and bytes of information around the network. Usually the physical transport mechanism in a digital network consists of the network interface cards of all devices on the network, together with the cables that connect them.

Plato's Dialogues: The collection of Socrates teachings, in dialogue format, set down by Socrates' student, Plato.

Playboy Bunny: A role made famous by the men's magazine Playboy during 1970's and 1980's. A Playboy Bunny was a woman who worked at a Playboy Club, a chain of private clubs that was part of the Playboy commercial empire. Playboy Bunnies are beautiful, big-breasted women who typically work as waitresses and club attendants. The Playboy Bunny costume consists of the following: a skimpy, tight-fitting, one-piece bathing-suit-like outfit that shows ample breast cleavage, a bunny ears headdress, two starched shirt-cuff bracelets and high-heel shoes. Also, the main part of the Bunny outfit has a bunny cottontail sewn above the buttocks. The Playboy bunny costume was known as a difficult piece of clothing to put on. It was painfully tight, in order to accentuate the bodily assets of the Bunny that it adorned. Over time, the role of Playboy Bunny became associated with sexist male behavior and the subjugation of women as a mere sex object. Gloria Steinem, a well-known feminist, was once a Playboy Bunny. Go figure.

Priority One Item: The most important thing; the thing to do first.

Project Management Institute: (PMI) The leading not-for-profit project management professional association, with over 100,000 members worldwide. PMI offers education, certification and research services to the professional project management community.

Proprietary: Something that is owned by a person or company under a patent, trademark or copyright; something that is the sole property of a person or company.

Prospero: A character in the Shakespeare's play, *The Tempest*. Prospero is an old man, possibly a magician, who lives with his daughter Miranda on an island upon whose shores a mighty tempest at sea has cast the play's characters. Arial is the spirit of the wind, summoned by Prospero.

Pull Through: a slang term used in the Information Technology consulting business which describes the act of getting more business from an existing client by identifying a need or shortcoming that the client has and then selling a solution that solves the identified problem. The consultant must have the trust of the client in order for a pull through opportunity. Without such trust, the consultant does not have access to the information, systems or people upon which to identify pull-through opportunities.

Q

Q/A: Quality Assurance, the department within a software development company or project responsible for testing and assurance that a given piece of software works as it is expected to.

R

Ranch-style house: A popular architecture style of the 1950s and 1960s in which the house is a single floor residential dwelling, similar to the Ponderosa as seen on the 1960's television show, Bonanza. Bedrooms are usually to one side of the house, while the living and eating space is on the side opposite.

Raytheon: A large technology company, headquartered in Waltham, Massachusetts, whose primary focus is the development and support of technology used by the military and Defense Department. Raytheon advertises that the company is a leader "in every phase of the Precision Engagement kill chain."

Richelieu, Cardinal, born Armand Jean du Plessis (1585-1642): Secretary of State and Prime Minister of France, considered to be the person who solidified royal authority in France using diplomacy, political repression, espionage, heavy taxation and providing the King of France with lovers loyal to the Cardinal.

Rigmarole: A complicated, most often petty, sometimes confused set of procedures.

S

Santa: Santa Claus, a fabled character, related to or derived from Saint Nicholas, who brings Yuletide gifts to deserving children and coal to children who are bad.

Santa's Elves: The helpers and associates of Saint Nicholas, whose primary responsibility is to make the gifts that Santa distributes on Christmas Day.

Shamu: The name of a set of popular killer whales held in captivity at the Sea World Theme parks in San Diego, CA and Orlando, FL.

Solipsist: A person who supports the theory or view that the self is the only reality.

SQL: (pronounced, See-Quill) Structured Query Language, the language that is used to program and control databases.

Static IP Address: The address of a computer on the Internet that is permanent to that machine. Using a static IP address is a sign of permanence, a location in cyberspace that is unchanging.

Sub-particle quantum physics: An area of study of quantum physics that is concerned with things sub-atomic, such as photons, unitons, etc...

Sweetheart deal: An easy opportunity, one that offers great benefit with little effort.

Switzerland: A country in Europe, not part of the European Union and historically neutral in terms of political alliances.

Systems Architect: An engineer who designs very large computer systems, sometimes involving hundreds of computers.

T

T1 line: A fiber-optic, or in some cases copper, network cable that is capable of carrying data at 1.544 megabits per second, which is about 60 times faster than a simple phone modem. T1 lines are used in most small-to-mid-size businesses. A T3 line can carry data at a rate of 45 megabits per second.

Test Plan: The formal document that provides step-by-step instructions on how a software product is to be tested. Usually a test plan will have a list of features and expected behaviors. The tester runs the plan according to the procedures described in the document, hoping to get the expected behaviors. Sometimes the software will behave as expected; sometimes it won't.

Time and materials: A way of billing for a project in which a customer or client is charged according to time spent on a project and materials used to fulfill the project.

Titan Rocket: The rocket used to launch intercontinental ballistic missiles (ICBMs), circa 1962. Later versions launched the Gemini spacecraft as well as the Viking and Voyager space probes.

Turbo-prop: A turboprop engine is a jet engine attached to a propeller. Turbo-props are usually used to power smaller aircraft that carry fifteen to thirty passengers.

V

VidNetSex: A slang term, peculiar to this book, for Internet-based Video Sex.

W

Wang: A computer hardware and software company founded by Dr. An Wang. Dr. Wang was a Chinese immigrant who started the company in 1951 with a $600 investment. At one point the company employed 32,000 employees. The company filed for bankruptcy in 1992.

Wang, Charles: Charles B. Wang was Chairman of the Board at Computer Associates International, Inc. (CA) from April, 1980, to November, 2002, and was Chief Executive Officer of the Company from 1976 to July, 2000. Wang was born in Shanghai, China, in August, 1944, and moved to the United States in 1952. No relation to Dr. An Wang. Charles Wang's father was a Justice of the Supreme Court in China, before the revolution. The term "killer instinct" has been used more than once when describing him.

Watson, Thomas J: Thomas J. Watson Sr. (1874-1956): first CEO of IBM, née Computing Tabulating Recording Company. He handed over the business to his son Thomas J. Watson, Jr. in the early 1950's. Thomas J. Watson, Jr died in 1993.

Windfall: Unexpected good fortune, a boon.

X

Xbox: A digital gaming console manufactured by Microsoft.

Y

Yokel: A non-urban dweller; a country bumpkin.

Z

Zits: Slang term for a facial blemish or pimple; typically used by (and about) teen-agers.